INVERCLYDE LIBRARIES

GOUROCK

HER SISTER'S GIFT

While her mother is at home giving birth, eleven-year-old Isa must look after her younger siblings, but when her little sister is killed in an accident on a train line she carries the guilt through the rest of her life. As Isa grows up, more tragedy strikes. Yet there is only so much Isa can endure over the years, and discovering her husband's affair is the final straw. Believing she has failed as a sister, a daughter, a wife and a mother, she makes an irrevocable decision ... but will she realise in time that her troubled past can also give her the strength to carry on?

HER SISTER'S GIFT

HER SISTER'S GIFT

by

Isabel Jackson

Magna Large Print Books
Long Preston, North Yorkshire,
BD23 4ND, England.

British Library Cataloguing in Publication Data.

A catalogue record of this book is
available from the British Library

ISBN 978-0-7505-4371-2

First published in Great Britain 2015
by Black & White Publishing Ltd.

Copyright © Isabel Jackson 2015

Cover illustration © Nik Keevil/Arcangel by arrangement with
Arcangel Images

The right of Isabel Jackson to be identified as the author of this work
has been asserted by her in accordance with the Copyright, Designs
and Patents Act, 1988.

Published in Large Print 2017 by arrangement with
Black & White Publishing Ltd.

Magna Large Print is an imprint of Library Magna Books Ltd.

Printed and bound in Great Britain by
T.J. (International) Ltd., Cornwall, PL28 8RW

For my grandparents, Isa and Peter
my mother, Margaret
and my aunt, Netta

1

She had not felt too good when she got up this morning. There was a tugging ache in her lower back. Waves of pain washed over her and now the contractions had started to come in earnest: every ten minutes, she reckoned. Mary clutched her sides as her breath caught. A low, prolonged moan escaped through her parted lips. It was hard to stand and she could no longer concentrate on preparing the vegetables on the chopping board in front of her. It was a bit early but it was time. She put down the knife and went to the window. The tiny, grassed-over yard was pooled in sunshine and her children's voices stirred her deeply. She leaned out, glad of the cooling caress of air across her face. She waited until she had enough breath.

'Isa,' she called, her urgency conveyed in the sharp and commanding tone.

The sweat gathered on her brow with the effort. She moved back into the room and held onto the table edge as she concentrated on regular short breaths. Her eldest daughter came into the kitchen from the garden, something serious in her demeanour and the way she carried herself, belying her eleven years.

'What is it, Mither?' She was a little breathless from her play with her young sisters.

Her mother gritted her teeth and bent a little

over her bulging belly, wrapped in the floral work apron. When the pain had subsided she whispered, 'Go and get Mrs Macleod frae next door. The bairn's comin'. She kens I'm near ma time. Tell Eliza to keep the ithers ootside.' She made towards the kitchen bed and tugged the woollen curtains aside desperate to lie down to ease the strong pains clawing deep in her lower back that were preventing her from keeping upright.

Isa took her mother's elbow and helped her to her parents' box bed in the kitchen recess. She undid her mother's boots and helped her loosen her grey serge dress at the back. She covered her with the feather quilt. 'I'll away and get Mrs Macleod now. It'll be aw'right.' She patted her mother's shoulder tentatively, not quite sure of herself in this new role of caring for her mother, but anxious to be of use and of comfort. 'Dinna wurry, Mither.'

She quietly closed the door behind her and ran down the short path and along the street to fetch the neighbour as asked. Her mind was buzzing. Would the baby be born soon? A boy or girl? Her mother must be in pain when she groaned like that. She hoped she would be all right.

Jessie Macleod, like all the women in the street, was always ready to aid her neighbours. The women were extended family to each other, but Jessie had a special attachment to Mary Dick since they had both moved in to the row of works cottages in the Camelon district of Falkirk on the same bright August morning in 1898. Back then she and Mary had been young brides setting up their first homes together. Everything was new:

looking after their husbands, cooking and cleaning, saving up gradually to furnish other rooms, adjusting to living away from home and coping with disagreements with their spouses. When their babies arrived they had delighted in their first steps and words and supported each other when times were tough. The important moments in their lives had often been shared.

She knew Mary and John Dick were a real love match. Everyone could see that: the way they held each other's gaze, the way she took his arm as they walked through the streets, the way his voice softened when he spoke of her. Such a love changed them for the better. John learned to read and write under Mary's patient tutoring and he took the pledge to stay off the drinking. Her family had thought she was marrying beneath her when she took up with a foundryman but John turned out to be a good provider and a great father.

Jessie knew right away what Isa wanted when the girl appeared on her doorstep panting, wide-eyed and anxious. 'It's yer mither, lass? The bairn on its way already is it? I'm ready as I am.' She grabbed a shawl from the chair and followed Isa out. 'Has yer mither awthin' laid by?'

'There's towels and a clean basin in the kitchen press and we've been keepin' water hot in the sway kettle on the kitchen range.'

'Hoo is she, lass?'

'She was grippin' her side, Mrs Macleod, and breathin' quick, like she did when oor Chrissie was born.'

'Aye of course. You'd mind her birth. Let's hope your mither has an easy time again.'

At the door to the house, Isa could hear her mother. It disturbed her to hear the whimpering moans. But Mrs Macleod was determined to be cheery.

'I'm here, Mary. Dinna you fret lass,' she called as she went through the front door into the kitchen.

From the bed Mary reached out and gripped her neighbour's hand. Jessie clasped it. She willed calm on her friend.

'How many births have we been through thegither noo, Mary? Your fower, my ain three and Belva's twa an aw'. We're becomin' dab hands at this.' And she smiled reassurance to her friend.

She looked over her shoulder to Isa, still hovering nervously in the kitchen. 'Noo dear. The water ready? And the too'els and basin?' Isa nodded. 'Great. Now you take the wee yins awaw for a bit and I'll see tae yer mither. By the time you're back there'll be anither sister or brother for the Dick clan.'

With that she turned her attention back to the figure in the bed. 'Noo Mary, let's get ye mair comfy,' and she eased the woman down on the pillows and arranged more under her knees, loosening the bedcovers.

Isa watched her mother in the bed and saw the pain sweep over her again, a pain which made her mother grip the bedding. Jessie had taken a cloth and wrung it out in cold water and was now carefully wiping away the sweat from Mary's brow. Isa could not get her feet to move to follow Jessie's instruction.

In a lull between the contractions Mary turned

towards her daughter, her pale face framed with wet wisps of auburn hair, and smiled encouragingly. 'Isa. I'll be fine now. You look efter the wee yins.'

Enabled by her mother's smile, she lifted the latch and headed outside.

It was warm for the time of year. Just beyond the rickety wooden fence marking the end of the tiny yard, a breeze played the leaves in a rowan into a gentle flutter. The dappling sunlight caused each layer of leaves to cast their shadows on the ones below. Isa loved this awakening of spring.

'Isa! Whaur hae ye been?' Her sister's voice seemed too loud and Isa's first thought was of her mother's need.

'Shh, Eliza. It's Mither. She's about to hae the baby. She wants peace and quiet, so we've tae tak' Chrissie and Margaret oot for a bit.'

'Oh. Is Mither aw'right?' Isa put her arm around her younger sister's shoulders and drew her close.

'Mrs Macleod is wi' her. She said they would be fine. We've just to stey oot o' the way for a bit.' Part of her longed to be included, to be with her mother, but childbirth was not a public affair. Children rarely stayed in the house while it was happening. She'd always been sent away. Maybe it had something to do with the pain and groaning. It might be a bit scary.

Isa looked down at her sister's worried frown. 'It'll be aw'right, Eliza. Mother's already gi'en birth tae aw' us and Mrs Macleod kens whit wey to help. They dinnae need us in their wey. Let's tak' the wee yins tae the parks.'

'That's guid thinkin'.'

13

They walked to the fence and found their two younger sisters digging in the earth with their bare hands. Four-year-old Margaret sat in the earth, her face wreathed in smiles. Chrissie, a toddler of some twenty-odd months, showed them her muddy hands, her own shock at their state registered in her surprised brows.

'What have you twaw been up tae?' Isa demanded in her big-sister-in-charge voice.

'We was diggin' fir worms, Isa,' Margaret chirped.

'For goodness' sake. Whit a mess.' She pulled out a handkerchief from the pocket in her pinafore dress and briskly wiped their faces and hands.

'Right. Eliza and I are takin' ye awf tae the parks noo. Tak' a haund each. Haud on tight.' And she set them on their feet again either side of her.

Eliza felt briefly the loss of her place at Isa's side. Before Chrissie was born she and Margaret had held their big sister's hands but now she was six and had to concede her place to Chrissie. Nonetheless there was the compensation of Isa including her as her second in command. She held on to Chrissie's other hand, completing their chain. The quickest way to the field was out the back gate, along the passage behind the row of cottages, through the gate at the end, and then down the embankment and across the railway line that ran into the Carron Works.

The Carron Iron Works was the biggest employer in Falkirk. Here in the sweltering heat of the foundry, hundreds of men sweated their days by the furnaces, making all kinds of goods from the cast iron: pipes, drain and man-hole covers;

fencing, lamp standards and pillar-boxes; even humble kettles, cooking pots and baths; goods that they saw as they walked the streets of the town and that they used daily in their homes, all a constant reminder of their debt to the company.

The girls' father, John, worked there as an iron moulder. He was a tall, broad-shouldered man of immense strength and stature, one of the best moulders the iron works had on their books. The moulder was tasked with following the pattern maker's measurements on paper and turning these into a three-dimensional sand mould into which the molten iron would be poured to cast all the various pieces produced at the foundry. Each moulder had a daily quota of sand box moulds to be made by the end of each shift. It was piece-work and they were limited to a maximum number to control the wage bill. John Dick regularly had his quota finished well before the end of his shift and with the energy he still had to spare, he would help younger moulders get nearer to their full quota too thus helping them earn the fullest possible wage. This strong man took some feeding and at meal times the girls were used to seeing their mother set a steaming ceramic baking bowl in front of their father. It would be filled to the brim with meat stew for breakfast and thick barley broth for supper.

The families who lived like the Dicks in the Camelon district, in the works' houses flanking the yards and grounds, saw the train loads of coke and coal and iron ore coming from the mines around Falkirk and further afield, in Fife: the necessary raw materials for the foundry. It was a dirty business and the men-folk arrived home at the end of their shifts soot-smeared and exhausted from the heat and their exertions, but it paid better than some other, cleaner jobs. At times the women bemoaned the dirt and grime on their men's work-clothes and the charcoal-black dust that the east winds blew onto the washing line from the coal wagons. Still, the steady wage meant there was always food on the table and a roof over their heads and the rent ready for the landlord at the end of the month.

Isa unsnecked the latch on the gate at the end of the path running along the back of the houses in Sunnyside Road and they filed through. Then it was a careful sidestepping operation down the embankment slope, Chrissie held by Isa and Margaret holding Eliza's hand. They were used to crossing the line, checking beforehand by looking and listening that no train was coming and then making the steep scramble up the other side. There was talk of how there should be a proper crossing for the tenants of Sunnyside Road but as yet nothing had been done and so everyone just came through the gate and crossed the line.

When the girls reached the field Isa let go of her sisters' hands and let them run free for a bit as she sat down to watch them. It was warm and the grass under their feet was springy, its fresh scent, sharp and green, filling her nostrils, heralding summer. Isa was aware of a constant tremor of excitement running through her body. The thought that right now, in the box bed in the kitchen, her mother's body was labouring to release a new child into the world: it was thrilling and terrifying, an awesome mystery to her, and yet Mrs Macleod had managed to make it sound almost mundane. Isa could remember Margaret's and Chrissie's births but not Eliza's. She had only been five then and had stayed at her grandparents' house for a few days. She remembered, on her excited return, desperate to meet the new baby, being shown Eliza, tiny, pink and wrinkled, peacefully asleep in her cot, much to her annoyance, as she had expected to be playing with this new sister immediately.

She had been seven when Margaret was born and she had made pom-poms from yellow wool to hang in between the cot bars. Someone had shown her how to make these. She remembered winding the bright thick wool round and round the two cardboard rings, then carefully snipping in between the rings to create the fluffy wool tufts. Before the rings were removed she had to pass the wool round and round the centre to hold the tufts together. Then the rings were eased off and the wool tufts ruffled by hand to complete the little balls. She had been thrilled with her handiwork.

She could remember holding Margaret, not long after she was born, while she sat on a chair. Sometimes Mother had wrapped Margaret in her carrying shawl and tied her to Isa, the shawl slung across her chest over her shoulder and tied around her back. She'd been surprised at how heavy the baby was but had loved being able to look down into her tiny face and see the little fists waving at her. Mother could get on with her work while she carried Margaret this way and she didn't even need to stop to feed her. It was a simple matter to open her dress and allow Margaret's hungry mouth to latch on to her breast. Isa remembered calling the rope for Eliza and the others in the street to skip while she had Margaret strapped to her in the shawl. Once Margaret was weaned, Isa was allowed to feed her sometimes with a spoon.

Chrissie's birth was only twenty-six months ago and fresh in her memory. Eliza had helped occupy Margaret and Isa had gone for Mrs Macleod then too. That was when Isa realised just how much older than Eliza she was, because she had been through the excitement and the thrill of caring for a baby sister before. She had the experience to keep Eliza right about how to support Chrissie's head in the early days and how to test the water in the bath. She knew how to tie the carrying shawl. And now here was Mother going through it all again for a fifth time.

Eliza came up to her and flung herself down on the grass at her side, oblivious of the green stains smeared on her pinafore by her slide to the ground. 'Dae ye think this time she'll have a boy, Isa? I hope she does. It would be graund to have a wee brither.'

'Faither would like that, I think: a son to carry on the Dick name.'

Every time a new baby was expected she remembered neighbours saying to her mother, 'Aye ye'll be hopin' for a laddie this time, lass.' She hadn't really understood the comment before, but now she knew that the son carries on the family name while daughters take the name of their husbands. With this fifth child expected any minute she was sure that Mother and Father would be hoping it

18

was a boy.

'Look, Isa, Margaret's picking daisies. Let's mak' daisy chains.' And without waiting for a reply Eliza was on her feet, mercurial as always, and humming a song she'd been learning at school. Isa sighed, tucked her knees under her long navy skirt and eased herself to her feet using her hands. She headed over to where the others knelt on the grass.

In the large spread of the meadow sprinkled with the white daisies and sunny yellow buttercups, there were now four heads bent over the task of nicking slots in the sappy daisy stems and threading the flowers through them to form necklaces, tiaras and bracelets. The afternoon sun caught the blue-black in Margaret's dark curls and Eliza's shiny locks, burnished the red and copper tones in Chrissie's hair, and set Isa's rich auburn aglow, highlighting the fine strands of honey, red and gold. The warmth went some way to easing her tension and she unclenched the muscles in her neck, and back. She stood up and stretched, leaning back from her waist with her arms up over her head, face up to the sunshine and blue sky. Maybe it was time to head back home.

All bedecked in their patiently made finery, they now linked hands in a row to re-form their chain, and singing 'Step we gaily on we go', they headed up the slight slope to the top of the field and the gate. Beyond it were the embankment and the railway siding.

Isa looked down at the line before she opened the gate. Nothing coming. She held Margaret and Chrissie by the hand and they scrambled safely down the slope. Eliza was just behind them. Isa led the little ones across to the other side, stepping carefully over the rails. They were at the top of the opposite embankment when she heard the rumble of a train approaching. Quickly she shepherded Margaret and Chrissie into the safety of the passage and closed the gate. She turned expecting Eliza to be right behind her but was exasperated to see her on the other side of the embankment.

'Wait for me, Isa,' she heard her sister call.

Isa could see the train now just twenty yards away; Eliza should not try to cross now. It was too risky.

'Stay there, Eliza,' she yelled. 'The train's comin'. Stay there! Stay there!'

But the roar of the engine was drowning Isa's voice. Eliza, a nervous, frightened six-year-old, anxious to cross the line and catch up with her sisters, had started to run down the slope so fast that her feet caught up in each other and she tumbled over, rolling down the slope towards the line.

Isa, on the opposite side, saw her sister trip, then the coal wagons passed by, obscuring her view. It took only seconds for the train to pass but for Isa time had stopped while her heart thumped in her chest the loudest she'd ever known, wagon after wagon clunking over the tracks. Finally the last one passed and she could see the line.

The air was shattered by a primeval scream, so loud it immediately drew some of the men from the yard at the works hurrying along the line, the hairs on the back of their necks standing on end at the sound.

20

Alongside the tracks was an auburn-haired girl staring at the ground. What on earth was she doing? One of the men ran down the line towards her. As he got nearer he looked on the line at the spot where the youngster was so fixedly staring and there he saw what appeared to be some clothing.

He focused on the girl and waved to get her attention. 'Get awaw frae the line lass. It's no safe. I'll fetch whit yer needin' awf the line.'

She didn't move, didn't turn her head, just stared at the track. Now that he was nearer he saw an arm, twisted, a leg at a terrible angle from the small body and blood on the tracks.

'Yer nearly there Mary. I can see the heid. Come on noo, lass. A couple more pushes should do it.' Jessie herself was exhausted. It had been two hours now since Isa had fetched her to the house but the labour was going well and it would soon be over. Mary had done a grand job working with the contractions but she was getting near the end of her energy reserves and Jessie hoped the baby would be here soon. She wiped the glistening brow again and took hold of Mary's hand. The labouring woman gripped it tightly almost to the point of pain. But Jessie didn't mind. She'd done it herself when Mary had helped birth her youngest.

She saw the rippling belly again and realised another contraction had gripped the woman. 'Go wi' it Mary. Push as hard as you can.'

Mary let out a long roar of sustained effort.

And there it was: the eel-like red slipperiness out of the labouring body and lying limp and wet on the sheets and towels. Mary lay back on the pillows in utter exhaustion. It was done. Jessie cut the cord. The baby was a strange, dark red. Why was there no wriggling? No arm movement? Why was the face so still? She checked inside his mouth to see if the airway was blocked. Nothing. She held the baby upside down and gave it a slight skelp. Nothing. Again... Nothing.

In the bed behind the half-drawn curtain, Mary asked in a whisper, 'Is it a boy, Jessie?'

'Aye it is, lass.'

'John'll be pleased.'

'Aye, he will.'

'And is he aw'right?' The voice so faint, so sleepy.

Jessie made a quiet reassuring noise and concentrated on trying to rouse the child but to no avail. The questions stopped from behind the curtain. Mary had slipped into an exhausted sleep. Jessie tried mouth to mouth. She pressed on the tiny abdomen to try to get the wee one to take a first breath.

She wrapped the child in the towels and ran to the door. She should send Isa for help but she was out of sight. She spotted Belva from down the road and called her over.

'Belva!' Her voice was hoarse, her breath coming in gasps. She could feel her heart pumping in loud beats throughout her chest as she crossed the street towards the other woman. 'It's Mary's new bairn. He's no breathin'. We need the doctor. I dinna ken whit else tae dae.'

Belva peered into the towels and saw the dark tinge in the skin, something she'd seen before on other unfortunate infants who never drew breath. 'Jessie ... he's long gone, dear. He surely was deid afore she went into labour, puir thing. There's naethin' tae be daen. We need to concentrate on her noo. Ah'll send Andrew tae fetch the doctor. You go in tae her. Watch for the efterbirth. Keep her calm. I'll be o'er shortly.'

Jessie looked down at the lifeless face in the towels.

'Oh my God, Belva. Whit'll I tell her?' But the other woman was already headed back to her own house to send her son on his errand.

The yardsman led Isa away from the track. He blew his whistle sharp and loud. Three long blasts. One of the signalmen and some other men from the yards came along the track. He waved them over and walked up the line to meet them.

'Somethin' awful's happened. There's a child on the line. She's badly injured. That lassie's wee sister. I think they're John Dick's bairns. We need to get the ambulance. Although I dinnae think there's ony hope, the state o' her.' It was taking all his strength not to weep.

Thomas Macleod looked at the dazed, bewildered child and saw James was right. It was the Dick girl, his neighbour's oldest. 'I'll tak' her, James. I ken whaur they stey.' Isa was shaking now, sobbing, incoherently moaning and clutching herself. He led her away from the gruesome sight of the child who still lay twisted and broken on the line.

'Isa we hiv tae get ye hame. We're phonin' for the ambulance for Eliza. Whaur are Maggie and

Chrissie? Are they at hame?'

Isa managed a nod in the direction of the path. 'Right then, come ye on wi' me, lass,' and he wrapped his arms around her shoulders and led the way back up the embankment.

Eliza's crushed body was still on the line, her dark hair shining in the sun, woven through with daisies, her face untouched, no sign of pain, as if her life had been snatched out of her body before the train struck. One of the men felt for a pulse, but they all knew from the twisted angles in the limbs, the mangled body and the almost severed leg there was no chance. They were glad her younger sisters had been out of sight. The older one was in a right state. The men were silent. There were no words for this. They took off their jackets and reverently covered the child, keeping vigil over her until the ambulance came. The signalman went back to his box and made sure the line would be left clear.

James, the yardsman who had recognised the girls, made his way towards the foundry to find their father. The heavy burden of the dreadful news he had to carry to this man gripped itself around his heart and he ached with the weight of it.

2

At the house in Sunnyside a shocked and silent lament shrouded the family and left them wordless and isolated. Only Chrissie and Margaret spoke. Chrissie knew little of what had taken place and in a subdued voice kept asking, piteously like a kitten mewling in the rain, 'Where Eliza?'

Margaret had heard the words 'she died' and repeated them in a whisper to her sister, but with no real understanding of what they meant she added, 'She'll be back soon.' Neither knew anything of the baby brother who never made it into the world.

Their mother lay in bed staring at the ceiling, and clutching the bedding. Jessie Macleod moved around quietly getting food ready for them, coaxing Mary to eat or drink a little. She picked up Chrissie when she cried and tried to keep Margaret busy with little jobs, drying pots and mixing things with wooden spoons. She did not know how to share her friend's pain, which went beyond her ken. She did what she could to keep everything else going and trusted time would work on Mary and bring her back to them.

John tried to comfort his wife but she was in a dark, lonely, painful place beyond his reach. He threw himself into his work and found some release in physical labour, emptying his body of the anguish he felt but could find no words to express.

Yet each time his shift ended, his body and mind were filled with grief and pain as much as before.

Isa had gone mute. She avoided eye contact and moved like an automaton. Inside the pain grew like a weighty cancer: it clung to her limbs and made them heavy and clumsy; it wrapped its tentacles around her chest and made breathing an effort; it took over her mind and replayed the scene on an endless loop – Eliza coming down the slope, tripping, sliding, disappearing from sight as the train passed. Isa felt her fear again, heard herself screaming, 'Stay there!' The long, long wait for the train to pass, and then the terrible sight of Eliza lying twisted on the track and her own piercing scream. Even in sleep there was no reprieve. Vivid nightmares took her back to the trackside every night. She would wake sweating, shaking, panting, terrified, reliving every ghastly moment. She was locked in to the event and there was no way to stop it.

It was something others could not understand. When she'd gone back to school, her teacher had greeted the class as usual and then on seeing Isa's wan face she'd voiced aloud the fact, 'Of course, you lost your sister on Friday. I'm so sorry.' Suddenly Isa could not breathe. She had scrambled clumsily out of her seat, tripping over the metal spar that held the three-seated bench to the desk, and had run out of the door. Like someone drowning, desperate for air, she had burst into the schoolyard, stumbling over the steps and running frantically for home. Until now shock had blocked her personal loss but today her teacher's words had allowed pain to ambush her from another direction. She no longer had Eliza. Her lovely shiny black hair, her deep-brown eyes ringed with dark blue, her freckles, her smile, all gone. Her singing and humming that had been the background to all their exploits silenced. Isa had no companion on the walk to school, no one to accompany her on errands, no one with whom to share her knowledge. Now there was this huge gap between Isa and her much younger sisters. She felt dreadfully alone with her pain. Her parents were stricken by their own grief and Margaret and Chrissie didn't understand. Suddenly she didn't want to go home. There was no comfort there, yet her feet had brought her automatically to Sunnyside Road.

She saw their neighbour, Mrs Macleod, heading back to her own house. Jessie had been in attending to Mary, persuading her to take a sup of porridge and a few sips of tea. The wee ones were down having a nap and Mary was dozing herself, so Jessie was checking her own home briefly. She turned on to her path, looked up and smiled quietly to Isa. When she saw the state the girl was in, she put out her arms. Isa ran to her and flung herself on Jessie's shoulder. Jessie wrapped her arms around the girl's shaking body and held her tight. She stroked the auburn head and gently spoke reassurance over her like an incantation. 'There there, lass. Let it oot. There's nothin' to be ashamed o'. It's aw'right. I'm here. Come in wi' me for a bit.' Still holding her close, she brought her into the living room and led her to the beaten brown sofa. They sat together, Isa with her head on Jessie's lap, her arms tightly around her waist, Jessie calmly stroking her hair. When her sobs had quieted, Jessie offered her handkerchief and Isa wiped her eyes and nose.

'Noo, lass,' she said. 'You've been dealt a hard blow. You're the only young one wha realises the twa losses tae your faimly. It hurts. But that's life. Eliza is no' the first to die on the line and yer mither's no' the first tae lose a bairn afore it's born. She'll be relyin' on ye even mair noo. It'll be tough for her the next while. And yer faither'll hae to be at his work. I'll be in bye to help as much as I can but I hiv my ain yins to see tae. But you can be a great help to yer faimly. You can dae a bit cookin' and cleanin' till yer mither's on her feet again and it'll help you tae. Work helps. It taks oor minds awf the pain, gies us some'at tae dae. Margaret and Chrissie will help you aw' as weel. They need tae be lovit and caret fir. Ye cannae just gie in to yer grief and forget aboot them.'

Jessie was heartbroken for the girl in her arms but she knew what she was proposing was the best remedy. When her mother had died suddenly, her grieving was put into perspective by the needs of her own young family. They still needed fed and walked to the school. Her husband still needed a meal on the table when he came home. She knew from experience how sorrow makes us selfish but the living call us back to the daily tasks that in the end can save us and show us a way out of the fog of grief.

'Noo here's whit we'll dae. We'll awaw back tae the hoose an' mak' some broth fir the denner. I wis fetchin' a leek tae mak' tattie soup. That was aye yer mither's favourite. I'm relyin' on you tae help me.'

Isa raised her eyes to Mrs Macleod's face. For the first time the grip on her chest seemed quieter. Some of the tension had found release. She was so grateful to this warm maternal woman who had understood her need to be comforted and had generously met it. She stood up on wobbly legs, took a deep breath and set off home with Jessie's arm on her shoulder, determined to be of use.

The day of Eliza's funeral was bright and warm, but inside the house, behind the drawn blinds, Isa felt shrouded in a dark, cold mist. She shivered in her black dress and stockings as she slipped on the black armband. Eliza's body had lain in the coffin in the bedroom she, Margaret and Isa had shared and so all the girls had been sleeping in the kitchen with their parents. It bothered Isa that her lovely sister lay in that awful wooden box. She could not bear to think about the terrible crushed body hidden from view under the shroud but forever engrained in Isa's memory. It was the first thing she saw when she woke and the last thing she remembered before sleep. Her sister's pale face looked at rest above the white sheet, her glorious wavy black hair framing her face, but she no longer looked like her real self. It was as if she were a shell, empty of its living being.

Her mother was distraught, pale and fragile. Despite trying to drag herself back into her life and its many duties, Mary often struggled to stand upright, and there were wet patches across her chest as she continued to lactate. Her body did not register the death of the baby, rendering this function useless, and it was painful both physically and emotionally to the poor woman. She bound herself with strips of cotton under her clothing to prevent the dampness reaching her outer garments.

Although there had been two deaths in the family there was no coffin or funeral for the stillborn baby. The undertaker had taken the tiny body away for burial. The place would have no grave marker. The Macleods and John's brothers had helped make all the arrangements for Eliza's funeral, and they were gathered with their wives and families in the crowded cottage, with the children spilling over into the backyard. The minister was coming to the house and then four of the uncles would carry the coffin, and family and friends would walk behind them up Sunnyside Road to the graveyard on Dorrator Road. They would return to the house for the funeral refreshment. Jessie was going to mind Margaret and Chrissie but Isa was determined to attend the ceremony and would walk with her parents behind the minister. Most of the women relatives would stay at the house, leaving their men-folk to stand at the graveside.

Isa, Jessie and Belva had helped Mary's mother, Ina, sweep and polish the house, and Isa discovered Jessie was right: physical work helped. Keeping her hands busy stilled the turmoil in her thoughts and she was grateful for the normally monotonous tasks. They had got her through these last difficult days. Jessie had supervised the food and all was laid out ready for their return. Now she helped ease Mary into her black mourning dress, which was too tight for her so soon after her pregnancy so Jessie had let out the back seam and inserted another panel of black woollen worsted to the dress bodice and waist. When Mary wore her shawl over her shoulders you would never know. The beautiful square black lace panel at the neck of the dress was what drew your attention and took your eye to the noble beauty of Mary's face with its cameo-like whiteness and still features. Even today, in all this sorrow and pain, there was nobility in her bearing.

The sound of a knock at the door meant the minister had arrived. The family all stood to welcome him. He shook each member of the family by the hand and expressed his condolences. Then the minister suggested they share a short prayer. In a gentle clear voice he began: 'Father of mercies and God of all comfort, look down upon thy bereaved servants. Fill their desolate hearts with Thy love that they may cleave more closely to Thee, who bringest life out of death, and who canst turn their grief into eternal joy.'

The mourners responded, 'Amen.'

The coffin, white and smaller and lighter than usual, was held aloft on the shoulders of Eliza's uncles, for whom this was a nightmarish task. The door was opened.

The minister proceeded to lead the mourners out of the house to their place immediately behind the coffin. In the street the neighbours had gathered, dressed in black, or wearing black crêpe tied around their arms, men, women and children alike. Solemn and tearful, they lined both sides of the street, heads bowed as the coffin passed them.

Eliza's death had touched the whole community. Parents felt for John and Mary. How could they not feel the horror of losing a child in such a way? Mothers who, like Mary, had lost stillborn babies, also felt a reminder of their own grief over the loss of these unnamed, unburied, unremembered children. Theirs was a secret grieving unacknowledged by others. Older folk recalled the pain of losses experienced over and over again in their families. Every funeral was a reminder of the fragility of human life and this death was felt sharply by all, the brutal tragedy of it written on every face.

John stayed by his wife's side. Mary had her veil down over her face and leaned heavily on her husband's arm. Isa walked at her father's other side, holding on to his hand, comforted by its strength and warmth, which was in such contrast to the shivering which still coursed through her body. With the minister leading the way, they began the short walk to the cemetery at Camelon Parish Church in Dorrator Road.

The men walked grim-faced along the short street, supported by the sense of the whole community grieving with them. Reaching the cemetery gates, they followed the minister to the grave, where they carefully lowered the coffin on to the ropes laid on the ground at the head of the grave. There was a brief silence as they all stood, heads bowed. Then the minister began.

'Our help is in the name of the Lord who made heaven and earth; For he knoweth our frame, he remembreth that we are dust. All flesh is as grass and all the glory of man as the flower of grass.

The grass withereth and the flower thereof falleth away, but the word of the Lord endureth forever.'

At the mention of the 'grass', Isa found her mind full of the sunny hour in the field making the daisy chains. How short-lasted the flowers were after they had been picked. They had indeed withered quickly, drooping and stretching, losing their colour and vigour. Jessie and Ina had taken the daisies from Eliza's hair and brushed it when they laid her out in the coffin. Isa's lip quivered, her breathing sharpened, she gripped her father's hand tighter.

The bearers took the ropes and raised the coffin once more, carefully stepping along the sides of the grave before lowering it steadily and slowly into the earth as the minister continued with the words of committal. 'Almighty and everlasting God, who has called out of this sinful and dying world the soul of our dear sister, Eliza, here departed, we commit her body to the ground, till that great day when the Lord Jesus Christ shall change our vile bodies that they may be fashioned like unto His own glorious body.' This he had said solemnly and softly but then he raised his head and firmly pronounced: 'O death, where is thy sting? O grave, where is thy victory?'

Sting, thought Isa. That is how it feels. An intense burning reminder of what happened. She heard her mother moaning and felt her father lean away from her as he slipped his arm around his wife's waist to support her more strongly.

The minister had begun his final prayer. 'Merciful God, Father of our Lord Jesus Christ, we give thee humble thanks for this Thy servant

Eliza, fallen asleep in the Lord. For all Thy goodness and mercy vouchsafed to her in her earthly
pilgrimage, we give Thee praise and thanks. We are
grateful that her trials and temptations being past,
her spirit is at rest with Thee, and her body awaits
the resurrection. Grant that, being animated by
her good example, we may run the race that is set
before us, not being weary in well-doing, that
when this transitory world is passed away, we may
again be joined with our dear friends, departed in
the Lord, in Thy kingdom of glory, where there
shall be no more sickness or sighing, pain, sorrow
or death...'

Mary's knees buckled under her and her legs
gave way. John let go of Isa's hand and caught
Mary before she fell to the ground. His brother
Frank came to the other side of her and between
them both they raised her to her feet, arms round
her waist and under her shoulders to help keep
her up.

Isa started whimpering and as the gravediggers
approached to begin shovelling the earth into the
grave she heard her mother's high-pitched keening
and her own sobbing under it. She knew this was
not how she was supposed to conduct herself but
she had no control. That was her sister in that box.
She saw again her broken mangled body. Why had
this happened? Why had she not waited till the
train had passed? She would still be here if she had
and they would be together looking after Margaret
and Chrissie and walking up the road to school,
chatting and laughing and sharing their day.
Instead she was gone. In a box in the ground.

As the other mourners were directed by her

uncles back to the house, the minister approached Isa and her parents.

'John, Mary, Isa,' he said. 'This is a most terrible time for you all. I hope and pray that your family and friends and our church congregation will be of comfort to you. Please accept our support and ask of us what you need. You will be in my thoughts and prayers every day. Remember the joys Eliza brought you when she was on loan to us from God, and know that she is now beyond suffering in His love.' Isa felt the wetness of his tears on her hand when he clasped hers in his.

'Thank you so much, Reverend Falconer,' she heard her father say, his voice trembling. 'Your words have been a great comfort to us today.'

Then they turned back towards the house, Frank and John struggling to keep Mary on her feet and almost carrying her home between them.

Isa was moved at how the minister had described Eliza as being on loan to them from God. She certainly hadn't been given long with them. But as he had said, her short life had been filled with joy. Eliza had been a happy companion, always full of fun and ideas to make the days lighter. Her cheerful smile and humming came from her contented disposition and positive nature. It had been a horrible death but it was over for Eliza now. The doctor had said she would have died instantly, unaware of what had happened. She was in heaven and Isa was so glad for her to be at peace. But for Isa, life had lost its shape, its sense, its simplicity. In its place there was this leaden heaviness, and a churning painful confusion.

Isa sat bolt upright in bed. What was that noise? It was like a throbbing, revving to a high pitch then dropping low again. It seemed to be coming from somewhere inside the house. She listened intently, anxious, alert, scared. Then she heard her father's voice soothing and the other sound turned into the more recognisable sound of sobbing. She realised it was her mother.

Mary was in a constant state of agony. It hurt to breathe, to think, to listen, to speak. It hurt to be alive when her two children had been robbed of their lives. During the day she was numb and solemn, but at night the pain was too great to contain. She rocked herself to and fro on the floor, her arms wrapped round her knees and John's shaking arms holding the counterpane around her shoulders.

'Ma bairn. Ma bairn,' she whimpered. 'Whit have they done wi' ma bairn?'

'Noo, lass, dinnae greet sae sairly,' John murmured as he stroked her hair. 'He's gone, Mary. He's wi' Eliza and their maker. They're both safe noo.'

'But I niver clappit ma e'en on him, John. I niver held him. I dinnae ken the colour o' his e'en or his hair.'

'It's for the best, Mary, love. It wisnae tae be. He wis niver gaun tae be wi' us. We hiv tae let him go.'

'It's too much, John. The baby and Eliza. It's too much. Eliza should still be here. I'm a useless mither, John. I didnae think properly aboot the weans that day. I should nivver hae left them tae Isa. I should hae gotten Belva tae tak' them.'

'It's nae use sayin' that noo. Whit's done is done. We hiv tae look efter the ithers noo. And you need yer rest. Come awaw, lass. Let me tak' ye back tae bed.' And he helped her to the bed, tucked her under the sheets, spread the counterpane over them both and held her in his arms until she slept.

Isa lay down beside her sisters but did not sleep.

Ma mither blames me, she thought. And she relived the terrible day and saw her mother was right.

3

Eventually, with John's and Jessie's prompting, Mary got up, put on her apron and took over the running of the house again. Soup was prepared, stew simmered on the range, the kitchen table was scrubbed, the floor swept, the children's clothes were washed and mended and John's boots were polished, but Mary as she had been, vibrant, witty and laughing, was nowhere to be seen. Mary's physical presence reminded them all of her spiritual absence and she was sorely missed by her family.

The girls missed the stories of her childhood on her parents' dairy farm in Tullibody. There was no gentle teasing, no playing or joining in with the baking. She wanted to know where they were so they had to stay within sight but they had to be quiet because her head hurt so much any noise irritated her.

John had lost his partner, his inspiration. He tried to interest her in stories about his day at work, to encourage her to notice Chrissie's needs, Margaret's exploits and Isa's schoolwork, but Mary was shut off from him, locked in her sorrow, numbed and isolated. There was no way to connect with her, except in the night when she sobbed her pain and sought comfort. Then he could feel close to her; and he held her, soothed her, and waited for her recovery.

Jessie was worried about her friend and neighbour. It was one thing to be grieving for her dead children, but what she saw was Mary abandoning the living ones. She'd call round in the afternoon and find Chrissie quiet and mournful, sitting on the floor sucking her thumb and pulling at the rag ends in the rug. Margaret would be chattering away to her doll but in hushed whispers and Mary would be involved in some mundane household chore but oblivious to where she was or what was going on. It wasn't right, but nothing Jessie said or did got through to Mary.

Instead Jessie played with the two youngsters for a bit and sometimes walked them up to the school to collect Isa and her own children at the gates. Then Chrissie and Margaret came alive. In the company of the other children they smiled, chatted, even sometimes laughed. And Jessie could see the three sisters hand in hand, tightly clinging to each other. If Chrissie ever let go of Isa's hand Margaret called her back too. Often they placed Chrissie between them to make sure she was safe. Isa had the air of being much older than her years.

Death had a way of doing that, Jessie knew. Some went under and never surfaced but others emerged stronger, able to swim ashore, determined to hold on to life no matter what. Isa had been under the cold wave of grief but was focused on getting back to the shore. Her mother, poor soul, was drowning.

'His she been like this every day?' Isa heard the disbelief in her grandmother's voice as she spoke in hushed tones to her father. Mary was having a lie down while the wee ones were asleep. Isa was supposed to be doing her homework but she needed a corner of the kitchen table and the adults were talking over at the fireside just within her hearing.

'Aye. I cannae get through tae her, Ina. I cannae shak' her oot o' it. God knows I've tried. I'm wurrit aboot the bairns when I'm at work. I dinnae think she notices whit they're daein' or whit they're needin'.'

'John this cannae ging on. She needs tae tak' a tummle tae hersel'.' There was a pause. 'Ah think she should come hame wi' me tae the fairm. The bairns an aw'. They need a break awaw frae the hoose; fresh air an' different things tae occupy their minds.'

'Aye that's a guid idea. And Isa can bide wi' me and—'

'Naw, John. She needs tae come awaw tae. She's worn oot. She's like a wraith. She's hairdly speakin'. She's been sair affected, John. She needs this as much as Mary does.'

Even as she listened to her father and grand-

39

mother finalising the details, Isa became aware of muscles in her chest loosening, her body reviving at the thought of the farm.

'Granny, can I hae mair Rupert jam fir ma toast?' Margaret asked and then added a belated 'please'.

'Of course, dear. The rhubarb jam is in the dish with the wee bee on top. Noo Chrissie, hoo are ye gettin' on wi yer egg?'

Ina Murray was in her element. She was in her well-ordered, productive kitchen at the heart of the farm, and she had her beautiful granddaughters with her. Her heartbroken daughter was asleep at last after an anguished night. She'd heard her moans and cries and gone through to her, crying with her, feeling her pain and suffering, yet fighting for hope and for renewal. She did not want to see Mary give up so completely on living.

Thankfully, up in her attic bedroom, under the soft down quilt, Isa for once had slept through her mother's trauma and been spared her own nightmares. After a long, undisturbed sleep, she had woken with more peace in her heart and a wistful desire to see what the day might hold. It was as if someone had removed a stone from the pile that had been weighing down on her chest.

'Isa! Isa! It's time to git up,' Margaret called gently as she opened the door and peeped round it.

'It's aw'right. I'm awake. Come on in, Maggie. Did you sleep well?'

'Aye, the bed was lovely and cosy. Granny says we can help bake the day. She's goin' to mak' gingerbread and scones and says we can dae it wi' her.'

Isa felt another stone slip off her chest as her sister prattled enthusiastically about the plans for the day. Her innocent joy in life had suddenly bounced back and it was medicine for Isa's soul to see her sister's smile.

'Chrissie's just finishing her toast. There was real butter curls. Granny says she'll show me hoo tae mak' them when the milk's churned.'

'I better get washed and dressed or I'll miss aw' the excitement.' Isa lifted back the quilt and swung her feet to the rag rug on the floor. Margaret skipped back downstairs to the kitchen. Isa poured water from the ewer on the dresser into the wide shallow enamel basin and splashed her face. She felt really awake for the first time in a long while. Previous days had been lived in a dwam. She'd been dazed, only partially involved in anything she did, and distanced from all going on around her. But now, as she stood looking out through the frothy white net curtain at the window, gazing over the neat vegetable plots and flower beds near the house and the fields of grain and dairy cattle beyond, she breathed more consciously in and out, aware that this was a turning point and that she was glad of it.

By dinner time the huge kitchen table, scrubbed clean and holding court in the centre of the kitchen, held trays of cooling gingerbread and scones at one end of its great length and at the other steaming bowls of broth for the midday meal. There was a plate of crusty bread already buttered and a dish of cottage cheese fresh from the dairy, covered with white muslin. Mary was up and dressed now and helped her mother serve the family. When the plate of bread ran low, Chrissie and Margaret were fascinated as their grandmother took the remains of the loaf on her crisp white apron between her knees and reached into the dish of butter curls with the large bread knife, which she swiped neatly over the white crumbly cut surface of the loaf, before carefully cutting to and fro to release the buttered slice for the plate. Her movements were practised, steady and deft and it was all rhythmically done as though to music. They'd never seen anyone else do it like this. Somehow it made the bread taste better and they asked for more, just to see the graceful movements again.

When everyone was replete and the dishes cleared away, it was time to check the cakes. A careful push with the finger into the sponge surface revealed a dimple that sprang away again, leaving the surface smooth. They were cool enough. Out came the glass bowls, the icing sugar, the sifter and wooden spoons. Sugar was sifted into the bowls and water added. The gingerbreads were iced. Fingers went into the bowls when the adults weren't looking and were licked surreptitiously. The task was soothing and absorbing. Chrissie was licking the bowl, her fingers and the spoons, and was now a happy, very sticky mess. The table was covered in fine powdered patterns from the sugar sifting but the gingerbreads looked good.

'Noo girls. The men will be bringin' in the coos soon for the milkin'. Will we get tidied up and go and watch?'

They did not need to be asked twice. Chrissie was down from her chair, her hands held high. 'Granny, My need wash my haunds. My don't want tae mak' the coos sticky.'

And suddenly the kitchen was filled with laughter. More stones rolled off Isa's chest as she spontaneously laughed at the picture Chrissie had created in her head. Instead of the clean, black and white jigsaw shapes covering her grandparents' Friesian cows, her mind had created Chrissie-sized palm prints on their backs. Her grandmother's heart leapt in relief. Her dear eldest granddaughter was coming back to life again.

In the byre, the cows had already been led to their stalls. Each had her own place and the names were on plaques on the sides: Clover, Daisy, Miranda, Gertrude, Emmeline, Flo. There was fresh straw on the hard-packed earthen floor and its honeyed smell lingered over the manure and warm milk. The milking had begun. They could hear the steady squirting as the first milk hit the metal pails. The women sat on the right side of the cow facing in to its flank sometimes so close their brow touched the animal's warm, suede-soft hide. Ina led the girls over to Flo's stall, where the dairymaid Ethel had just sat down.

She stroked the udder and wiped the teats with a clean wet cloth, then, humming gently to keep Flo calm, she took a teat in each hand and gently, using her fingers, squeezed the udder teats rhythmically one at a time, left hand then right hand. She was careful not to pull or stretch the teat as this caused the cow pain and stopped the milk flow. Gradually the sound changed as the bottom of the buckets filled and the milk rose to greater depth. The girls loved the sounds and the smells: the gentle mooing of the cows, their sweet breath and the splashing of the milk in the buckets. It was so soothing. When the cows had finished letting down their milk the dairymaids carefully wiped the teats and clapped the cow gently in thanks. They got up off their stools, draped the milk cloths over the tops of the pails and carried the milk through to the dairy.

'Can we go tae the dairy too, Granny?' asked Margaret.

'Of course,' said Ina and she led them back out through the byre and across the yard into the dairy. The farm at Tullibody was mainly a dairy farm and was known as The Doocot Dairy. They supplied the milk for the local shops and hotels and their butter and cheese were well sought after in the area. They took their products round the streets on a horse-drawn cart. The milk was kept in large, shiny urns with taps at the bottom. Customers could come with their jugs and cans and have them filled with milk from the tap. For a small farm it was well organised and the dairy shed was kept scrupulously clean. The children all had to wash their hands in hot, soapy water at the sink near the door before they went near the tiled shelf where the dairymaids worked.

Betty and Ethel carefully poured the milk through the milk cloth into shallow earthenware trays. The girls were fascinated. 'Why are they haudin' the clooties o'er the pails?' asked Margaret.

'That stops ony dirt that micht hae gotten intae the pail gettin' intae the milk or the butter,' answered Isa, having seen this process before. 'Then the milk lies in they shallow dishes ... they're called pancheons, aren't they, Granny?'

'That's right, Isa.' Ina was so glad to see Isa take an interest in things again that she left her to explain the process.

'The milk lies here till the mornin', when the cream will hae separatit oot and be floatin' on the surface. Then Betty and Ethel can skim off the cream fir the butter.' Isa looked over to her grandmother, who nodded to confirm she was doing a good job.

'So does that mean we'll hae to wait till tomorrow tae see the butter bein' made?' They could both hear the disappointment in Margaret's voice.

'Naw,' Isa reassured her. 'This mornin's milk is ready tae skim. It's o'er here.'

They moved over to the other end of the shelf, where the morning's pancheons were covered with muslin. 'Can I do some skimmin', Granny?' asked Isa.

'Ah dinnae see why no'. Let's get the skimmer doon,' and she reached up to the hooks on the wall and brought down a short-handled, saucer-shaped wooden skimmer, which she held low down so that Chrissie and Margaret could see the tiny holes in it. 'See they holes? They let the milk back through whilst the skimmer catches the cream.'

Then she handed the implement across to Isa, who dipped it carefully into the pan, gently dragging it through the milk, then lifting it out. Caught in the saucer of wood was the pale yellow cream

45

and dripping out from the holes came the bluish milk. When the milk had finished draining, Isa scraped the cream out of the skimmer and into another dish ready to go to the churn.

Margaret peered into the dish. 'There's no' much there. Will it be enough, Granny?'

'Yer right there's no' much. But ye see we collect some every milkin' and we've a few pans o'er here from yesterday and the day afore. When we put today's in with these there'll be enough fir the churn.' Ina took the cream from the different pans and tipped them into the wooden churn. Then she replaced the lid and the plunger and, grabbing the handle, started to push the plunger up and down in the sloppy cream.

'Can I try?' Margaret asked, practically jumping in excitement at Ina's side. She was given the handle of the plunger and guided to bring it down into the cream and then to pull it back again. Her arms were like wee pistons to start with, but fairly quickly slowed to a stop. The top of the plunger was level with her head and the action was particularly tiring for a wee one.

However, having seen her sister allowed to use this fascinating object, Chrissie too wanted to help and clamoured for her turn. 'My do it.' So Ina got a stool and stood Chrissie up on it, holding her firmly around the waist and assisting her to dunk the plunger down and pull it up again. Isa had her turn too and so did their mother, and with the dairymaids helping as well, the churning was soon done. Ethel called their attention to the different sound the cream made as it changed from liquid to semi-solid.

'That's hoo we ken it's near ready,' she told them. 'Then we tak' awf the lid and have a wee keek inside. Sometimes it needs a bittie mair workin'. Let's see hoo we're daein'.' She lifted off the lid and let the plunger move over to the side of the churn. 'Aye, that's no far off. Another minute or so and we'll be grand.' She replaced the lid and continued the plunging and shortly there was a real sticky, sucking sound, different from the swishing and slushing of earlier in the process. Now the lid came off and the plunger was scraped free of the butter grains and the churn was drained into muslin draped over a large bowl. The muslin caught the butter solids and the buttermilk drained into the bowl.

'Noo,' said ma, 'that's the buttermilk for the scones on Thursday. We'll just lay it by covered wi' the muslin. And noo we hiv tae get tae work on kneadin' the butter. Clean hands only fir this job.' And they all washed again. Then each had a go at beating and kneading the butter until the surface was covered in tiny droplets, glistening like beads all over the creamy yellow butter. 'That's the water and buttermilk that was still inside the butter. Noo that it's oot the butter will stay firmer and smoother.'

Chrissie had wandered over to a low table, which was covered with lots of round butter moulds. She was about to roll one on the floor when her mother caught up with her and rescued the mould. She picked Chrissie up in her arms and held her close. Ina held her breath. She hadn't seen her daughter reach out for Chrissie since they'd arrived. This was what had been worrying John.

'Chrissie, come and see what these are for,' Mary said and she handed it to Isa and then provided a commentary for them all. 'Watch how Isa fills the bottom part with the butter and then puts the moulded lid on top. Now she squeezes it down, twists it off.'

'Oh,' said Margaret and Chrissie together as the pattern was revealed on top of the circular pat of butter. Another twist and the bottom part of the mould was taken off too and the butter was ready to be wrapped in greaseproof paper, ready for sale.

Margaret puzzled at the pattern. 'What's this shape, Granny?' she asked.

'That's a doocot: the old tower house the pigeons used to be kept in, the ruin the farm is named efter. That way the customers ken whaur the butter was makit. Noo let's tak' some butter in for oor tea. The scones are waitin' for this and there's the gingerbread for efter.'

Isa stayed on for a bit, helping the dairymaids wash the pails and cloths and talking with them.

As she left the dairy, Margaret's hand in hers and Chrissie still in Mary's arms and cuddled into her mother's neck, Ina's spirits leapt a little. She'd been right to bring them all here. The darkness was beginning to lift.

Over the next few days, Ina let them each sleep until their own wakening bodies brought them out of bed. She fed them with her home-grown produce and she kept them busy with the farm tasks. They fed the hens in the morning and helped the dairymaids. Then there was kitchen cleaning and cooking. On nice afternoons they weeded the kitchen garden and picked vegetables for their meals and packed the remainder for the weekly market. The children were all more relaxed and Isa especially was transformed. Some of her old confidence was returning and she was communicating more naturally again, taking an interest in the little ones and getting involved in all the jobs Ina set before her. Although Mary had made some progress she still had a long way to go and Ina was still worried about her when she took them to the station to see them off.

She helped them into the carriage. Along with the suitcase they'd come with there was another, lined with greaseproof paper and filled with fresh fruit, vegetables and new-laid eggs wrapped in newspaper, scones and gingerbread in extra layers of greaseproof paper, and jars of raspberry jam and apple chutney.

'Noo girls,' she said firmly. 'You all be guid and tak' care o' yer mither. I want to see these rosy cheeks still bloomin' when I visit next month.'

They responded with a chorus of, 'Yes Granny, we will.'

Then Ina turned to Mary and wrapped her arms around her, folding her head onto her ample bosom. 'Mary, my darling girl,' she said into Mary's ear, 'be strong, be well, for those you still have wi' you. I will be praying for you night and day. God bless you.'

Mary released herself, stifling sobs. 'Thank you, Mither, for awthin'.'

They held each other's gaze for some time, Ina willing strength and peace to her daughter and

49

Mary desperate to take it. The guard blew his whistle and Ina reluctantly stepped off the train. As it pulled out of the station she waved and waved a white handkerchief until long after the train was out of sight, unaware they could no longer see her for the tears spilling from her eyes unabated.

John was delighted when he met them at the station to see how well they all looked. The two wee ones were back to their old selves, bouncy, chattering and contented, full of all their exploits at the farm. Isa was at least speaking again and looking much more positive and engaged with life. And Mary looked as though she had been eating properly and had reconnected to her role as the children's mother. She had Chrissie in her arms and had a hold of Margaret's hand while he helped Isa with the cases. He felt a load lift from his mind as he brought them home.

The children had just started to wear grey clothes at the end of the five-month full mourning period when Mary became unwell and took to bed. She was pale, weak and feverish and her pulse was erratic. The doctor thought it was her heart and advocated rest. John's sister-in-law, Thomasina, known as Auntie Teenie to the girls, came to help for a while but when her own daughter took ill she had to return home.

Isa stayed off school and kept things going as best she could, seeking help from Jessie when she was unsure. Mary hardly spoke. She drifted in and out of a restless sleep, fevered and breathless. Sometimes she sat up a little on raised pillows with staring eyes, listless and mute. Her sleep was disturbed with terrible dreams that caused her to moan and sob even as she slept.

And then one morning, very early, Isa was wakened by a different sound. It was her father sobbing, 'No. No. *No!*'

Isa got out of bed and went anxiously to the kitchen door, her heart thumping. 'Mither. Faither.' Tentatively she opened the door. Her father was holding her mother, rocking her to and fro. Her mother's arms were trailing beneath her and her head lolled on her husband's arm. There was something strange about the whole thing. It was not the usual scene of her father comforting his inconsolable wife.

'Mary. Oh ma Mary,' he sobbed as he brought Mary's face close to his own.

'Faither?' Isa tried again. 'Faither? Whit's wrong?'

Her father raised his head, his face flooded with tears, 'She's gone from us, Isa. She's gone, lass.'

Isa's legs gave way and she slumped down against the wall. As if she had been hit a hammer blow, her breath seized in her chest in a loud gasp and her whole body felt wrapped in chains. How could her mother be dead? Her mind just would not take it in.

John, overwhelmed with grief, kissed Mary's face and held her to his chest, rocking her. As his own tears subsided, he saw his grief-stricken daughter shaking against the wall. Gently he laid Mary back on her pillows and rearranged the bedding around her. Then he came over to Isa, lifted her in his arms and took her across to the rocking chair, smoothing her hair in a comforting rhythm and shushing her as he had done when she was a baby.

'Isa, dinnae greet sae sairly, lass. Yir mither couldnae thole the loss o' Eliza and the bairn. She'll be at peace noo she's wi' them. It's up to you and me noo tae look efter the ithers. Oor tears winna help onybody. We've to be strong noo,' and they both held on to each other until the sobbing ceased and they fell into an uneasy sleep.

4

When Margaret and Chrissie were told, it was clear they did not understand the emotional impact. They were both sat at the kitchen table before breakfast. Margaret realised the loss of her mother's role in the house and tentatively said, 'Does that mean you'll be the mither noo, Isa?'

Before Isa could answer, her heart heavy with loss and confused at the idea that she should be seen in her mother's role, her father answered for her.

'Aye, lass, it does.'

Chrissie, already sitting with her spoon in her hand, tapped the table with it and in her toddler's egoistic state of hunger, pronounced, 'If yer goin' to be the mither, *be* the mither.' So Isa dished out the porridge, intensely aware she was entering a new phase in her life and determined to do it well for her mother's and Eliza's sakes. What was it the minister had said? That those left behind must be inspired by those who had died and live by their good example and not be weary in well-doing. That's what she had to do now. No looking back, no more grieving. There were tasks to be done and she had to do them. And so she shut her pain and grief deep inside and turned her mind and body to her new role.

Tuesday afternoon was her mother's turn for the wash-house. Isa had often helped her on returning from school so she knew the routine. Her mother had always done the whites – sheets, shirts, nightshirts – first off, when the water was just off the boil. It had to be taken from the boiler into the tub, soap grated and then the clothes added. Wielding the wash dolly, which was like a paddle used to swish the clothes around in the water to release the dirt, was quite some task for Isa, but standing on the duckboard, the raised wooden step beside the tub, helped her get more purchase on it. Into the final water for rinsing the whites she added the 'dolly blue', which helped give the whites an extra-bright white look.

One day, not long after Mary's death, Isa was in the wash-house. She was just finishing running the heavy sheets through the mangle, to squeeze out the water from the last rinse, when there was a 'cooee', and Maisie Macpherson from down the street put her head around the door.

'How are ye, Isa? My, yer fair gettin' on. Is there onythin' I can help ye wi'?' Maisie was a big-built woman dressed in black serge and a floral wrapper. Isa knew her mother had not really liked her, finding her to be as nice as ninepence to your face but liable to decry you as soon as your back was turned. So Isa was keeping her wits about her.

'Well, Mrs Macpherson, no' really. The worst is daen. I'll just hing oot the sheets and get the coloureds washed noo. I'm daein' fine. Thank you for askin' though.'

'That's just grand. Yer faither must be right proud o' ye, Isa, fillin' yer mither's sheen sae weel.'

There was a tense silence. With a slight quiver in her voice, Isa replied, 'I'm daein' my best, Mrs Macpherson, but I cannae fill her sheen. She was a much better mither than I am. We all miss her sairly.'

'Oh I didnae mean tae offend ye, lassie. It wis a compliment tae ye. Yer managin' awfa weel. In fact, I hiv a proposition that micht make life easier for ye. I wis wonderin' if my time in the wash-hoose would be better suited to ye. Ye see my turn is Friday mornin' and that would mean ye'd have awthin' cleaned for the weekend. And ye wouldnae hae the scrubbin' o the flair tae dae at the end o' the day. Ye'd hae more time in the efterneen to get yer faither's supper ready as weel. Whit de ye think? I'd be glad tae gi' ye ma slot.'

Isa felt under pressure. How could she decide that right now? 'Well, Mrs Macpherson, that's very kind o' ye thinkin' aboot me. I'll talk it over wi' my faither and see whit he says.'

'Oh. Right ye are then. If yer sure.' She sounded almost peeved. 'I'll leave ye tae it. Looks like ye've awthin' under control,' and she walked stiffly out of the wash-house and clicked the door shut behind her.

When she left Isa continued to mangle the sheets

and transfer them into the basket, all the while mulling over what Maisie Macpherson had proposed. She walked out to the green and pegged the sheets up on the washing line, strung between the two iron poles placed diagonally opposite each other to give the longest hanging space. As she was bending into the basket for the last one she realised that one of the reasons her mother had liked the Tuesday afternoon slot was that they could use the wash-house into the early evening as long as they tidied up. It meant they had more time to do all the washing, and then her mother had boiled up another lot of water, filled the zinc bath tub and they had all had a wash in it. If she swapped with Maisie, the morning slot would be far more rushed and Margaret wouldn't get a wash, for she had started the school now. No: she would keep her mother's slot and they could all still have a bath. She was pleased she had seen through Mrs Macpherson's wily plan. Dressed up as helping Isa, it had really been about helping herself to the better slot.

Mrs Macpherson was not the only neighbour who tried to take advantage of the young girl trying to be mother and housewife, but most of the women on the street were good to her, keeping her right about shopping, store cupboards, cooking, cleaning, childcare. But it was Jessie she always turned to first, and she was on hand with sound, practical advice and wise counsel. Her grandmother, Ina, was a great help too, but she was a half-hour's train journey away and much needed on the farm, so her visits were often spread apart. Isa took to writing her grandmother a weekly letter with news of the family, which she loved to do and which Ina loved to receive. Sometimes Isa would ask a practical question about household issues: perhaps how to darn her father's socks so they weren't so lumpy when finished, or how to cook a particular cut of meat she'd seen in the butcher's shop. However she soon discovered the butcher himself was happy to give his customers tips on how best to cook his produce. He'd often keep aside special pieces for Isa, aware of how hard she was trying to keep up her mother's standards for the family.

'Here ye go, lass,' he would say, when other customers had left the shop. 'I've kept this bit o' plate for ye. Just you broon that gently then pop it in the slow oven in the range wi' whole skinned onions and carrots aroond it. Leave it hotterin' for twaw, three hoors and it'll be fine and tender. Ye can mak' a braw gravy wi' the juices that'll hae aw' the flavour o' the beef and the veggies. Yer mither aye said it was one o' your faither's favourites.' And she'd be handed the beef wrapped in brown paper and tied with string. The price he'd pencilled on the paper would always be a bit cheaper than he'd charge wealthier customers.

It helped, she supposed, that her father and his eleven brothers were well known in Falkirk, notorious even. They were nicknamed the Fighting Dicks due to their prowess in taking on the travelling fighters who arrived with the fairs, knocking most of them senseless to walk off with the prize money. But John Dick was now respected as a hard-working moulder and family man despite the notoriety of his fighting brothers.

56

His wife Mary, had been of gentler breeding, as the daughter of a businessman and farmer who owned his own land and had kept his children on at school until they had passed their leaving certificate. Her influence had left its mark on John and he was able to read and write, and keep abreast of current affairs in ways other workmen could only admire.

However an old problem was beginning to rear its head. Since Mary's death, John had taken to the drink again. At first it was just a quick glass of beer after his shift. But after some months it became an all-out marathon on a Thursday payday. Thankfully he went home first and gave Isa the housekeeping money, so they never went short of food, always had the rent money and were never in debt. But then it was straight to the beer shop to drink the rest away, and he was very well paid. Isa's uncle Tommy was the wages clerk and told her that her father was the top-paid man on the books at the foundry. Yet vast sums were used to buy rounds for his mates down at the beer shop.

Sometimes her father would come staggering home with one of his brothers, equally well oiled. If the girls were still up, John would get them each to do a party piece for entertainment. At a family occasion they usually loved to do this, and each had their favourite bit of poetry or song to perform. But when the audience was men you knew to be your father and uncle made rough and uncouth by drink, it was a different affair. Worst of all was when John Dick sat in his chair and bellowed orders at his girls. 'Stand up!' They stood up as quickly as they could. 'Sit doon!' They sat down and just as they were relaxed, again would come the command, 'Stand up!' Then he would turn to his brother: 'See how I've got them dancin' tae ma every command.' Then the men would roar with raucous laughter. The girls hated this more than anything. They felt humiliated but there was no way they could refuse. Any disobedience would only anger their father when he was in this kind of mood.

One Thursday Isa had just finished settling her sisters for the night and was tidying up in the kitchen when she heard her father's footsteps scrunch the gravel on the path. The door opened and before she knew it he was in the kitchen. His huge bodily presence seeming to fill the room.

'Isa my lasss,' he slurred. 'Yer no sshtill at the sink? Come and sit ye doon wi me fur a bit.'

Truth be told, Isa was very tired. It had been a long day and she was very keen to get to bed herself. 'Father, I'm awfae tired. I wis jist aboot tae go tae ma bed—'

'Sit ye doon,' her father insisted. 'I want tae talk tae ye.'

She felt she had no option but to join him at the table. All his married life, her father had kept the pledge to be teetotal. She found it very disturbing to be in the presence of this large, strong man who seemed to be quite other than the stable father she had known.

She sat down on the far side of the kitchen table, her eyes cast down at her hands tightly clasped in her aproned lap.

'Can ye no' look at me, lass? It's yer faither here sittin' across frae ye, no' a stranger.'

58

Immediately Isa raised her head and looked him in the eye.

'That's better.'

He seemed calmer then. 'Noo. We'll jist hae a bit chat. How are ye getting' on wi' awthin'?'

Isa was taken aback. 'I'm fine, Faither.'

'Chrissie and Maggie are no' giein' ye ony problems?'

'No, Faither.'

'An Maggie daein' fine at the skuill?'

'Aye, Faither.'

'Mercy lass,' his brawny fist thumped the table, 'it's like gettin' bluid oot o' a stane tryin' tae hae a bit conversation wi' ye. "Aye, Faither, no, Faither." Whit's wi' ye? Hae ye forgotten hoo tae spik tae yer faither?' He was leaning across the table and Isa was scared. She felt the simmering anger. Her heart was thumping in her chest. Instinctively she sought to pacify him.

'Maggie is gettin' on weel. Her teacher says she'll be ready for a new reader next week and she can coont up tae twenty.'

As quickly as he had flared he settled down, leaned back in his seat and smiled across at his daughter, who was to all intents and purposes now the substitute mother for her siblings.

'Aw that's grand, so it is, Mary. We can be richt prood o' oor girls.'

Isa was dumbstruck. Had she heard aright? Her father had just called her by her mother's name. Surely he had not confused her with her mother?

'Come ma bonnie lassie and gie me a hug.' He patted his knee as if to signal Isa should come and sit on his lap. She knew he'd not done this with her

59

since childhood, except for the night her mother'd died. She realised therefore that in his drunken mind he was still confusing her with her mother.

'Faither,' she said tentatively. 'Shall I make ye a cup o' tea?'

Her father looked up at her in consternation. He had not expected the term 'Faither' nor had he expected Isa's voice. For a few seconds puzzlement furrowed his brow. Then she saw the realisation of who she was cross his features, but she was quite unprepared for his reaction.

'Where's yer mither? She wis here a minute ago.'

Isa put down the kettle and braced herself.

'Faither. Mither passed away, months ago. It was her heart, remember?' Isa's lips were trembling as she spoke the words, and she was filled with the pain of her grief, so much so that for a few moments she did not see her father drop his head to the table over his folded arms, his shoulders heaving as his body was racked with the renewed pain of loss. Isa drew near his side and sat beside him with her arm around his shoulders. It was some time before they were both at peace again. Then she helped her father into his bed in the kitchen and she lay down beside her sisters. At last the house was quiet.

The experience had shaken her. It left her feeling a little wary of her father. They had been through so much together. This common grief they shared had created complex bonds between them. From then on, she did not relish paydays and sought to avoid being up when her father came home drunk. She did not think there was any real threat or danger but the situation was just too adult for her to predict his mood or where it might go. At times she could hear him singing noisily if he was in a good humour, or swearing loudly if something had irked him. But he never hit any of them, though he could be bad-tempered. Young as she was, the very fact he was not his usual self was enough to scare her. A bad mood could often last over to the next morning and that made her very tentative in her dealings with him.

The main problem was asking him for any money over and above the usual weekly budget. Chrissie and Margaret were still growing and would at times need new shoes or clothes. Isa did her best to adjust clothes, letting out seams and dropping hems, using hand-me-downs from Margaret for Chrissie. She'd even used some of her mother's clothes and cut them down to fit herself, working out the techniques with help from Jessie. Chrissie grew out of her shoes every six months. So Isa always had to pick her time right when tackling her father.

Payday was a Thursday. So on a Wednesday night she'd make sure she had a good meal ready: liver and onions or a piece of frying steak, with a nice steamed pudding to follow. She'd mention how Chrissie was growing out of her shoes and say she'd seen some in the Co-op. Her father would say, 'No bother Isa. I'll gie ye the money the morn when I get my pay. Noo, are there ony mair onions in the pan? Mak' sure the wains hae enough first.' Isa would breathe a sigh of relief.

Her days were kept very busy. Margaret had started the school after the summer and so it was just Chrissie she had to occupy during the day.

She tried to involve her in the daily chores, giving her a duster to dust the furniture or a cloth to wash the windows. She always had a bowl and spoon on baking days and although it made a mess she was happy and it all got cleaned up afterwards. She kept tricky tasks like ironing until Margaret was home and could amuse Chrissie. Then she'd heat the two irons by the fire, lay down the folded blanket on the kitchen table and set to.

One day she remembered a song her mother used to sing to her while ironing and she began to sing it.

'Twas on a Monday morning, when I beheld my
  darling
She looked so neat and charming, in every high
  degree
She looked so neat and nimble, O, A-washing o'
  her linen, O,
Dashing away with the smoothing iron, she stole
  my heart away.

It had a great ironing rhythm for sweeping the hot iron over the sheets and shirts and the kitchen soon filled with a lovely damp warmth, and the fresh smell of the newly washed and ironed clothes and linen was as comforting as anything she knew. Chrissie and Margaret stopped their play to listen to her and she went on to the next verse.

'Twas on a Tuesday morning, when I beheld my
  darling
She looked so neat and charming in every high
  degree

She looked so neat and nimble, O, A-hanging out
    her linen, O,
Dashing away with the smoothing iron she stole
    my heart away.

She gave the girls some tea towels to smooth with
their hands and they joined in the other verses,
which took them through all the days of the week
and all the processes of washing, hanging out,
starching, ironing, folding, airing and finally, on
Sunday, the wearing of the linen. Before she knew
it, the ironing basket was empty and everything all
folded neatly, ready to air on the wooden clothes
horse spread in front of the range. It became a
weekly ritual for many years.

One of the hardest things to accept about her
new life as 'Mither' was giving up school. Isa had
always loved learning and relished Miss Watson's
compliments on her essays, which sometimes she
was asked to read aloud. And she missed the
playground chats with friends. So she was always
glad to see Jean, Jessie's oldest daughter, who was
the same age as her, who sometimes called in
after school if her mother could spare her.

One afternoon, eighteen months into her new
role, Jean arrived as she was spreading bread with
jam for the after-school piece that Margaret and
Chrissie always craved, which they needed to keep
them going till supper time. She spread one each
for herself and Jean, poured out milk for them all
and they sat round the table. The wee ones were
quickly finished and asked to play in the backyard,
which Isa granted, provided they did not get their
clothes dirty.

Elbows on the table, out of sight of her mother, Jean sighed wistfully. 'Oh, Isa,' she pined, 'I wish I could be like you. You look so grown-up here in charge of the kitchen and the weans; nobody bossing you about, no boring lessons and homework. Me, I've either got Miss Watson on my back or ma mither. I canna win–'

Isa banged down her glass of milk so hard that half was spilled over the rim and pooled on the table. She pushed back her chair roughly, grabbed a cloth from the sink and scrubbed vigorously at the mess as she rounded on her friend. 'Don't you go envyin' my situation, Jeannie. I'm up early lightin' the fire, makin' the porridge and washin' the weans while you're still in bed. All day I'm cleanin' or cookin' or washin' or mendin' and ironin' while you get the chance to learn about the world and read and do fancy things wi' numbers.'

'Oh Isa I–'

'Ah'm no near finished,' Isa yelled. Her face was red, her fists were clenched and the cloth in her right hand was dripping milk, it was so tightly gripped. 'You think this is easy? You envy *me*? Me wha lost my sister, wha has nae mither to listen tae me?' She broke down in sobs, her chest heaving, then she sat down at the table, her head on her hands and wept, angry bitter tears that stung her cheeks and deafened her to Jean's attempts to console her. Jean could see nothing else for it but to go and get her mother. And so it was that once again Jessie took into her arms her best friend's firstborn child whose birth she'd aided, and held her till the sobbing subsided. She spoke no words. Isa's tears fell on Jessie's shoulder and Jessie's ran through

Isa's hair.

Over the years there would be more outbursts of anger at the situation imposed upon her. She rarely said aloud, 'I hate this life,' but it ran through her mind often enough. If she kept busy and saw the fruits of her labours, she could take a pride in what she was achieving. But if her efforts were thwarted, it was hard to keep control of the resentment and grief she felt at her impoverished ambitions. What options did she have now? No leaving certificate. No job as a governess or secretary. Childhood over, and catapulted straight into a married woman's life, running a household and looking after children – exactly the life she'd have to lead when she *was* married. All her contemporaries meanwhile could moon over the handsome boy in the row behind them, or talk excitedly about the new fashions in Mrs Weir's drapery store. They were getting the chance to grow up gradually and to be young and carefree for at least part of the day before they came home and helped their mothers.

It was things like sending the girls out in clean dresses and pinafores, newly washed and ironed, and their coming home with them spotted with dirt. She'd practically tear the aprons off them, ranting at how stupid they were. Couldn't they see how much work it made for her? They were confused. Their mother had never made such a fuss. She would take the aprons off gently, sponge them at the sink and dry them at the range. They were trying to keep them clean but it was difficult with long skirts and petticoats plus an apron. Even walking along the road kicked up dust and got the hems dingy.

Early on, there were times she'd tried to cook a new recipe from a neighbour and had left the meat a bit long in the top oven of the range, instead of putting it in the bottom oven where it was cooler and the meat could cook more slowly and keep its juices. When she took out the casserole and lifted the lid, they could all catch the acrid smell of charred meat and they knew what would happen next. The casserole would be set down noisily on the table in front of her father. He would spoon out portions onto their plates, say grace and they would try to eat it. But if it was undercooked and raw underneath its blackened surface, he would say, 'Noo, Isa, I dinna think we can eat this. It's no richt cookit. We'll hae a bit bread and drippin'.'

Isa would stomp off to fetch the bread, lift some cheese from the press, if there was any, and burst into an angry diatribe. 'It's aw' Margaret's fault, Faither. She distracted me when I was pittin' it in the oven and I didnae notice I'd pit it in the top. She's aye interruptin' me when I'm busy.' Or Chrissie would be blamed for crying over something, or a neighbour for interfering in how she was doing things. She could never just put it down to a mistake easily made, as her father always did. Somehow he knew she was under huge stress and he grieved for her and so never chided her when things came unstuck. It was to be expected, after all. She was only learning.

As the months went by, John worried for the girls managing without their mother and was glad of neighbours' help and that of his mother-in-law. He knew he could go to them and ask their advice on how to look after his girls and how to handle Isa. But most other girls forced into caring for their family through the death of their mother settled into it without too much complaint, realising this was what a woman's life was about anyway and that the practice they were getting earlier on in their life would help when they were married themselves. Somehow Isa's resentment was much stronger than any of the others he'd heard about.

But then there had been three deaths within six months. He knew Mary had cherished ambitions for her daughters to do well at school and to take as much education as they could. She had hoped they would get training as governesses, teachers or secretaries, able to earn their living independently and enter more genteel society. Isa had wanted this for herself and could see it happening when she was doing so well at school. Now she was nearly fourteen and all such hopes were dashed. Yet he could see that in lots of ways she had become a very competent homemaker.

What he could not know or see was the constant burden of guilt and pain that plagued Isa's sleep and dreams. Many nights found her again at the side of the track, watching the approach of the train, willing Eliza to stay still and wait for it to pass. But then the train passed and she saw the broken body, torn apart by the train, sprawled across the ground. She carried this stress with her into every day. She was not consciously thinking about it, but the feelings it had re-evoked were the background to most days. It only lifted when she was involved in more demanding tasks, which fully occupied her mind.

Her father wondered about Margaret and Chrissie. This was no real life for them either. Isa was so unpredictable at times that he feared she was not always coping well with the role as substitute mother. He needed to sort this out, but how? They could not impose on neighbours and family any more than they were already doing. After all, they had their own families and difficulties to face. He needed some advice. Maybe he should talk to his sisters-in-law and see what they thought.

He was closest to Tommy and Teenie, so he went there first. When he told them what was happening and how he felt he needed to do something their suggestion shocked him.

'There's a children's hame in Stirling has a good reputation, John. It's run by a woman name o' Crail. Whinhill it's cried. They've a school there an' awthin'. Mebbe we should ging an' hae a look at it, see whit it's like.'

'Oh, Tommy, I dinnae want tae pit my girls in a hame.'

'Well there's naebody in the faimly has room, John, an yer efter sayin' Isa's no managin'. Whit else can ye dae?'

John's head fell to his chest in weariness and despair. 'Aw'richt then. Will ye come wi' me next week tae see whit's whit?'

'Aye, John. I'll ging wi' ye.'

So the two brothers took the train to Stirling and made their way to Whinhill Home. It was indeed a fine building and well equipped and there would be schooling organised. The matron, Miss Crail, was sympathetic to his plight.

'Mr Dick, a man cannot hope to look after his

daughters by himself without his wife. A mother is essential to their upbringing. Here, they would have a housemother who will treat them kindly and guide them with a firm hand. Your two younger daughters would be well provided for here for a reasonable remuneration. Unfortunately we have no place for your older daughter, since we only cater for girls to the age of twelve and as your daughter is fourteen she won't be eligible.'

John was having difficulty taking all this in. 'But whit would happen to my older daughter? It's too late for her tae ging back to the skuill.'

'Might I suggest the domestic-service training school in Glasgow, Mr Dick? A girl can make a very good career in that line. All the best houses are employing bright girls as cooks and house-keepers and if your daughter has been keeping house for you then she already has useful skills in this area. She could earn a good wage and would of course be living in.'

'I'll need tae think aboot it, Miss Crail. I thank ye for yer time,' and he shook her hand.

As he thought about it he wasn't sure it was the right thing. Isa seemed to be coping better, and Margaret and Chrissie were happy, so he decided to leave things be. However, months later, in August 1914, shortly after Isa's fifteenth birthday, world events contrived to force his hand, when it was announced that Great Britain was at war with Germany and all able-bodied men were being en-couraged to enlist in the forces. Although foundry workers were a reserved occupation, John found himself drawn to the idea of getting away from all his troubles and using his strength to defend his

69

country. His volatile drunkenness was not good for the girls and perhaps looking after the family had been too big a burden for Isa. Domestic-service training might be a way for her to build a life more suited to her ambitions. It would be a new start for all of them.

5

Isa was not at all sure about her father's plans. She did not like the idea of Margaret and Chrissie being sent to the home. She and her father had taken them there and seen them settled in the room of little beds, each with a side locker for their things and a laundry basket at the end of the bed for each day's dirty apron and the weekly wash. Although they were both quiet and stood almost woodenly by the beds, holding each other's hands, there had been no tears, both accepting this was what their father had organised. Told they would have to be brave, do as they were bidden and not let their father down, they held in their anxiety as Isa hugged them each goodbye and promised she would see them soon when she had time off. But she felt a strangeness in them as she held them. Isa did not like leaving them, and yet she felt Miss Crail was a good woman who wanted to help children who had fallen on hard times. Many of the other residents were orphans with no parents, whereas Maggie and Chrissie had her and her father and all their relatives. Why had none of their aunts offered to take them in? In fact, why was her father leaving for the war and abandoning them to strangers? But she could not let any of them know she was thinking like this. She told herself that the home would take good care of them.

As she travelled with her father in the train carriage to Glasgow, she was unsure about his arrangements for her. If truth were told, she was frightened about going in amongst students she did not know in an unfamiliar city. She worried about how clever the others would be and that she would appear to be stupid. As they approached the city she could not believe its size. A vast sprawl of factories, foundries, shipyards and tenements appeared in the windows looking most uninviting, the brick and sandstone blackened with soot.

Her father escorted her to the college entrance hall and was allowed no further. Their parting was tense and brief. Isa felt numb. She watched him head through the door and set off to a war everyone said would be over by Christmas. Perhaps they would all be together again in a few months. Somehow she just had to get on with things.

After registering she was shown up to her dormitory, a long, well-lit, wooden-floored room with tall windows along one side, hung with thick black curtains. Each cot bed had a pair of clean sheets, two rolled blankets and a pillow laid on it in a pile, ready to be made up by each girl. A small locker by each bed had a set of drawers in which folded clothing and personal items could be stored. No one else was in the room. The timetable said to report for the first lesson at two, so Isa quickly unpacked her small suitcase into the locker at her bedside.

The Glasgow and West of Scotland College for Domestic Science had been set up with the aim of teaching young girls and older women already married with children how to cook for their families using fresh, cheap, nutritious ingredients. Filling soups with barley, peas or lentils, stews using cheaper cuts of meat, cooked slowly with vegetables, and milk puddings such as rice and semolina were all designed to provide vitamins, calcium and protein in the cheapest form possible. It was intended to improve people's health in the slums. Isa, however, had been producing these basic meals for four years in her father's home. Her six-week course was to prepare young girls like herself to work in domestic service in the big houses, where the cooking would be more demanding, as would the standards of housework. Most of it would be learned on the job.

She tidied her hair, put on a clean apron and headed through to the first class. The door was open and she came in to a long, wooden-floored room with tall windows facing the door. To her left was a series of raised steps with desks and benches. Ahead of her under the windows were sinks and ranges and in the centre of the room were big wooden tables like her grandmother had in the farmhouse kitchen. To her right stood the teacher's podium, desk and blackboard. Isa felt her spirits rise. She was back in a classroom again. There were some other girls sitting at desks already, somewhat stiff and unsure in their starched aprons. Each desk had booklets, pens and ink ready for each student. Isa found a seat beside a rosy-cheeked, dark-haired girl who sat upright on the bench. She smiled at Isa and introduced herself as Bettina Gray.

'But awbody caws me Betty,' she whispered. 'Isn't this excitin'? I'm right glad to be here, awaw frae hame for a bit. I dinna ken hoo ma maw survives. Four wee yins there is the noo and my next oldest sister is just twelve and nae that strang. Still. Whit about you? You're nae frae roond here.'

'Naw. Ah'm frae Falkirk,' Isa said hesitantly. The places were filling up around them.

'Weel. Tell us about yer faimly, then.'

So Isa briefly outlined her situation, not mentioning Eliza or the stillborn brother. It was hard enough to voice the fact of her mother's death, her two sisters put in a home and her father away at the war. As the words came into her mouth to tell this stranger about her life, they felt all wrong.

'Oh,' said Betty, 'That's awfy hard on yez all, so it is. Ah've a big brother awaw in the war but ma da's in a reserved occupation wi' the railway. So he's still at hame wi' us.'

Before Betty could prise anything more out of her, the door swung wide open and in came the teacher, her dark skirts rustling over the wooden floor. The girls all stood to attention at their desks.

'Good afternoon, girls. My name is Miss Mackenzie. This afternoon we will be making baked custards. Please copy the recipe and method from the board.' She turned away from them and picked up a piece of chalk and began writing on the board. Isa and Betty picked up their pens, dipped them in the inkwells and began to copy their first lesson into their books.

After they'd written down the ingredients and the method, Miss Mackenzie then came forward to one of the big kitchen tables and proceeded to demonstrate just how to prepare the custards, calling their attention to the eggs being at room temperature, the glass dishes being placed in a deep oven dish and the eggs whisked with a specific wrist action to avoid the mixture becoming frothy. Then it was their turn. In pairs they came down to the tables, assembled the ingredients, measured them out and followed the teacher's instructions. The oven dish was then filled with an inch of boiling water and the dish of custards carried carefully to the ovens to bake. While this happened, the girls tidied up the tables and took their places at their desks again. Meanwhile, the teacher told them some variations on the recipe, such as how to make the custards savoury rather than sweet and how to flavour them differently, with vanilla, nutmeg or cheese. Miss Mackenzie also informed them that the custards were nutriious light meals suitable even for young children or invalids. This may prove useful to them if helping in the nursery in their employer's home.

Then it was time to check them. Each pair had to fetch their dish of custards and stand beside them while Miss Mackenzie came round to check them. She inserted a clean knife into a sample on each tray and if the knife came out clean they were done. Some had been done with too heavy a hand and had sunk. Others had not set right because the measuring of ingredients had not been accurate. When she came to Isa and Betty she pronounced theirs perfect. Isa was glowing inside. She just knew this was the place for her. She was going to love it here.

Over the six weeks there were lessons on etiquette towards their employers: how to curtsey, keep their gaze low, how to address their employers – Ma'am, Sir, or even Your Lordship or Ladyship if they worked for those so titled. Isa and Betty practised curtseys and bobs with bowed heads and a 'Yes, Your Ladyship', 'No, Your Lordship', and even, in fits of giggles, 'Why, of course, Your Highness', just in case.

Other sessions were held on cleaning. The everyday kitchen cleaning Isa knew inside out but it was new to some of the girls from homes where not much attention had been paid to scrupulous scrubbing. Of course, Isa's grandmother had to have high levels of cleanliness on her dairy farm and this meant her mother's routines had been thorough too.

Some lessons focused on cleaning and polishing of finer furniture and ornaments and on various recipes for cleansers and rubs. Isa used some of these already: white vinegar and salt to clean kitchen surfaces and baking soda to clean the zinc bath. She was intrigued with the mix of lemon juice, olive oil and warm water to polish wooden furniture. It smelled so good. She also loved the tip to remove stains on wallpaper by rubbing bread over the stain to lift off grease and dirt.

Isa began to realise how capable her mother and grandmother were, as she had already learned so much from watching them. She began to feel capable herself, receiving good reports and compliments from her tutors. Freed of the extra responsibility of looking after Margaret and Chrissie, and the emotional burden of her father's bouts of sadness and drinking, she was discovering herself as a person distinct from her father and sisters. She met other girls who had had similar experiences. None had seen a sister die in the way she had, but none were untouched by death, illness and flawed families. She found again the camaraderie she'd had at school.

Occasionally she had a letter from her grandmother telling her about the farm and asking her about her lessons. Isa wrote back with her news about what she was learning and about her new friendships. She also began to write to Margaret and Chrissie, hoping the letters would be read to them although she was sure Margaret would be getting good at reading now. She was coming up for nine and Chrissie nearly seven. So she kept letters short and simple and not too personal, including little funny stories she hoped would make them laugh. She imagined their two heads together on the bed carefully deciphering the words and could hear Chrissie's infectious giggle as she wrote of the day when another girl had taken her soufflé out of the oven. When the girl reached in for it, the soufflé had been perfectly risen and fluffy, but when she laid it down on the cold, marble-topped pastry board, the coolness in the surface transferred into the dish and the soufflé collapsed in on itself. All this happened before the tutor was able to see the fine specimen it had been on first leaving the oven. The girl was crestfallen. She couldn't understand what had happened. She had just turned her back on it to shut the oven door and when she turned round her perfect soufflé had been replaced, by someone jealous of her success, she claimed! The class soon put her right and the tutor showed her where she had left the dish. She was all apologetic and was very careful about the surface she laid her baking on after that.

They were given a holiday late in September and Isa headed off to get a train into Stirling to visit her sisters in Whinhill Home. She had never travelled on her own before and was terribly nervous. She checked over and over that she had her ticket, her money, her gloves and the cake she'd baked the day before in class. She had asked the tutor if she could take it to her sisters. Miss Munro knew about her situation and was especially fond of her pupil, who had clear talent. She felt for Isa, alone with no mother or father around to guide or protect her, and she admired her mature concern for her young sisters left in the home, so of course she agreed Isa could take the rich fruit cake and even found a tin and extra greaseproof paper to wrap it in. Many of the tutors were keen philanthropists, trying to do something to help people trapped in poverty improve their lives. That was often what attracted them to work in the college. They understood and had compassion for the young girls and did everything possible to support them.

The train was busy and Isa had to walk along the platform, staring into carriages to see if there were any seats. Finally she saw one, opened the carriage door and climbed in. She greeted the other passengers briefly and sat down with her cake tin on her lap. The journey to Stirling was not long – under an hour – and she amused herself looking out the window at all she passed: the backs of tenements with washing strung out on pulleys were followed by the factories and mills with their tall brick chimneys belching smoke into the grey dusty air. There was the occasional park surrounded by trees and then the posh, three-storey villa houses of the wealthy, where she might eventually be employed, and then Glasgow was behind them and the fields began.

Isa was lulled by the swaying train and the steady clicking of its passing over the rails. She was concerned about how she would find Margaret and Chrissie when she arrived. Would they be much changed? She was excited to be heading there now to see them face to face. She had written to arrange it all and she was going to be able to take them out. Her father had left an allowance for them and she would use this to give them all a treat.

Stirling was approaching. The young man nearest the door opened it when the train came to a halt and they all descended politely one after the other, the men offering the ladies a hand to step down on to the platform. Isa was shy when the young man near the door offered her his hand as she was used to her father or mother doing this for her, but she accepted it graciously and felt very grown-up doing so.

The home was situated on a hill on the edge of the town and Isa set off to walk there. Carrying the cake tin was quite awkward and she constantly shifted it from one side of her body to the other. When she and her father had accompanied Margaret and Chrissie here a month ago, she had been too concerned about the girls themselves to notice much about the home itself. Now as she came through the gate, she realised what a huge amount of land there was around it. There was an orchard over to the left, lots of grass on all sides, and vegetable plots round the back where she could see some people digging. The house itself was a stout, square-built sandstone building, with bay windows on the ground floor and sash windows on the three upper floors. There were mature beech and elm trees along the drive and everything looked fresh and tidy, as though the house felt a need to take a pride in its appearance. Isa was almost intimidated by it all but she stepped forward bravely, clutching the cake tin and the letter confirming all the arrangements she had made.

She climbed the front steps, rang the bell and waited, her heart pumping loudly in her chest. A maid in a black dress and white cap and apron answered the door and showed her a seat in the lobby, asking her to be so good as to wait for Miss Crail, who would be with her shortly. It was not long before Miss Crail arrived to greet Isa warmly and lead her into a room immediately off the lobby. It was furnished with a dark-green and gold patterned carpet, a desk and chair at the window and several gold upholstered armchairs facing the desk. Isa was beckoned to sit down on one of them, where she perched a little nervously.

'Isa, I am so glad you managed through. Did you have a pleasant journey?'

Isa was aware she had to present herself in the very best light and so she was careful to speak correctly, as she had taken to doing with her tutors in college.

'Yes, thank you, Miss Crail. How are Margaret and Chrissie?'

'Both very well, as you shall soon see. I sent Frances to fetch them. They have settled well and are no trouble at all. I think it helps that they have each other. And how are you, my dear? I hope the college treats you well?'

'Yes, thank you. The tutors are very kind and helpful. I have a cake here I made that they allowed me to bring for Margaret and Chrissie,' and she proffered the tin.

'How lovely, my dear. I shall see they get this for treats. And are you enjoying the course?'

'Very much. It suits me well, I find.'

'I am so glad. I did think having kept house for your father and sisters would stand you in good stead for the course. Ah, here they are,' she broke off, as there was a knock at the door. Isa rose from her chair, heart racing.

Frances opened the door and led in Margaret and Chrissie, holding each other's hands and beaming smiles when they saw her. Then they ran to her and hugged the parts of her they could reach, burying their faces into her in joy. Isa bent down to hug them back with tears in her eyes. She felt relaxed and at peace. This was home, this was her family: the three of them together.

'Now girls, I expect you want to head off for your outing. Have a lovely time and we shall see you at tea time.' So saying, Miss Crail shepherded them to the front door and waved them off. Isa took each of them by the hand and squeezed tight, then they set off down the drive into Stirling. Chrissie and Margaret were desperate to tell of all their exploits and had so much news; there was no end to their chatter. Isa loved it. She felt so much more assured than when she had left them here a month ago. It was good to be their big sister.

'Isa, Chrissie is so clever. You wouldnae believe how often she has her haund up in class or in church ready to answer questions. This Sunday she was answerin' sae mony that Miss Crail had to ask her to not put her haund up for a bit to gie ithers a chance to answer the minister's questions.'

'Gosh, I hope she wisnae tellin' ye off.' Isa did not like the idea of anyone else finding fault with her little sister, especially not the founder and matron of the home.

'Naw, Isa,' smiled Chrissie. 'She tellt me she was prood o' hoo weel Ah wis answerin'. It was jist to let ithers hae a chance in case they kennt the answer tae. So noo I wait a bit, in case. And sometimes someone else can answer. So that gies them the chance to be praised too.'

A gentle lesson in humility, then, thought Isa, and looks like it has been well learned. 'Guid. Ah'm richt gled you're daein' sae weel.'

'And Margaret passed her maths test,' said Chrissie, proud of her sister's achievement.

'Well done, Maggie. Oh I'm sae proud o' you baith. And are you happy?'

'Oh yes. Oor hoosemither, Annie, is lovely, isn't she Chrissie? Like Jessie Macleod. And we hae nice friends in oor room.'

81

'Yes and efter lights-oot we can still whisper to each other and reach over to hold hands because Maggie moved oor beds closer thegither. She pit ma locker on the ither side.'

'And if there's enough light to see by we do the dummy alphabet.'

'The what?' asked Isa, her brows furrowed as she tried to make out what Maggie had said.

'I found it in a book. It's for people who are deaf and dumb to communicate with each other. You use your hands and fingers to make shapes and each shape is a letter in the alphabet. See I'll show you.' Maggie then proceeded to go through a series of shapes touching the fingers and palm of her left hand with the fingers of her right one. Each finger was a vowel, starting at the thumb for A, then index finger for E and so on. Clasped hands were for the letter W. Pinched index fingers and thumb on both hands were brought together like spectacles to make the curved shapes in the capital letter B. It was ingenious. Chrissie had been learning it too and so the two sisters could communicate silently when they did not want to be overheard or when they had a secret to pass on to each other. Maggie was not revealing to anyone else in the home what she had found in the book in the library, but by the end of the afternoon Isa was included in the secret too.

They had reached the town now and Isa suggested they look for somewhere to find lunch. They walked up the main street past a butcher's, a draper's and a small greengrocer's with boxes of fruit and vegetables out on the pavement to tempt his customers in, and finally they found a baker's with a small tearoom attached.

'This will do nicely,' Isa decided. 'Let's see if there's a table.'

She led the way in. The tearoom was popular but there was a nice table near the back, to which the waitress showed them. It was warm inside and there was a quiet background buzz of chatter, so the girls felt comfortable and very posh being out in a tearoom for their lunch. This was a rare event indeed. The waitress brought them a menu.

Isa scanned the card, noticing the prices. She made a quick calculation about what they could afford. 'Let's see,' she said. 'We could have the sausage casserole or the liver and onions. What would you prefer?'

Margaret scowled. 'I really wantit the steak pie,' she said.

'Well,' said Isa, 'that will cost more so you can't have ice cream as well later.'

'That's okay,' she replied. 'I dinnae want ice cream onyway.'

'I do,' said Chrissie. 'So I'll hae sausages. I like them.'

'So do I. I'll have that too,' Isa decided. A smartly dressed waitress came over to take their order and it was not long before the food arrived, steaming hot, on white plates rimmed with silver. The girls all thought this was incredibly exciting as eating out had never been a regular feature of their family life. The waitress arrived again with a pot of tea and a tray of cups and saucers. She put the pot beside Isa and Margaret said, 'You can be mither, Isa.' In the home this phrase was tripped out over and over when someone got the job of pouring the tea, but here it brought upon the sisters a sombre moment of shared loss. Isa organised the cups and saucers, took the teapot firmly by the handle and began to fill them.

'You're a guid mither, Isa,' Chrissie whispered.

Isa looked into her sister's warm brown eyes, her own misty with tears, and smiled. She realised that Chrissie's memory of their mother would be very dim indeed and that in fact she had been the only mother her youngest sister would remember. 'Thank you Chrissie. I think I was very hard on you at times.'

'But you always loved us, Isa.' Margaret squeezed her hand. Isa took both her sisters' hands and they held each other's gaze. Rising within their hearts were memories of the love and tragedy that was woven through their lives, short as they were, and as they sat at the little table in the busy café they were grateful for their togetherness.

Afterwards they walked further along the main street into the park by the river. All too soon it was time to head back up to Whinhill. Over the six weeks that Isa was at college, Margaret began to write her letters, short at first, on sheets torn from the back of her school jotters. She would ask her housemother for an envelope and stamp and post the letter at the bottom of the hill. But then she took to spending her small allowance on notepads and envelopes, and thus began a lifelong habit and love of letter-writing.

Isa loved receiving these letters, telling of their lessons, their friends and exploits. Margaret had an easy, friendly style of writing and describing things, which sounded as if she was in the room talking to you. Isa could just see her and Chrissie in bed at night, whispering to each other after lights-out, or hear Chrissie's giggle when they shared a joke. Although she missed them, she felt sure they were happy and cared for. This allowed her to concentrate on her course and to get high marks for everything.

Miss Munro was impressed. Isa was capable in all areas: laundry, cooking, cleaning. Moreover, she was an organiser. She could see her in charge of a household staff one day. She was polite and intelligent, and she could hide her broad Scots accent when required and speak excellent correct English. So when a request came from London from Lord Tolquhoun of Abernethy's household for a girl to start on the staff of his London house, Miss Munro knew just whom she would recommend for the post.

6

King's Cross Station was enormous. The platform was crowded with passengers and their luggage and those coming to greet them. Porters scooted around, bundling cases and trunks onto their trolleys in teetering piles, tilting them back and pushing them along at some pace, with their owners trailing behind holding on to hats and hand luggage. The hall was filled with steam, as trains let out hoots of arrival, their engines not yet cooled down. The steady clatter, of footsteps, hissing of trains, porters' calls and whistles echoed all around her and Isa stood somewhat bemused with her trunk at her feet, unsure of how to attract a porter's attention. Gradually, as the passengers from her overnight train from Edinburgh dispersed and the steam rose to the high glass ceiling, she got her bearings, spotted a uniformed porter and raised her gloved hand when she caught his eye. Soon her trunk was propped on his trolley and he was leading her down the platform to the main area of the station.

Her instructions said the Tolquhouns' driver would be there to meet her and take her to the house on Cadogan Square. He would be holding a card with her name on it. So she told the porter he was to look out for a uniformed driver. Very shortly she spotted him, the card held in front of him declaring grandly 'Miss Isabella Dick'. He was tall and dressed in grey, with a flat-brimmed cap trimmed with slate-grey ribbon and bearing the Tolquhouns' coat of arms on a badge at the front.

Isa approached shyly. 'Excuse me. I am Miss Dick. I am to start with Lord and Lady Tolquhoun of Abernethy.' She thought they should have their full title since they had given her hers.

He touched his cap. 'Pleased to make your h'acquaintance, Miss Dick. I'm 'Arry Jamieson, chauffeur to the Tolquhouns. I 'as the cab waitin' out front. Follow me please.' He signalled to the porter to bring the trunk out to the cab. Isa was not sure what his first name was. She'd never heard of anyone being called Arry before and assumed she had misheard. Perhaps he had said Larry.

A lovely chestnut mare was in the harness and the cab shone and sparkled in the autumn sunshine. The driver and the porter got her luggage secured. The driver paid the porter, then opened the carriage door for her, flipped out the step and held his hand out to assist her climb. When she was safely sitting on the leather seat he shut the door and climbed up to the driver seat, untied the reins and called, 'Walk on,' to the horse.

Isa could not believe she was sitting in a horse-drawn carriage. She had always walked everywhere in Falkirk and carriages had not even been hired for the funerals. This was such a new experience. She was filled with excitement and leaned forward so she could look out of the window. As they drove through the streets, she looked out at the people: gentlemen with silver-topped canes, top hat and tails; workers with patched jackets and flat caps; ladies with long skirts and fitted peplum jackets, smart in elaborate hats with feathers; poorer women bedraggled in dirty petticoats and black worsted with shawls wrapped round their shoulders. Buildings she'd heard about went past and she gasped as she read the street signs for Oxford Street, Regent Street, Piccadilly and Hyde Park. To her these had previously just been names from books, advertisements and newspapers. They moved away from the crowded areas into the quieter, tree-lined streets of Victorian red-bricked terraced houses in Knightsbridge, their tall windows beautifully dressed in lace, silk and brocade. Finally the carriage drew to a halt outside number forty-two Cadogan Square. It was a five-storeyed building with basement, situated on the corner of the terrace, with bay windows. On the second and fourth floors, these windows led on to railed balconies supporting plants in clay pots. Isa had never seen anything like it.

Five steps led up to a porticoed entrance. Black iron railings ran along the front of the building either side of the steps, except for a short gap to the right of the portico where another series of steps led down to the basement. Jamieson came round to the cab door and opened it, flipped out the steps for a second time and aided Isa down to the pavement. He fetched the trunk down from the rack and then indicated the stairs to the basement. He turned the handle on the brown glossed door at the foot of the stairs and held it open for her.

'After you, Miss Dick,' he said. As he watched Isa gracefully walking along the corridor, head held high, her light auburn hair gilded in the autumn sunshine, his eyes took in her shapely form approvingly. Aye she's a looker. Ye could do worse and that's a fact, he thought.

Unaware she had created such interest in her colleague, Isa walked through the corridor, which was tiled from the floor up to waist height in white glazed tiles, and then painted in white. Where the two surfaces met, there was a row of narrow dark-green curved tiles. Brown lino covered the floor and off the narrow passage she could see several rooms, which Jamieson identified for her as they passed. There was a broom cupboard, where a young maid was filling a basket with polish and cloths ready for her cleaning tasks; a scullery with sinks, where another maid was washing basins and ewers used for early morning ablutions in the bedrooms; a pantry for the butler with a winged armchair, fireplace, books and writing desk; and one she assumed was the housekeeper's, with a chintz-covered chair, fireplace with photographs on the mantle and an open sewing basket, filled with bright threads and tiny scissors. Further along, the corridor opened out into the kitchen, floored with pale-green linoleum, which gave the room a peaceful light despite being in the basement. In central position was the huge deal table at which stood a short, rotund figure wrapped in a spotless white bibbed apron. She had curly brown hair only just tamed by her white mob cap, and her hands were in a large ceramic baking bowl, sifting a butter and flour mixture through her fingers. Isa guessed this was the cook.

The woman turned to look over her shoulder at Isa. Shaking the mixture from her hands and wiping them on her apron, she smiled a broad smile which crinkled the corners of her bright, berry-black eyes and said, 'Ah, you must be the lassie comin' doon frae Edinburgh for to start wi' us. Another Scot like mysel'. Come on in. I'm Mrs Roberts.' She stretched out her hand and Isa shook it, nervous but glad to hear an accent she understood.

'Pleased to meet you, Mrs Roberts. I'm Isabella Dick. But everyone calls me Isa.'

'Isa ye shall be then. Noo. Sit ye doon and we'll hae oorselves a cup o' tea. Harry'll tak' yer trunk up tae yer room, and later one o' the lassies will show ye whaur it is. Right now ye'll be needin' some breakfast in ye efter yer journey. Pull up a chair.'

As Mrs Roberts busied around, making the tea and rustling up some eggs and toast for her, Isa realised the mistake she had made about the driver's name. She looked around her carefully. There was a large porcelain sink at the window, with a wooden drainer to the right. A huge range stove ran the length of the short wall, giving out warmth to the whole room and offering several heats for cooking on different hotplates and ovens. Near it was a basket she assumed contained the wood for stoking the fire at the centre of the range. Rails at the ovens held an array of cream-coloured kitchen towels and oven cloths. Opposite the range was the pantry, lined with cupboards and dressers in which the dry and tinned stores would be kept, and next to it a door she assumed would lead into the cool pantry, which would be tile-lined and used to store fresh food such as fruit, vegetables, fish, dairy foods and meat. Onions plaited onto strings hung from hooks, alongside bunches of herbs, away from the steamy side of the kitchen. She was impressed. It all looked just as she had learned about in class in Glasgow. Mrs Roberts clearly was good at her job.

A plate of eggs and toast was laid in front of her, beside a steaming cup of strong tea, and after a grateful thanks to Mrs Roberts, Isa began to eat, careful not to spill or make a noise or in any way to appear clumsy or inept.

'Nae doot ye'll feel a bit strange the day, Isa, but we all get along fine here and Lord and Lady

Tolquhoun are very fair employers. Ye'll be introduced to them baith in time. Where is it yer from, lass?'

Isa wiped her mouth on the napkin provided and replied, 'I come from Falkirk, Mrs Roberts. I studied at The Glasgow and West of Scotland Domestic College.'

'Ah right. That'll be much like the one in Edinburgh I went tae masel. It's grand tae hae anither Scott here. I can feel quite homesick for the accent, ye ken. Is it yer first time doon tae London?'

'Aye it is, Mrs Roberts. I hiv tae confess I'm no understandin' whit folk are sayin' tae me. I can speak good English but no' like Mr Jamieson.'

'Harry doesnae speak good English, lassie!' Mrs Roberts exclaimed. 'He's a real Londoner. He tones it doon a bit fer His Lordship and Her Ladyship, but he can't even say his own name properly. They all drop their h's down here. Took me some time to get used to, I can tell you. But ye'll soon get the hang of it. Mind you, they'll hae a go at yours. They don't hear much Scots down here. Even though Lord and Lady Tolquhoun are Scots like oorsels they don't talk braid in front of us. So try yer best English. I usually do.' She cast her eye down at Isa's empty plate. 'Feel better now?'

'Oh, yes thank you, Mrs Roberts. It was very kind of you to make me breakfast.'

'Well now, we could hardly be asking you to do a full day's work on an empty stomach, could we?' She dusted down her apron. 'Anyway I'd best get on. The housekeeper, Mrs Williams, will be through shortly to tell you your duties. Mr Westfield, the butler, would normally meet you

91

but he's up in Scotland with Lord Tolquhoun on the estate. No doubt Sally will show you up to your room after she's finished with all the bedroom service.'

Isa wondered if Sally was the young fair-haired maid she saw washing the ewers as she came in. 'Can I be of help to you, Mrs Roberts, while I wait?'

'You can fetch the pitcher of buttermilk in the pantry for the scones, Isa,' suggested the friendly, chatty cook, who had taken a shine to the newcomer. She watched Isa get up and assuredly go to the door next to the dry pantry, locate the pitchers, identify the one with the buttermilk and carefully carry it over to the table, shutting the door behind her. Aye, she thought, she's quick. This lass'll do well. Provided the others don't tease her to death. Just as well she's tae hae a room tae herself. It'll gie her somewhere tae get awaw frae the blighters. And she turned to her mixture, sifting until it was ready for the buttermilk.

When she looked up, Isa had taken the flour shaker and prepared a board and roller ready for the dough. Impressive indeed!

'Ah there you are, Miss Dick.' Isa looked up to see before her on the other side of the table a tall, slender upright figure with grey hair plaited and wrapped tight around her head, dressed top to toe in black, with a belt at her waist from which hung a chain of keys which swayed and clinked as she walked. All of this created the impression of someone used to giving orders and being obeyed. This must be the housekeeper, she thought. She curtsied a little in respect.

92

'My name is Mrs Williams. I am the house-keeper here and you will be working in my team today. I trust Mrs Roberts has seen you had a cup of tea after your journey.'

Isa nodded and was about to say something in reply but Mrs Williams had continued, 'Very well. Let's get you kitted out with uniform and then up-stairs to your duties. This way please.' She turned on her heel and with a swish of her skirts she led the way through a different corridor, running parallel to the one Isa had used to come into the kitchen.

Along this corridor were several doors on the right and at the third, Mrs Williams stopped, knocked briefly and introduced Isa to Miss Higgins the laundress and seamstress. 'Miss Higgins, this is Miss Dick, who needs a uniform for work-ing upstairs. I'll fetch her again in quarter of an hour. Thank you.' Isa was unnerved by the woman's imperious tone and the nice warm calm she'd felt from Mrs Roberts' welcome was ebbing away.

Miss Higgins got up from her chair behind her sewing table and came toward Isa, brandishing her tape measure. As she approached, Isa could see she was being closely scrutinised from beneath arched brows as the seamstress eyed the new-comer. There were no words of welcome from the thin lips aligned as if to sneer. 'Right. Let's see what size you need.' Isa's arms were raised, the measuring tape brought round her chest, then slipped to her waist and lower to round her hips, then from the nape of her neck to her waist and from there to her ankle. In no time, it seemed,

Miss Higgins had decided what size would do and she went to a large wardrobe, where she rummaged through hangers till she found what she was looking for, then through shelves and drawers for caps and aprons. She handed Isa a bundle of clothes and indicated they should be tried on behind a screen. Feeling totally out of her depth and flustered by the hostility she had felt oozing from the seamstress' appraisal of her, Isa was nervous and clumsy with buttons and strings, but the clothes fitted well and she came out looking the part.

Miss Higgins gasped a little. Truth be told, Isa looked amazing in the black serge uniform dress with her striking red hair and milky skin and her upright bearing. Good deportment for a young working lass, thought the seamstress.

'You'll do,' she said. 'Where are you from?'

'I'm from Falkirk,' she blurted out nervously, letting her broad accent escape.

'I'm sorry, from where?' Miss Higgins asked again, smirking.

'Scotland,' Isa tried.

'Oh yeh, the frozen norf.' Isa could not believe it, but she thought she heard the woman snigger. 'Well, you'll soon see how we do fings down 'ere. A civilised nation, we are. Our men don't run around in skirts like girls.'

Isa felt her face flush with shame. Who did this woman think she was to berate her country in this way? She stood speechless, clutching the spare uniform and aprons. Along the corridor she could hear the purposeful stride of Mrs Williams and her keys coming back for her and she turned to face the door. She did not know which would be worse: to stay and face the stinging sarcasm of Miss Higgins, or to be taken off by the imperious, steely-faced Mrs Williams. She felt very lost.

'All set? Let's be off, then. Leave your spare things here. You can collect them after lunch, when Sally will show you to your room. Follow me.' Isa laid her clothes in a pile on a chair and followed the housekeeper out.

They set off up the back stairs and arrived in the front hallway of the house. Isa could not believe her eyes. Her family's home could fit in this hallway, along with their next-door neighbour's. The floor was black and white marble, with an intricate star pattern inlaid in the centre. A beautiful chandelier hung on a long chain from the high ceiling, its faceted glass catching the sunlight and creating tiny rainbows. Stairs led up to a balustraded balcony, from which many doors led off. From either side of the entrance hallway ran two corridors. Mrs Williams led her down the one on the left and into the first room on the left. Isa could hardly contain herself. Persian rugs lay on the floor and a huge mahogany table was polished to a gleaming shine. In the centre, on a lace cloth, stood a silver bowl filled with gold and cream roses whose scent filled the room. Bay windows straight ahead looked out on to the street, but long lace curtains, thickly draped gave the house privacy from the outside world. A large dresser and sideboard stood on her left and trays, decanters and various pieces of crockery stood at the ready for serving meals.

'This is the dining room, Isa, where all family meals are taken.' Mrs Williams spoke brusquely.

'Cutlery and crockery are kept here in the dresser. You will set breakfast and luncheon normally. Today, of course, breakfast has passed. You will also dust and polish here after breakfast each day. Now I want you to show me a setting for luncheon.' And so saying she stood, hands clasped over her starched black dress, and waited for Isa to begin.

Isa tentatively moved over to the dresser, conscious that everything she did was being closely watched for the slightest mistake. She had no doubt that Mrs Williams would have many and awful ways of making you realise you had failed in some small detail. Yet she also remembered she had been recommended for this post by her tutor. She needed to take confidence in having been selected for the job with the Tolquhouns. So she opened the drawers to find table linen, noting where cutlery was for later. She laid out a linen table mat in cream bordered with green, chose a crystal water glass and wine flute and placed them near the top right edge of the cloth, then – approximately twelve inches apart, as she had been taught – she laid the silver fish fork on the left and the fish knife on the right, then the meat fork and knife inside on their respective sides. Along the top of the setting she laid a dessert spoon, with the bowl facing to the left and a dessert fork, with the prongs facing to the right. Lastly she laid a soup spoon on the outside right of the setting. Then she ran through it all. Had she forgotten anything? Of course, a napkin. She returned to the linen drawer and located a matching napkin in cream linen trimmed in green, then hunted in the silver drawer and found a napkin ring through which she threaded the rolled napkin. This she placed to the left of the setting. A last check. She needed a side plate and butter knife for bread which, once retrieved from the dresser, she placed to the left of the setting. She stepped back, her hands held together in front of her.

'Good. And what else would be required on the table?' the housekeeper quizzed her.

'The cruet sets, ma'am, bread basket, water jugs.' Isa thought that was all. She paused.

'Good. Check with cook what is on today's menu just in case finger bowls are required for seafood. Now. When cleaning in here after breakfast you must dust each ornament or piece of crockery carefully and replace it just where you found it. So no lifting everything off at once and then muddling it all. Each object has its place and must be returned there. Understood?'

'Yes, Mrs Williams.' Isa was so relieved. She had passed the first test of her suitability. But there was no time to enjoy the relief, for Mrs Williams was already moving on.

'Right. Off we go.' The next room was a drawing room done in beautiful pastels and creams with a white carpet patterned in reds and blues. The walls were panelled and papered with tropical birds flying on a cream background, their jewel colours echoing those in the carpet. China cabinets displayed exquisite pieces of porcelain and silver. A chaise longue, upholstered in red velvet, was flanked by gilded-backed chairs with satin cushions in pale pink, damson and peach. It was a peaceful, bright, tastefully decorated room and

Isa's senses were thrilled by it. She could not believe such opulence existed. What would her sisters, friends and neighbours think of this?

'You will also dust and polish the drawing room. Same rules apply in here. The items in the cabinets will not be dusted every day. They are taken out and washed once a month but I shall supervise that. Small rugs are rolled and taken to the back garden to be beaten over the washing line on a Friday only. On other days they are swept with a dustpan and brush. Surrounds of course are polished twice a week. Any questions?'

'No, Ma'am.'

'Right then. Back to the kitchen. I'll pair you up with Sally today. She'll sort you out with cleaning materials.' The swishing skirts led the way and Isa dutifully followed. Her mind was full of all the beautiful things she had seen in these two rooms and the hallway. It was like the films. Better. It was in colour. She had no idea people really lived like this. Possibly every house on this square was similar. It was so much to take in.

Back in the kitchen she was introduced to Sally, the girl she had seen in the scullery. She seemed friendly and soon equipped Isa with a basket of cloths and polishes plus a feather duster and then it was off to start her first task of cleaning the dining room. The morning passed quickly and after a lunch of soup, bread and cheese around the kitchen table she was shown her room in the attic.

The back staircase they had used to get from the kitchen to the hall had further sections leading eventually to the attic bedrooms for the staff. Isa could not believe she was to have a room to herself as she had fully expected to share one, even a bed, which was an idea she had not relished. She was used to sharing a bed with her sisters, but it was another matter to share with a stranger. When Sally opened the door on the plainly furnished room, with a tiny window in the sloping roof, she felt a thrill in anticipation of independence and her first taste of privacy. She thanked Sally and shut the door, scanning everything: the bed with its feather quilt and pillow, the small wardrobe for her clothes, the little chest of drawers and the rag rug at the bedside. She sat on the bed and sighed in pleasure. She did not have long, since she would have to set the table for 'luncheon', as they called it, but she took a moment to savour her joy. She should be all right here. She knew she could do the work and she had this lovely room. If only she was not so far from Chrissie and Margaret. But she would write and she would try to visit on her holiday. Both Miss Crail and Miss Munro at the college had told her they would watch out for them and she was not to worry. She stood up, smoothed down her apron and set off for the dining room.

7

Although Isa could speak the King's English and rarely used her Scots vocabulary in her new environment, she was faced with mimicry of her accent, which was soft and had a lilt to it quite different from the London cockney. When she was at the market fetching orders for the household the stallholders understood her and respected her. It was the other servants who constantly imitated her with an exaggerated intonation, or who made her repeat things, insisting they hadn't quite got that, regardless of how carefully she pronounced her words. Then it was worse, of course, because they made out she sounded like a toff and thought she was better than them. Isa had a strong character underneath this shyness of being new, but their teasing hurt her pride. She was already feeling very alone, so far from what was familiar to her. Sometimes, as she came into the kitchen or the scullery, she would hear two or three servants giggling and laughing and when they saw her they went quiet. She began to think they were laughing at her behind her back and rather than intimidate her it was beginning to rile her.

One morning, Isa was in the broom cupboard fetching the polishes and cloths she needed for the morning cleaning. She was bending over to reach a bucket to wash the floors when behind her she heard the door shut.

'Caught you alone at last, Isa,' said a voice behind her. ''Aven't had much chance to chat since you got out of me cab. 'Ow are ye settlin', like?'

She stood up and turned to face him, holding the bucket in front of her. 'Oh, fine thank you, Mr Jamieson. Getting used to the house and the work just fine.'

'Oh now. Why so formal, Isa? You can call me 'Arry. We've been introduced.' Harry took a step nearer and looked her straight in the eyes. 'You've got lovely hair, Isa. I'd love to see it down.'

Isa brought the bucket she held up to her waist, instinctively protecting herself and keeping some space between her and Harry. She had no idea how this was going to go. Completely naïve about men, having no brothers and spending most of her time with her sisters and then at the girls' college, she did not have a flirtatious bone in her body and had no idea how to play the game Harry had embarked upon. She felt frightened.

Harry moved towards her and took her elbows. 'Pity it's so cramped in 'ere. We could have us a bit of a dance. Bet ye'd look good in a nice dancing frock wi' yer hair all up and no cap on it.' He moved as if to touch her hair when there was a gasp as Isa pushed the metal bucket against his diaphragm and winded him. As he bent over, clutching himself, she pushed past and wrenched the door open. She ran along the corridor straight into Mrs Roberts coming out of her pantry.

'Goodness, Isa. What on earth are you doing? Ye can't go running along these corridors like that.' Then she looked into the girl's face. 'What's happened, lass? What's upset you so?'

Before Isa had a chance to say anything, Mrs Roberts looked over her shoulder and saw Harry come out of the broom cupboard, bent over and shocked as he looked after Isa. Mrs Roberts did not need any explanation now. It was all quite clear: Harry had been flirting with Isa and the poor girl had had no idea how to deal with him. She'd known the lass would have a hard time with the staff: teasing, mimicry ... and now pestered by Harry Jamieson. She put her arm on

Isa's shoulder and led her into her pantry and shut the door.

'Sit down, lass,' she said. 'You don't need tae tell me whit happened. I saw Harry Jamieson come out the broom cupboard. He wis pesterin' ye, wasn't he?' Isa nodded. 'The blighter. He's like that wi' aw' the girls. He winnae hurt ye, Isa. It's jist his way. But he shouldnae hae done that tae ye when he could see fine ye were nae used tae they goin's-on. He's all right really, means well, but too much of an eye for the girls. The others are all used to him and are playful back at him. Ye'll need tae watch yer back, Isa.'

Out in the corridor, Harold Jamieson had seen the protective arm go round Isa's shoulder as Mrs Roberts took her into the pantry. She was different, this Scots lass, obviously not one for messing around with. Well, maybe there were other ways he could attract her attention.

About three weeks after Isa's arrival, Mrs Williams came down to the kitchen as they were taking their morning tea. She was holding a black cloth in her hand and her face was set the firmest Isa had yet seen it.

'Who cleaned the drawing room this morning?' she demanded. Isa stood up and said, 'I did, Mrs Williams.'

Mrs Williams then laid the cloth on the table and opened it out to reveal a broken porcelain shepherdess figurine. There were gasps round the table as all eyes focused first on the damaged figurine and then on Isa's blushing face. Isa could not understand this. She recognised the figurine, but it was kept in one of the cabinets by the window and

she had not dusted inside since that was not her
job.

'I thought I distinctly told you Isa, that the contents of the cabinets were not to be touched.' Isa
was speechless but nodded her head. Mrs Williams' chilly tones had frightened her, making her
almost feel guilty. What was going to happen
now? But she knew it was nothing to do with her.
Suddenly anger flooded her veins as she thought,
I am not to blame so I will just have to stand up
for myself, because no one else will.

She looked straight into Mrs Williams' eyes and
slowly and firmly stated her case. 'Mrs Williams,
I can assure you I did not open nor have I ever
opened the cabinet to touch or dust anything in
it. That figurine was whole and undamaged when
I left the room. I know your instructions were not
to clean those pieces and therefore I have not
done so. I will not be blamed for something I did
not do. There must be another explanation for
this damage.'

The faces round the table registered shock and
disbelief: Isa, the newest staff member, from
north of the border, if you please, standing up to
Mrs Williams. They could not believe it. This was
unheard of. No one dared disagree or argue with
the housekeeper.

Mrs Williams herself was nonplussed. Staff did
not answer her back. Who did this girl from Scotland think she was? She was about to tear a strip
off her when she looked again at the girl's face.
Although she had said her piece calmly and in a
controlled way there were now tears rolling down
her cheeks and her lip was quivering. Mrs Wil-

liams had seen plenty of dramatics from staff over the years, but this girl was something quite different. She had courage and she was honest. She could see that in how the girl had conducted herself over the issue.

But she herself needed to save face.

'Come with me please, Isa,' she said, and she led the way through to her parlour on the back corridor.

Isa pushed back her chair and left the kitchen without saying a word.

In the kitchen the servants waited till they were both out of earshot and then the room was buzzing with their comments.

'Well, what d'you make of 'at?' said Sally, her eyes wide in disbelief. 'Isa definitely did the drawing room this morning.'

'She admitted that 'erself. But God she was convincing in her "I didn't do it" speech,' sniggered the kitchen maid Elsie, her hair tumbling out of her cap and her apron as scruffy as always.

Miss Higgins smirked spitefully, delighting in the thought that had come to her. 'I don't fink she'll be 'ere this afternoon once dragonface has finished wiv 'er. The nerve of 'er. Can tell she's a rookie. Got no idea about 'ow fings work down 'ere. Can't go round arguin' wiv the 'ousekeeper and get away wiv it.'

Harry leaned back thoughtfully in his chair and slurped another mouthful of tea, his features tense. He said nothing.

'Enough, the lot of you,' interrupted Mrs Roberts at the head of the table. 'She's worth ten of you. Don't you see that took courage? She could

104

only do it because she knew she was telling the truth. Mrs Williams will see that. You mark my words. Someone else is to blame. I just hope they weren't trying to fit her up. Now, tea's over. Get back to your work.' She started to gather the teacups from the table and took them across to the sink.

In Mrs Williams' room, once the door was shut, a chair was indicated for Isa to sit down. Isa took a handkerchief from her pocket and dried her eyes. Her body was tense and she was shaking all over, but in her mind she felt she had done the right thing. If she lost the job then too bad, she would have to find another, but she was not going to become a liar for anyone. She had to stay true to herself. She would have to stay calm and stick to her story. There would be no false confession from her.

Mrs Williams sat opposite her in an upright chair, her hands on her lap, the cloth with the figurine on a small table beside her. 'Isa,' she began. 'I am sorry. Clearly you have spoken the truth. I do not believe it was you who broke the shepherdess.'

Isa could hardly believe her ears. She was believed. She was not to be held responsible. Relief flooded her. 'Mrs Williams, thank you.'

'You were right to defend yourself, Isa. When we know we speak the truth we have nothing to fear. Did anyone else work with you in there this morning?'

'No, Mrs Williams. Sally was checking what I was doing up till last week but she lets me do it all by myself now. I am so sorry about the figurine. I always thought it was so pretty.'

'It is also very expensive. Her Ladyship will not be pleased. However, you are not to worry about that. I am very pleased with your work here and glad you had nothing to do with this business. Now, I shall allow you to get back to your duties. I need to do some further investigating. That will be all, Isa.'

Isa curtsied. 'Thank you, Mrs Williams.' She left the room and shut the door behind her. Her legs felt like jelly after all the stress she had been under in the short space of time: accused of breaking an expensive ornament, forced to defend herself and then called to the housekeeper's room, only to be told she was reprieved. Mrs Williams and Mrs Roberts were 'people of quality', as her mother had often called such folk. You could trust them, they were honest, respectable and genuine. They may be tough on you but they were straight. And she had earned their respect. The thought stiffened her spine and strengthened her legs and she re-entered the kitchen with her head held high, her footstep firm.

'Well, Scotty. Give ye yer books, did she?' The seamstress made no attempt to hide the sneer in her voice as she gathered up linen for mending.

'Indeed not, Miss Higgins,' Isa replied coldly. 'Mrs Williams knows I am not guilty of causing any damage and that the culprit is still to be found. Excuse me. I have work to do.' She glided past her to the back stairs to attend to laying the table for luncheon.

Watching her cross the room, Harry felt glad she was still here. He had not relished the thought of her disappearing out of his life so soon.

Gathered around the kitchen table in the evening ready for their supper, Isa realised Harry and Polly Higgins had made the others aware of the situation. She could palpably feel the enmity towards her from Sally and Elsie who clearly believed she was guilty and that somehow she had wrapped 'dragon-face' Williams around her finger. Mrs Roberts dished out plates of mutton stew and they were to help themselves to potatoes and turnip out of bowls on the table. Isa could not reach a bowl of potatoes and no one made to pass one to her so she was going to make do with the turnip rather than have to make a request of anyone. She got on with her meal, quietly hugging to herself the knowledge of Mrs Williams' respect for her and what she had said about having nothing to fear when you speak the truth. The others would eventually see this. She just had to 'bide her time' as her father would say. Then Harry passed her a bowl of potatoes. She looked up at him in surprise and mouthed a silent thank you.

The butler, who had been with Lord Tolquhoun on his estate in Scotland, was present for the first time since Isa's arrival and introduced himself, breaking the silence. 'Isa, I am Mr Westfield, butler to Lord and Lady Tolquhoun. Delighted you have joined us here and sorry I was not here earlier to welcome you. I am sure Mrs Roberts and Mrs Williams have settled you in. I believe you are from Mrs Roberts' part of the country?' He was giving her an opportunity to speak. Well, she would not hesitate. There was no need to hide or apologise for her birthplace.

'Yes, sir, they have indeed welcomed me. I come from a town called Falkirk between Glasgow and Edinburgh. This is my first time in London.'

'Indeed.' He smiled to her at the far end of the table from where he and Mrs Williams sat as the chief authority figures on the staff, with Mrs Roberts sitting nearby on their right. There was a very definite hierarchy in the seating arrangements below stairs and Isa, as the new girl, was at the bottom of the heap.

'And do you have family there, Isa?' Mr Westfield continued.

Isa was not ready to talk about this in much detail in front of all the others, but she could hardly ignore the butler's question. 'Yes, sir, I have two sisters who at present live in Stirling and several aunts and uncles in Falkirk itself.'

'Your parents?' he enquired with a quizzical raise of his eyebrows.

Isa paused, continuing to look at her plate. 'My mother died four years ago and my father has gone to the war, sir.'

There was a hush in the room. Mr Westfield coughed slightly to hide his embarrassment at having put this young girl on the spot in front of everyone. 'Well, we are glad to have you in the household, Isa.' A change in conversation was needed. He turned to Mrs Roberts to compliment her on the stew.

'Thank you, Mr Westfield. I'm sure it would have been better if it had been a nicer cut of lamb, but mutton was all we could get today. Thank goodness for the carrots and onions from the garden and Fred's herbs. Wouldn't have much flavour otherwise.' And so the conversation around the table turned to the usual hubbub, giving Isa the chance to merge into the background of things.

When she was finally in her room that night she could not believe the day she had had. Often at this time she would write letters to her sisters or her grandmother, but tonight she was in too much turmoil. She knelt at the side of her bed, looking up to the window in the roof that was angled so that no buildings or streets were seen, only a tiny patch of sky. She wanted to pray, but she could not put into words how she was feeling, so she just let it all flow through her: her anxiety about being accused of damaging the ornament, the rage and pride that had led to her self-defence, the relief of being believed and respected, the sneering of the staff and the pain of revealing her situation to these strangers. She laid her head on the quilted bedspread and wept. As her sorrow seeped from her, she became aware of a calming presence around her, formless yet knowing. It felt as though her sorrow had been shared. The sobbing ceased. She felt drained but cleansed, freed of the emotions of the day and more at peace. Slowly, her limbs heavy and clumsy, she undressed and fell exhausted into bed, where she slept deeply until morning.

8

Mrs Williams was sitting in her pantry the next day after the evening meal when there was a gentle knock on her door. 'Come in,' she said crisply. As the untidy head of Sally appeared round the door edge she added, 'What can I do for you, Sally?'

The girl curtsied a little, respectful of the room's occupant, who so often had scolded her for this or that not done just exactly how she wished.

'Mrs Williams, I am sorry to disturb you but I 'ave somefing to tell you.'

She hesitated, not sure she could find the right words. 'It's about that h'ornament.'

Ah, thought Mrs Williams. The confession she was looking for at last. 'Do go on, Sally.'

'Well. I was doing the drawing room today and when I comes over to the cabinet to dust the top. I looked inside the cabinet and the h'ornament is back in its place as right as ninepence, ma'am. I had to look for ages cos I couldn't believe me eyes, bu' it is there, right next to the shepherd it matches.'

The housekeeper stared at the girl in utter disbelief. 'Sally, if as you say the shepherdess figurine is back undamaged in the china cabinet in the drawing room,' and she paused, 'just what do you think this is?' She took from the drawer in her bureau the black cloth she had brought that day to the kitchen and there, nestling in its folds, lay the shepherdess figure, still in its broken state.

'Mrs Williams,' whispered the girl, 'you must believe me. It's back upstairs. I don't know what that fing is bu' it's not Lady Tolquhoun's shepherdess.'

Mrs Williams could not understand the girl's persistence, but she knew what they needed to do now. 'Come on, girl. Show me.'

In the drawing room, Sally led the way across to the window and to the china cabinet and there, clearly displayed in its usual place beside the shepherd boy, stood the delicate shepherdess with her crook, ruffled pink skirts and bonnet, a tiny lamb curled at her feet. At first relief flooded Mrs Williams, as she realised there would be no need now to tell Lady Tolquhoun one of her favourite porcelain pieces had been broken, nor to doubt her faith in Isa's innocence. However, what did it all mean? What was this broken ornament she held in her hand? Why had it been left to look as if someone had broken it? Who had a devious mind to think up such a prank and to endanger others' employment as a result? These thoughts were as uncomfortable as her original ones regarding breaking the news of the damage to Her Ladyship.

'Thank you, Sally, for noticing this. You have saved a lot of trouble calling on the wrong doors. Well done for being so observant. Not a word of this to anyone. I'll deal with it in the morning. That will be all.'

'Yes, Mrs Williams. Thank you, Mrs Williams.' Sally returned to the kitchen and Mrs Williams stood holding the cloth that was now the evidence in a completely different story she needed to fathom out.

It was clear the culprit had to be someone able to buy the replica, intending to break it and then plant it where it could be found, where indeed she herself had found it under the folds of the curtain hems, which trailed the ground at the windows. The more she thought the more she realised there really was only one possible culprit.

'You wanted to see me, Mrs Williams?'

'Yes, Harry. Do come in. We need to have a chat. I believe you used to live near the market. Indeed you have some relatives who trade there.'

'That's right, ma'am.'

'In particular you have a cousin who runs a stall selling second-hand bric-a-brac.'

'Right again,' he said.

'Well, Harry, I wondered if you could have him value this for me,' and she opened out the black cloth on the side table near her chair to reveal the china shepherdess which she had glued together. Mrs Williams could see a faint red blush creeping over Harry's normally pale skin. 'I'm afraid she did have a little accident recently and you can see some hairline cracks, but nonetheless I think she might still be valuable. In fact it is quite possible your cousin may even recognise her.'

Harry sighed, 'All right, Mrs Williams. Game's up. Yer on to me, right enough. I just fought it would be a bit of a lark, like. I fought Sal or Isa would find it and she'd just get teased a bit below stairs and then I'd come clean. I never wanted to cause all this fuss.' He tried an apologetic smile, hoping to charm his way out of this.

The housekeeper fixed him with her fiercest stare. 'Harold Jamieson, how dare you trifle with other people's employment. You nearly cost a young girl her job and livelihood, just for a lark? I think not. I will be informing Her Ladyship about this matter. That will be all.'

When the door had shut, Mrs Williams sank back into her chair. How was she going to sort this out?

The cook and housekeeper to the Tolquhouns had both held their posts for over two decades. They knew and respected each other and worked together on most staff matters, often sounding each other out before taking things to Mr Westfield. Regarding Isa, they were agreed that changes needed to be made. Mrs Roberts called Isa into her parlour at the end of dinner next day. She looked at the girl and pondered for a bit. 'How much cooking have you done, Isa?'

'I've been cooking for my family since my mother died and I was trained in cookery at the college as well.'

'I knew fine ye were no novice the way ye kent whaur the cool pantry would be and could identify the buttermilk.'

'My grandparents have a dairy farm in Tullibody so we're used to all that.'

'Well, I'm goin' tae ask that you help me in the kitchen and that useless Elsie can ging up the stairs wi' her polishin' cloth, for she hasnae a clue. I've tae tell her a'thin' twice and even then she gets in a muddle. Dae ye think ye could cope?'

It was all agreed while Isa waited in Mrs Roberts' pantry. Both older women felt Isa had had a rough deal from the other staff and realised keeping her in the kitchen would provide a safer environment and one where she could fully use her skills. After all, most girls could lay a table and polish floors, but not all could learn to make a soufflé or roast beef to perfection. They would see how Isa did under Mrs Roberts' tutelage. At least it would give her a bit of respite from the vindictiveness of the servants.

Lady Tolquhoun prided herself on keeping good staff, looking after them and taking an interest in their well-being. She saw it as part of her duty as a member of the wealthier classes, just as she considered it important to tend to the poor. Her husband was also mindful of the plight of others through his work in the House of Lords. As a Liberal peer he was instrumental in getting Lloyd George's legislation passed, which could lead to improvements in the lives of the country's poorest citizens: bills connected with factory reform, minimum wages, tax allowances for children to help families on low incomes and pensions for those over seventy.

When Rowena Williams appeared at Lady Tolquhoun's study and asked if she could have five minutes of her time on a staffing matter, she happily laid aside her correspondence and beckoned Mrs Williams to be seated.

'What can I do for you, Mrs Williams?'

'Well, Your Ladyship. I thought we had found a broken porcelain ornament knocked over by one of the domestic staff, but it turns out all the ornaments are in fact safe and in their rightful places.'

'I don't understand. There is still some problem?'

'Indeed. The problem is not careless damage but rather deliberate framing of a member of staff. The broken ornament I found was deliberately purchased and broken to implicate the new girl from Scotland who's been with us nearly a month now. I'm afraid to say one of our staff thought it would be a lark to frame her.'

'So who is the culprit, Mrs Williams?'

'It's Harry Jamieson, the chauffeur, Your Ladyship.'

There was a silence. Mrs Williams knew that Harry was a very capable driver who had worked for the Tolquhouns for three years now. It may well be that Her Ladyship would not like having to take action on this. She had had to tell her. What he had done could have tarnished the young girl's reputation and even cost her this job. It would have been difficult for her to find another position with neglectful damage written as the reason for dismissal on her reference. That was definitely a step too far in her book. It was up to Her Ladyship now. She had said her piece.

'I have here the broken ornament that he planted, Your Ladyship. You can see it looks at first glance like the shepherdess in the drawing room cabinet, but it is in fact a cheap replica he got from his cousin's market stall.'

Lady Tolquhoun sighed. 'Leave that with me, Mrs Williams. How is the new girl taking all this?'

'She has courage and stood up for herself with dignity, Your Ladyship. I think she has great backbone. Mrs Roberts and myself decided she'd be better working in the kitchen, where we can keep an eye on her. The others have given her a bit of a hard time.' Here she paused, not sure how much to tell her employer. However, knowing the Tolquhouns to be fair-minded, she continued, 'I'm not sure if you were aware, Your Ladyship, that Miss Dick lost her mother four years ago and her father has gone to the war. She's virtually an orphan and her young sisters have been put in a children's home in Stirling up in Scotland.'

Lady Tolquhoun looked her housekeeper in the eye. 'Poor girl. I think I had better introduce myself. Do ask her to come and see me when you return to the kitchen. Perhaps you could escort her up, Mrs Williams. My husband will see Harry later. No word to him about this, if you don't mind, thank you.'

'Certainly, Your Ladyship.' Mrs Williams closed the door behind her and headed off to the kitchen to fetch Isa.

When Isa was told the news she was shaking. She realised that Harry Jamieson was a longer-serving member of staff and that she was just the newcomer. Despite Mrs Williams' assurances that she had got to the bottom of everything and that nothing had been broken after all, Isa was trembling when she arrived at the door to Lady Tolquhoun's study on the first floor. She had never been here before and the whole summons had about it a terrifying mystique. Still she knew she had done nothing wrong and therefore had nothing to be ashamed about and nothing to hide. She must hold her head high and trust Mrs

Williams' interpretation of events. She knocked gently on the door.

'Come in,' she heard, and turned the handle. 'Ah, you must be Isa.' Lady Tolquhoun greeted her smiling. 'I have heard very good reports of you from Mrs Williams which makes me so sorry to hear about this horrid prank of Harry's. My husband and I shall be dealing with that matter later. I believe you came down from Scotland.'

'Yes, Your Ladyship.' Isa curtsied.

'And apart from this little trial are you settling in?'

Isa in fact loved the housework and even more so the work in the kitchen. She felt Mrs Williams and Mrs Roberts were true allies and though the others were hard going she felt she was beginning to earn their respect, so it was quite truthfully that she answered, 'Yes, thank you, Your Ladyship. Mrs Williams and Mrs Roberts especially have been very kind. I am enjoying the work.'

'Good. Now, when you are with us so far from home and with your father away in the war, I do hope you will look upon Lord Tolquhoun and myself as your protectors. If there is anything we can help you with, you must not hesitate to ask.'

Isa could hardly believe her ears. Lord and Lady Tolquhoun offering to look out for Isa Dick from Falkirk. What would her father say about that, or her neighbours back on Sunnyside in Camelon? She was lost for words at first, then remembered her manners. 'Thank you, Your Ladyship. That is most kind of Your Ladyship and much appreciated.'

Lady Tolquhoun was amazed at the girl's bearing. Despite her youth and her working-class background, someone somewhere had taught her carefully. Most of the London staff would do well to take a leaf out of her book. This girl was definitely worth holding on to.

'Well, Isa, if there's nothing else? I had best let you get back. It has been nice to meet you and I do hope you will be very happy here.'

Isa curtsied again. 'Thank you, Your Ladyship.' In somewhat of a daze she left the room quietly, shutting the door behind her.

The following morning, when the staff breakfast was finished, Harry came over to her.

'Excuse me, Miss Dick. Migh' I 'ave a word?'

Isa was embarrassed at this public approach in front of the staff, but she caught Mrs Roberts nodding across to her and realised it must have been permitted by her.

Isa got up and followed Harry through to Mrs Roberts' parlour, where Harry left the door open and turned to face her, his head hung low.

'Isa, I was seen by His Lordship last night and told I could lose me job. I've served the Tolquhouns for three years now and they've no complaints about my work: never a scratch on the carriages, horses well looked after, routes carefully planned, always smartly turned out. But they've docked a day's wages off me for what I did to you and I'm heartily sorry. I never fought it might mean you could lose your job. I s'pose I hoped for tears or a tantrum or somefink and then I'd tell you what I'd done. I never fought dragonface would find the wretched thing.' He ventured to raise his head to look at her face. 'Isa, please forgive me for bein' so stupid and unkind. I want to stay here and I want us to get along.' Here he paused. 'Can we start again, do you fink?'

'What do you mean, "start again"?'

'I want to show you I'm really a decent bloke. I wants us to be able to work alongside each other. I don't want us to be h'enemies.'

'As long as there's no more messing about like in the cupboard that day. I don't want that. I won't put up with that, Harry.' Isa thought she might as well make things clear when she had the chance.

'I'm really sorry.' There was another pause, then he dared to look up at her. He wiped his hand on his trousers and held it out to her. 'Friends?' he asked tentatively.

Isa waited a second or two, looking in his eyes and then at his hand. There seemed no point in being enemies and she didn't want the rest of the staff hating her for threatening Harry's employment. Besides there was a new deference in his manner towards her that seemed genuine. He appeared to have realised the possible effects of his 'prank'. She shook it. 'Friends,' she said.

Harry breathed a sigh of relief. 'Fank you, Isa. You won't regret this. I'm going to make it up to you. You'll see.'

9

It was October 1914 when Lord and Lady Tolquhoun received a telegram informing them that their son, Simon, who was serving with the Gordon Highlanders regiment, had been taken prisoner by the Germans. It was the talk of the kitchen for the next few days, as most of the staff knew him. Many, like the cook, the housekeeper and the nanny, had known him since he was a boy. Isa saw the shock etched on the faces of her employers a few days later when the staff were assembled to see them in their full regalia, ready to leave for the State Opening of Parliament. They were both pale and drawn and there was a sadness in their eyes.

The staff, in their various greys and faded blacks, with white caps and aprons or black ties, were all lined up in the hallway, shoes polished, hands scrubbed and held crossed in front if female, clasped at the back if male. Both Lord and Lady Tolquhoun came down the grand stairway, their scarlet velvet robes rippling over each step, the ermine collar and trim snowy white with the regular spots of black sealskin. They both wore coronets encrusted with crystals and gems whose every facet sparkled in the light from the gas-lit chandelier. This was a first for Isa and it took her breath away. Other staff members were used to the annual ritual but for Isa it was as if she was in the presence of royalty. It put her in mind of all those curtsies she and Betty had giggled over in training and made her want to address her employers as 'Your Majesties'. Yet these were the people who had said they would be her protectors whenever she needed them. Quite unbidden, she found tears welling in her eyes and a constriction in her throat. Her father would be so glad to know she was here under their safe patronage. She hoped he too was safe. She bowed her head and curtsied deeply as they passed her. Truly these were people worthy of their titles and worthy of her respect.

Christmas was approaching and so began a very busy time, with preparations of Christmas puddings, cakes and preserves underway. Despite the war there was no shortage of foodstuffs. From the estates in Scotland they had received hares for jugging and several brace of pheasant and, for the main course, a massive haunch of venison. Fred's vegetable garden had been harvested, the carrots layered in sand boxes for the winter, the apples laid out in the attic and potatoes in sacks in the cellar. Mrs Roberts had preserved plums and pears back in September, when there was a glut in the orchard, and these would now be opened to provide colour and contrast with the heavier puddings. Isa had been helpful in making crowdie and cheese, using her knowledge from the farm. All in all there would be a worthy feast.

Following the fashion set by the royals, which had started with Prince Albert, a huge Norwegian spruce had been set up in the hallway, its topmost branches scraping the ceiling. Staff had assisted the family with its decoration, which had taken hours. Hundreds of tiny coloured wooden and silver ornaments twirled on its branches in amongst yards and yards of ribbons and silver garlands. Candle holders had been fitted to the lower branches and the candles would be lit on Christmas Eve. Isa loved it: the tangy smell of the pine needles, their dark blue-green a perfect backdrop for all the shiny colour of the decorations.

Isa was terribly excited, because on Boxing Day the staff would be presented with a box to take home to their families and she was taking the train up to Stirling to see her sisters for two whole days. The Tolquhouns were to be guests of the Hamiltons for a seven-day period and were releasing most of the staff for that time, since they would not be needed in Cadogan Square. The thought of seeing her sisters and of being in Scotland with the comforting familiarity of landscape and tongue around her kept Isa buoyant and cheerful.

Christmas Day itself was a day of intense work for the staff at Cadogan Square. Upstairs the main reception rooms had to be thoroughly cleaned and dusted, the dining table set with elaborate white linen cloths, damask napery folded into swan shapes and the best silver cutlery polished and laid at each place setting for the five-course dinner, which was being prepared in the kitchen. Long fronds of ivy and white lilies were garlanded on the table and the low silver urn centrepiece was filled with dark laurel greenery, white lilies and chrysanthemums tumbling in all directions and splaying on to the white cloth. Small red poinsettia

122

plants in silver pots were placed strategically in amongst the white flowers in striking contrast. It was spectacular.

Downstairs had been a hive of activity since four in the morning. As well as the big early dinner for family and guests, there was the elaborate breakfast and cold supper buffet. All had to be prepared, served and cleared up afterwards.

The ovens were on all day, grilling the breakfast kidneys, bacon and sausages, and roasting the pheasants and venison for the dinner. Thankfully the ham and roast beef, which would be served in the cold supper buffet, had been cooked and chilled the day before. The kitchen maids were stirring pans on the stove from morning to night. First it was the porridge and scrambled eggs for the breakfasts; then the pan of soup for staff lunch. Their fingers were numb from peeling vegetables all morning. Then towards dinner there was more soup, cream of cauliflower, which Isa had had a hand in preparing. It was velvety, creamy and slid down like silk, according to Mrs Roberts when she tasted it. The Brussels sprouts, carrots and potatoes steamed away, while parsnip and beets had been added into the roasting pan, soon followed by the parboiled potatoes. Next it was gravy for the meats and vanilla sauce for the pudding that needed stirred. The kitchen was very hot and sweat was dripping from their faces, but the atmosphere was good. Mrs Roberts had everything organised. All was going according to plan and so there was a positive feel despite all the hard work. There was enough space for each to move about their tasks without getting in each other's way and all were willing to follow instructions. They knew too that they would have a share in what they had prepared.

Upstairs, the butler, Mr Westfield, was kept busy ensuring everything was served properly on the right dishes, that the correct wines were offered at each course to complement the food, that glasses did not remain empty and that dirty plates were carefully cleared away. It was a relief when the coffee and petit fours were served and the ladies withdrew, leaving the men to their brandy and the staff to the clearing up.

When the washing up was done from upstairs, the staff sat round the kitchen table and made a feast of what was left of the dishes. There was Isa's lovely cauliflower soup sprinkled with cheese. Next came roast venison with trimmings of vegetables, roast potatoes and gravy. And finally the Christmas pudding and vanilla sauce. Lord Tolquhoun had given Mr Westfield instructions to ensure the staff had wine and so they did. It was a very happy feast. But everyone was very tired. When all was carefully cleared away and stored, Mrs Roberts signalled for Isa to follow her through to her parlour.

'Come in, Isa. I wanted to give you a little something.' She reached into her bureau and drew out a small package wrapped in tissue paper and narrow red ribbon. 'Here. I hope you like it.'

Isa was overcome. Presents had never been a big thing in her family. They had an orange and a threepenny bit and maybe a pennyworth of sweets in a twist of paper in their stockings. Carefully she undid the ribbon and opened the tissue paper and there at its heart she found a beautiful needle case in tooled leather. Inside was a tiny pair of scissors, rows of needles, tiny spools of thread and a thimble. 'Thank you so much, Mrs Roberts. This is beautiful. You have been so kind to me. I never would have lasted here without your kindness...' She put her finger up to her eye to catch a tear.

'Now, now. You have done very well, my dear. You've got talent, you have. You need to concentrate on your cooking. That's where you can make a decent living for yourself. You'll be in charge of a kitchen yourself one day, that's for sure. Now it's time we were both in our beds. You've a big journey ahead of you tomorrow, my girl. So have I.'

'Thank you, Mrs Roberts. You trusting me has meant the world to me.' And after a brief hesitation, Mrs Roberts moved to hug this capable, sensitive girl who to all intents and purposes was alone in the world. Isa realised she was in a safe place here under the Tolquhouns' roof and protection and with Mrs Roberts as an ally. Things were turning out well.

Her brief time in Scotland was spent in the family house, which was freezing from being unused. She soon had the range lit and huddled close, still wearing her travelling coat. Isa felt somewhat sad back in the house without her father and without Margaret and Chrissie. Her life seemed on hold, somehow, up here. In London she had tasks and constant goals to do everything better and become more skilful. There were people around her and a buzz of activity. Here she was on her own with no clear purpose in the house and too much needing done.

The first night she lay in the double bed in the room she had shared with her sisters. Tired from the work at Cadogan Square and the long journey north, she fell asleep quickly under the warmth of the heavy quilt. In her dreams she was in a beautiful field so green she ached with the pleasure of it, warm sun on her back and her hair loose around her shoulders, hanging in waves to her waist. She could hear voices around her, happy and distant. She ran her fingers through the meadow grass and noticed now it was thick with daisies. She began to pick them and thread them to make chains for her hair and neck. She lay back in the lush grass and breathed happiness. Opening her eyes, she saw three smiling faces around her, made rosy by the sunshine. A dearly loved voice she had missed so much called her to get to her feet. Hands tugged at her until she was upright. Within her a nagging fear had begun to build in the pit of her stomach. She wanted inexplicably to stay where she was, with her lovely sisters in this grassy meadow, forever. Yet they had succeeded in pulling her to her feet and now, joined together, they were running towards the fence and the embankment. She should be enjoying this togetherness, this freedom. Why was she so leaden, so fearful? She could see the fence at the edge of the field and beyond that the railway line. Foreboding filled her with dread. Why did she feel this way?

They were through the gate now and scrambling down the embankment. She held Chrissie in her arm on her left hip and held on to Margaret with her right hand. They crossed the line and started up the other side. She got them safely into the passageway behind the cottages and turned to speak to Eliza but she was not behind her. She felt herself sweating in fearfulness when she saw her sister still on the opposite embankment. At the same moment she became aware of a train coming round the bend. She heard herself yell, 'Stay there!' She saw Eliza continue down the slope. She turned to check on the train, only yards away now. Turned back to Eliza in time to see her trip and lose her footing, her body tumbling and sliding down the slope. The train hurtling past, blocking her view. Panic clutching the breath out of her chest. Her gaze frozen to the spot. Terrified. Praying. Let her be safe. Let her be safe. The last wagon passing...

She woke screaming, sobbing, broken anew at what she had witnessed and relived in every painful detail. Why? Why had this awful thing happened to Eliza? When would all this guilt and pain leave her? She had worked so hard to suppress these memories. She kept herself busy, she made sure there was no empty space in the day when she was not on guard. But at night it was impossible. She could not control what happened as she slept. Isa had a sudden, terrible realisation. The dreams might never go away. They were her penance for not looking after her sister that day. And in the empty house she howled in desperate grief.

Jessie Macleod had taught her the living call us back to the tasks of life and those tasks fill the void of grief. So the next morning Isa tidied up the house and set off to visit her sisters in Stirling. The box she had been given by the Tolquhouns contained surprise after surprise. There were gloves, scarves and bonnets for all three girls and two hand-me-down winter coats for Margaret and Chrissie, treats of cake and treacle toffee made by Mrs Roberts, and neatly edged handkerchiefs Isa had made from an old ripped pillowslip that was past mending, which she had saved from the duster pile. She had cut the squares out of the area that was still sound and hand-edged them, embroidering their initials after borrowing needles and thread from Mrs Roberts, who no doubt realised a sewing kit would make a suitable present for her as a result.

Margaret and Chrissie were, as always, delighted to see her and this had been a long separation for them all so there was much to catch up on. They were desperate to hear more details of the stories Isa had related in her letters about ''Arry' and the smashed ornament, for instance. Isa saw that they were well cared for and happy and this set her mind at rest. Being so far away was really hard because she felt responsible for them still. She felt angry with her father for leaving them to go to the war when he could have stayed at home in his reserved job as a foundryman.

She wondered where he was and what was happening. Staff often discussed newspaper reports of how the war was going around the breakfast table, but it was impossible to imagine what it was like to be in the midst of the fighting. She knew they were using trenches in France and many had been injured and killed there. The Tolquhouns' son, Simon, had been taken prisoner in France and they assumed imprisoned in Germany, but there was no detail of where, or under what conditions.

Back in London it was difficult to settle again. She found she was crying herself to sleep thinking of her sisters and her father. Nightmares woke her, sweating and trembling, and she was left with a feeling of horror when she opened her eyes. Eliza's death was vividly re-enacted in her dreams and now there were the added horrors of what might be happening to her father. Sometimes her fears were for Margaret or Chrissie needing her and being unable to reach her. It was hard to shake off the feelings these nightmares aroused in her, and at times she moved through her work the next morning pale and distracted. Thankfully Mrs Roberts did what Jessie had done and gathered her into her arms, allowing her to weep and release the stress.

On January 20th 1915 the staff awoke to the terrible news of a new threat to the country. It was all over the papers that a German invasion was imminent. Several towns in Norfolk had been bombed by mysterious airships, which drifted silently through the night skies like huge whales, if the photographs were to be believed. They were calling them Zeppelins. Only two people had been killed but sixteen had been injured. People were terrified by the suddenness of the attack and the fact they could do nothing to protect themselves.

In April she read that her father's regiment, the King's Own Scottish Borderers, had been sent to

Turkey, to the Dardanelles, to try to secure the sea route to Russia. From the school map she remembered Turkey was far to the east in Europe and that there was a narrow strait at the entrance to the Black Sea on the Mediterranean side. This was the area referred to as the Dardanelles. She thought of her strong father delivered to a beach shouldering his pack and weapons in a strange landscape. She hoped he would be safe and that the area would be quickly secured by the British and French troops. This war that had been supposed to last six weeks had now endured for close to nine months.

Isa's daily life that year took a more peaceful turn. The staff had got used to her and the teasing diminished to the same level they all received from each other. Her prowess in the kitchen was quickly recognised and the cook often let Isa prepare the staff meals, which involved the kind of wholesome homely cooking she had been doing for years. After the success of the soup for Christmas Day, she was allowed to contribute to the meals that went upstairs, preparing soups and sauces or vegetable dishes at first. Mrs Roberts was quickly satisfied that she could train Isa to be a decent understudy to herself.

One day she approached Isa with some books in her hands.

'Isa, when I first started as a cook's assistant up in Edinburgh, the woman who trained me, Mrs Mackenzie, gave me a book and told me to write down in it every recipe, every hint, every bit of planning, especially for big occasions, so that I would always remember what I was learning and be able to show to new employers just exactly what I was capable of. This is it. I still refer to it even now. Although I'm on to a third book now with all I've gleaned over the years.'

She got Isa to sit beside her at the table and she opened up the book, turning the pages over carefully. In neat black ink and pencil, Isa read recipes for soufflés and puddings, roasts and stews, instructions on how to dry herbs and which ones complemented which dishes. Some had been written in directly and others were on different paper, pasted in to the book.

'It's amazing, Mrs Roberts.'

'And this one is for you. It's time you were thinking about your future. You'll be in charge of a kitchen yourself one day, so here's a book to get you started.' She passed into Isa's hands a large blue bound book. Inside, each page was ruled with faint blue lines, ready to be written on.

'Thank you so much, Mrs Roberts.'

'You make sure to put in there every little thing you learn. It all mounts up. Every recipe or hint on how to do something. It becomes your very own manual, unique to you.'

In her own peaceful room in the late autumn evenings Isa could rest briefly, read over letters from Chrissie and Margaret, and write replies to them. There were always plenty of tales about the staff to tell and descriptions of the grand rooms in the house and new recipes she was learning. She wished she could convey to them the strange accents that surrounded her but she had no idea how to write the London twang on to the page. She contented herself with trying to mimic it in her head, ready to reproduce it when they were next face to face. And now there was her own kitchen book, where she could write up the recipes or what she had observed during the day that she did not want to forget.

10

One Wednesday evening in December 1915, just as she was finishing storing leftover dishes from the family's dinner in the cool pantry, Elsie came into the kitchen wearing her shawl, ready to go out.

'Isa,' she said excitedly, 'I'm going to a séance.'

'You're going where?'

'To a séance. You know. You sits round a table 'olding 'ands while a medium tries to contact the spirit world.'

'You mean the spirits of dead people?' Isa asked incredulously, never having heard of such a thing.

'Yes. Joanna Foster from the staff at number four'een has been and she says Mrs Forpe, the medium, is really good. Joanna's been twice and Mrs Forpe put 'er in touch wiv 'er grandmovver and uncle. The messages she got from 'em were really comforting. Why don't you come? Joanna says the h'atmosphere is unlike anyfink else. Do come. You're all done 'ere. It'll be such fun.' Elsie was putting on gloves and checking her purse.

There were strange, powerful stirrings in Isa at the thought of contacting those she'd lost. What would it be like to receive a message from her mother that she was all right now, that she was with her baby boy and Eliza and they were all happy, no longer weak, ill or maimed? Longing filled her as she allowed herself to feel the yearning for that contact and that reassurance. Suddenly this yearning was replaced with an icy chill that crept through her chest like a fog and her mind was flooded with dark pictures of her mother sick and despairing, her stillborn brother in the towels and blankets Jessie had wrapped him in. Then Eliza's brutally mangled body on the tracks. And then, swiftly after these, a new and shocking picture of her father catapulted through the air and lying face down in a battlefield, with smoke and carnage all around him. Isa was gasping for air.

'No. I won't come, Elsie,' she managed to say. 'That's not for me.'

'Oh well then. I'm off. I'll tell you all 'bout it when I get back.'

'I'd rather you didn't, Elsie. If you don't mind,' Isa replied stiffly.

'Oh!' Elsie stopped and turned at the definite tone in Isa's voice, thinking she was about to be lectured by a prudish colleague about why she was wasting her time on such nonsense, but when she turned and looked at Isa's face, pale and drained of all colour, the line of her mouth and her wide eyes, what she saw was immense sadness and fear, not priggishness. Remembering what Isa had told them at the table about losing her mother, she suddenly realised Isa could not take the séance lightly as she could.

133

She touched Isa lightly on her arm. 'I'm sorry, Isa. I didn't think.'

Isa looked into Elsie's face and saw the realisation written in her eyes. She said nothing but nodded acknowledgement of her colleague's contrition. Elsie wondered anew at this serious-minded girl, who was sociable enough but who clearly kept much to herself. There were unhealed wounds there for sure.

As Elsie left, Isa collapsed into a chair, her head in her hands, willing away the unbidden memories and shaking with fear at the image of her father, which had been as intense and real as the deaths of her mother and siblings she had actually experienced.

About six weeks into the new year, Mr Westfield, the butler came down to the kitchen asking for Isa.

'Straighten your cap, Isa. Lady Tolquhoun wants to see you in her study on an important private matter. Nothing to do with your work.' He spoke softly and quietly and although she felt a little flustered she was not panicking. She followed him upstairs.

At the door to the study he knocked.

'Excuse me, Your Ladyship. I have Miss Dick here for you as requested.'

'Ah yes, Westfield. Show her in please.'

Isa quietly slipped into the room as Westfield retreated and closed the door behind her. She curtsied and nodded. 'Your Ladyship.'

'Come and sit down, Isa.' She indicated a tapestry-upholstered high-backed chair near the desk and her own chair. 'Something arrived for you today, which I thought might best be opened here.'

Isa sat on the edge of the chair, her heart beginning to beat faster. Lady Tolquhoun reached down to the salver where Westfield collected the post. She picked up what was clearly a telegram and handed it to her young employee.

A telegram? Isa looked at the address. Her name was printed on it: Miss Isabella Dick. She could feel her pulse racing as she clumsily began to open it, a sense of dread gripping her.

'We regret to inform you that Corporal John Dick of the King's Own Scottish Borderers is reported missing presumed dead in the Dardanelles.'

'Oh God,' Isa gasped. The terrible image of her father pushed through the air and lying face down in the burned, smoking grass, moaning incoherently came to her again and overwhelmed her. It was as if she was there, as if she was her father – seeing the war-torn landscape, smelling the burning, hearing the gunfire and explosions, feeling the impact of a force pushing her to the ground, winding her, feeling his confusion and the cold, clammy mud in her own face.

Gradually the experience retreated and faded and she heard once again the tick of the French clock on the mantelpiece and Lady Tolquhoun's anxious voice.

'Isa? Isa, dear, are you all right?'

Then Isa heard the tinkle of a bell and Mr Westfield returned to the room.

'Some tea I think, please, Westfield.'

'Right away, Your Ladyship.'

Isa could not speak. She passed the telegram to Lady Tolquhoun so that she could read the news for herself.

'Oh my dear, I am so sorry. I had a feeling this would not be good news. Mr Westfield sensibly thought to consult me before passing this to you. We did not want you to be on your own.'

'He's not dead,' Isa managed.

'They do not know for sure, my dear,' Lady Tolquhoun said gently. 'The phrase means he is missing and there is no body identified as his … yet.'

'No. I mean I know he's not dead.' Isa was definite.

'What do you mean, Isa?'

'I felt it. I saw it happen. He was forced to the ground by something but he's not dead. I saw it a few weeks ago. I thought I had imagined it. But I just saw it again.'

Lady Tolquhoun was completely at a loss. What was the girl talking about? She did not appear hysterical. On the contrary, she was very calm. Was this wishful thinking? Denial? She had already been through too much for one so young. But that was what this war was doing. Her own dear Simon had been captured by the Germans and was being kept in God knows what kind of conditions, she knew not where. The girl clearly needed more than tea. So did she. She would get Westfield to bring some brandy.

Isa was allowed some time off away from the kitchen and she lay on her bed, the telegram still clutched in her hand, looking up through the skylight window at the clouds crossing the tiny

136

patch of winter sky. Gradually her body calmed and her mind stilled. What was the meaning of these strange experiences of her father? The first time in the kitchen had been brief but intense and she'd cast it aside as born out of her grief, the reliving of her traumatic memories and her fear for her father's safety. Today's looked the same, but it was no longer something playing in front of her eyes like a film. Instead it was as if she and her father were one and the same. She had felt a huge blow in her back and legs, throwing her to the ground. She had felt the impact of the ground on her face, smelt the burning grass, heard the cries of other men, then confusion and blackness.

She was calm now, and in this quiet state knew even more strongly that her father had not died on that battlefield. She now felt restless, as though she must do something. But what could she do? She knew from the newspaper reports that all the Allied troops were evacuated from the Dardanelles. The whole attempt to maintain the Bosporus and Black Sea as routes into Russia had failed. But the men had left. Just after Christmas.

Suddenly she knew what she had to do. She took off her cap and apron, grabbed her shawl, pinned on her hat and ran downstairs. She had only one thought in her head: to get out and start looking for her father. She headed down the back stairs and crossed the kitchen, oblivious to Mrs Roberts calling after her. She was halfway down the street when Harry caught up with her.

'Isa. Where do you fink yer going?' he asked her, as he stood himself in front of her, blocking her way.

She made as if to pass him but he held her shoulders gently. 'Isa what's the ma'er? You can't just take awf like this in the middle of your day's work. What are you finkin' of?'

Isa was speechless and suddenly her legs gave way under her. Harry caught her under her arms and led her round to sit on the wall, leaning against the railings for support. He fanned her face with his hand. Slowly Isa recovered and her eyelids fluttered.

'That's it. You'll be awlright now. I've got you. Don't worry.'

Isa opened her eyes and saw Harry's concerned face looking into hers. She gave him a slight push. 'What are you doing here, Harry?'

'I saw you runnin' out've the kitchen like you was possessed or some'at so I came after you to see you was awlright. What's happened? I ain't never seen you like this.'

Isa began to come to properly and realised she must have fainted. Why was she out on the street? Then it came back to her.

'I have to get to the hospital,' she said.

'You feelin' poorly, like? 'Er Ladyship would send for 'er doctor if you wasn't feelin' well. You don't have to go to the hospi'al.'

'Not for me. It's my father. He's reported missing presumed dead. But I know he's alive. He'll be in one of the hospitals with the other troops back from the Dardanelles. I have to...'

'Now hang on a minute. You can't go round hospi'als looking for your farver by yourself. Do you h'even know which 'ospital you're going to? Or how to get there? Look, we'll go back to the house and I'll ask her Ladyship if I can accompany you. I knows me way round. I'll keep you right. Come on.' He tucked his arm under her elbow and helped Isa to her feet. Steadily they retraced their way back to the house, where he got Isa sat in the kitchen and then informed Mrs Roberts of what had happened. Then he headed upstairs to find Lady Tolquhoun.

When she heard what had happened she was sympathetic and realised the girl would not be at peace until she had gone to the hospitals and checked for her father. She was not at all convinced about Isa's certainty that her father would be found, but she knew the pain not knowing her own son's whereabouts was causing her. So she gave permission for Harry to accompany her when not needed in the evenings and on their afternoon off. She consulted her husband regarding the most likely hospitals and gave a list of suggestions to Harry. Everyone dismissed the search as futile wishful thinking, but Elsie remembered a maxim of her mother – that it was as well to hope for the best until you knew the worst – and secretly hoped Isa would not be disappointed.

11

They had already been to St Thomas's on Lambeth Palace Road, King's College on Denmark Hill and St Gabriel's in Camberwell. Harry decided they should head next for the Royal Victoria Patriotic in Wandsworth. Isa was bearing up remarkably, he thought. He could not believe what they were seeing as they walked through the hospitals. Isa had not been satisfied just to be told there was no record of her father's admission; she had insisted on looking around the wards in case he could not be identified or had lost his dog tags. So they had gone through ward after ward of men with their legs in plaster, their arms in slings, men encased in bandages, men whose limbs had been amputated, men who had been burned, men moaning, men smiling, men trying to walk again on crutches. Each time she had asked, had anyone seen her father, John Dick, she had been met with silence or shaking heads. Some of the men who were further on the road to recovery smiled and tried to engage them in conversation, but Isa was on a mission; she was not there as a ward visitor.

Now they'd turned on to Trinity Road and ahead of them, set in grassy lawns and fenced round with iron railings, lay the impressive Victorian building of the Royal Victoria Patriotic Hospital, which before the war had been an orphanage and was commissioned for use as a hospital the day after war was declared. The children were re-housed nearby and now their class-rooms and dormitories were filled with beds for wounded servicemen. As they came through the gates, Isa gazed at the building with its towers and turrets and thought it had the look of a stately home about it. Only the windows were small and school-like. Above the central archway through which they passed to reach the entrance hall, there was a statue of St George killing the dragon, his sword held high, ready to strike. Isa shuddered.

At the desk they spoke to a white-capped nurse who checked her records and told her that no John Dick had been admitted. 'However, we do have a number of patients who have been victims of shell shock who came from the Dardanelles ships a few weeks ago. Many of them have not been able to give us their identity and their ID tags were blown off in the blasts. They are in ward ten upstairs and to the left. I should try there first.'

Isa's heart began to sing. This was sounding so hopeful. She practically ran up the staircase, with Harry hot on her heels. At the entrance to the ward they were met by a smiling nurse, the white bib of her apron printed with a large red cross to show she had been trained by the Red Cross as a volunteer.

'Can I help you?' she asked.

Breathless after the quick climb, Isa told her, 'We were sent here by the nurse on reception in case my father might be on this ward and not yet identified. You see, I had a telegram reporting him missing in action presumed dead in the Dardanelles, but I don't believe he is dead. I feel sure he is alive.'

The nurse touched her arm gently. 'You're not the first to feel that, my dear. Let's go and have a look, shall we. What is your father like?'

Isa felt suddenly calm in the presence of this nurse, who didn't think she was mad or strange. She let her lead her on to the ward and answered her questions, all the while looking around her. But what a different series of sights met her eyes.

The men on this ward were not all obviously injured. True, some had plaster casts and amputated limbs, but others sat drooping in chairs or propped on pillows in bed like dolls, lifeless, taking no notice of anything around them. Some sat staring straight ahead, eyes wide in terror, and yet they were safe in the hospital, away from the horrors of the battle. Isa felt a huge surge of empathy for these men. From the place deep within her, scarred by Eliza's grotesque death, she recognised the men's pain for what it was: fear, shock and horror. Responses to what you should never have seen being imprinted on your mind and memory forever. Their bodies were safe in their beds, but inside their heads they were still in battle, surrounded by their injured friends, with death lurking everywhere they turned, just as she still stood by the railway track.

Coming into the ward, she saw another man, supported by two orderlies, with his head bowed, his feet dragging along the floor while the orderlies tried to encourage him.

'Keep your head up, now. Try to look ahead and let your legs lift your feet. Good man. One foot in front.'

The man slowly moved his left foot and pushed it a little in front of him, then brought the other foot up alongside it. He raised his head and looked at Isa. Despite the dishevelled, greying hair and the brokenness of his large, strong frame, she recognised the bright-blue eyes of her father and saw the pain in them that had brought him to this state. She'd found him. She'd been right. He was alive – but only just.

'It's him,' she said to the nurse, her voice quivering. 'This is my father, John Dick.'

She walked towards him.

'Faither. It's Isa.'

At the familiar sound of his daughter's voice, John raised his head further and looked into her eyes. A smile flickered around his lips. 'Isa?' He whispered. 'Isa. Isa.' And then at the realisation of who this stricken young woman was, memories came flooding back and he collapsed in tears and sobs.

The two orderlies helped him to his bed, and when he was comfortable Isa came and sat beside him and held his hand. Neither took their eyes off the other's face. It was not a time for words. Relief, joy, pain and hope surged between them through the clasping of their hands and the steady gaze that locked them together in deep communion. John knew he was home at last. Isa knew her father was alive. They anchored each other amidst the confusion and horror.

'It'll be all right, Faither,' Isa whispered. 'I'm here now. Yer home. Yer safe.'

'Isa. My Isa,' her father managed, the tears still gently falling.

For John, seeing his eldest daughter brought the beginnings of a return of speech and the recovery of his identity. This was a huge turning point on his long recuperative journey, for now he knew who he was and began to remember his life. It took weeks of physiotherapy and occupational therapy before his speech became clear, but the fog in his head lifted, unlocking his memory. The will to live demanded that he drew on every ounce of his strength to make himself learn to walk again, and to make the shapes with tongue and lips that would allow him to communicate once more.

Isa visited on her days off and every evening she was freed of duties in the kitchen. She brought her photographs of the family and talked to her father about Margaret and Chrissie. She wrote to them and told them what had happened and they wrote letters for her to read to their father about their exploits and lessons. He loved hearing their news and gradually was able to respond with questions as well as smiles and laughter. They had no idea how essential all of this was to his recovery, since it gave him a reason to improve, a reason to live, to fight to regain his faculties.

As a result he made speedier progress than many other patients who had begun in similar circumstances. By April he had been in hospital for four months. Isa arrived one afternoon on her day off to find him alert, lucid and ready to tell her what he knew of the events leading up to his arrival in the Royal Victoria.

'Some o' it has come back tae me noo an' the nurses hae filled me in wi' whit they ken. Seems I somehow got separatit frae ma unit and wis caught in heavy shellfire frae the Turks. Ma dog tags wis blawn off in the blast an' I'd bin thrown tae the groond wi' sic a force I wis oot cold.'

Isa shivered as she heard this because it was just as she had seen it in her strange experience.

'Apparently I was foond later, efter the shellin' subsidit, by lads frae Australia and New Zealand – the ANZAC unit – wha were headit doon tae the

144

beach. They were due tae evacuate on the ships waitin' in the bay fur the retreat at the end o' December. They takit me wi' them an' got me tae a British hospital ship on accoont o' reco'nisin' the uniform, whit was left o' it. They savit me or I could hae bin left for dead for I didnae come roond fur days. I slepit maist o' the journey hame an' I dinnae mind much until ma ee'n clappit on yer face, ma bonnie lassie. Then I kent I wis yer faither an I hid tae get weel.' He reached out for her hand and held it tight.

There was something very special between them. It was as if all the traumas they had shared had knitted them together: grief and hardship and having to look after the others had imbued them both with strengths they would otherwise never have found and somehow they fed on each other's will to survive. Isa knew her father was flawed – the drunken bouts had been hard on her – but she also knew his warmth, his love, his pride in her had helped make her who she was. They might at times disappoint each other but they would never let go, never turn their back on the other, it was like an unspoken promise, a trust that had already been tested and held firm. Perhaps that was why she had known, even though separated by thousands of miles, that he had been in danger and yet had survived. It was a special secret that she did not yet share with him, but she held it close to her.

In June her father was about to be discharged and Lord and Lady Tolquhoun expressed a wish to meet him, and so John was given an invitation to take tea with them at Cadogan Square. He was very nervous at the thought of meeting a lord, but Isa reassured him that the Tolquhouns were very fine people and from all her stories he knew they had been wonderful to his daughter and therefore he wanted to thank them for their care of her.

The day arrived and he left the hospital wearing his new suit carefully brushed, shoes highly polished to a shine and his cap. They had sent the car for him and Harry greeted him with a handshake. On the journey Harry told John what great employers the Tolquhouns were, how impressed he was with Isa and how glad he was personally to meet her father. John relaxed in the car talking to this chatty Londoner, though part of his mind was jumping ahead to what he would say to Lord Tolquhoun.

In the event he need not have worried. Lord Tolquhoun was a Scot and could speak in the vernacular, which was exactly what he did, to put John at his ease. He was shown into Lord Tolquhoun's study and plied with whisky and soon he was telling this member of the nobility about his life in Falkirk, his work in the foundry and what he could remember of the Dardanelles campaign. Man to man, he could talk of the terrible heat and flies in the summer months when he arrived, the overcrowding in the tents, the poor sanitation; the thirst, dysentery and exhaustion which killed more men than the bullets from the Turks; the heartbreakingly small gains of ground which were quickly lost again; the bitter, stormy winter prior to the heavy bombardment in which he had been injured; the wounded men he'd known as comrades; the dead and maimed bodies he'd seen strewn on the battlefield and left to go putrid and which now peopled his nightmares. Such details he'd never share with his daughters.

When he met Isa briefly on his way out he was full of admiration for Lord Tolquhoun, who had spoken to him 'like a Scot in ma ain tongue'.

By the end of the month of June, John Dick was installed once again in 22 Sunnyside Road, Camelon, Falkirk, and Margaret and Chrissie could come home. Margaret was now a very fine-looking, confident girl of nine with a mop of glossy dark curls and a delightful smile. Chrissie was seven and a little shy, always holding Margaret's hand, but when she laughed it was impossible not to laugh with her, her giggle was so infectious.

That summer Isa was able to see much more of them all because the Tolquhouns had decamped to their Scottish home at Pitskellie Castle near Dunfermline in Fife. Parliament was in summer recess and the family came to relax and shoot grouse on the estate. Isa was given a room at the top of the house. It was really more of a stately home than a castle, built originally in the seventeenth century and extensively remodelled in 1885, but very grand and huge in comparison to the house in Cadogan Square. The castle was surrounded by extensive lawns and woodland. When she had a few hours off, Isa loved to walk by herself, enjoying the fresh air and the quiet, which she had much missed in London. From the foot of the sloping lawn, Isa could turn back and admire the symmetry of the house, the grand bay windows of the dining room and drawing room on the first floor and above them the bedrooms with the balustraded balconies overlooking the sweeping lawns. Her own room had a window up in the roof and she could see how tiny it looked compared to the grander family accommodation in the castle, but if she stood on a stool at the high window she got an amazing view past the lawns and woodland over the surrounding countryside, and to her it was perfect.

Within a few days of the household re-establishing itself in Pitskellie, there was further upheaval. Rose Nelson, the assistant nanny, had taken ill and needed leave of absence. There was great consternation as to who would take her place. Mrs Roberts, ever mindful of her protégée, had a word with Isa.

'How long was it that you looked after your two sisters, Isa?'

'I was eleven when ma mother passed and I looked after Maggie and Chrissie till ma father went tae the war so that would be nigh on four and a half years, Mrs Roberts.'

'You'd fairly be experienced then.'

'Aye, I suppose. I saw them through a few illnesses and I always cooked for them and heard their lessons. Truth be told, Mrs Roberts, it wis hard at times, but I liked it. I fair miss them. It's grand bein' nearby now. I think Chrissie doesnae really mind ma mother. It's as if I had that role in her life.'

Mrs Roberts had a word with Mrs Williams.

'I know Her Ladyship is worried about the departure of Rose, but you know, Isa looked after her own sisters for four and a half years when they were just little ones. I think she will be very capable. Perhaps she could cover in the nursery till Rose recovers?'

'But what about her help in the kitchen? I know you have come to rely on her.'

'Oh yes, very much so, and I'm not suggesting a permanent move. I need her back. But for now, to help Miss Rutherford out? It would be good experience for Isa and the children know her.'

'Very well. I shall mention this to Her Ladyship. We'll see what she thinks of the idea. Thank you, Mrs Roberts.'

And so it was that for a period of three months Isa transferred to work in the nursery with the Tolquhouns' youngest children: Agatha, who was four, and James, who was six and who would next year be off to boarding school. She soon discovered looking after wealthy children was different in lots of ways. She was taken aback at the books and toys the children had at their disposal. This was a far cry from what she and her sisters had had. Most of their games had taken place outdoors in the fields, playing with twigs and stones, imagining themselves as shopkeepers or farmers, taking it in turns to invent stories and characters. Then there were the games where they played at being mother, with rag dolls made from stockings with embroidered faces and clothes made literally from rags of cut-down or worn-out clothing. Here in the nursery there were beautiful dolls with porcelain faces and rosebud mouths, long hair, frilly petticoats, silk dresses, fur-trimmed bonnets and little leather shoes. There were rattles and tambourines, building blocks,

149

miniature cars, a wooden rocking horse, jigsaw puzzles. There were mechanical toys: tin soldiers that marched when wound up with a key, monkeys that climbed a ladder rung by rung then flipped over the top and climbed down the other side. There was a huge doll's house, one whole side of which was hinged and opened out to reveal three floors of rooms with tiny exquisite furniture, little plates and knives and forks, even candlesticks and vases of flowers, everything replicated as in a stately home.

What Isa loved most were the books. Fond as she had been of writing stories and reading them out loud in class she had not had books at home. Now here she was surrounded with all the children's classics. There were collections of fairy tales, illustrated books of nursery rhymes plus novels such as *Treasure Island* and *The Water Babies*. Miss Rutherford, the senior nanny, a somewhat frosty spinster in her forties, was quite put out at first to discover that this girl from the kitchen could actually read, and do so reasonably well.

Isa would look back on this time as one when she learned much about child-rearing that her own mother had not known. It was here she learned about table manners and what was not done in polite society, for as Miss Rutherford instructed the young Tolquhouns she was also unwittingly instructing Isa. Knowledge was power and Isa knew she was being shown into a very different level of society from the one she had previously known. She stored every tiny detail in her thirsty mind: new approaches to hygiene that could keep germs at bay, different ways of treating

150

a fever, polite ways to ask questions or to say no to something, how to hold one's cutlery, what to do with the table napkins, the correct way to hold a teacup and saucer. It was a revelation that one could give away one's breeding so easily by the way one held one's knife. But now she too had those secrets of noble breeding.

On one of her evening walks, Isa was returning towards the house in the summer dim. The light was just beginning to fade but darkness was a long way off and it was already past ten o'clock. She loved these Scottish summer evenings that seemed to last forever. As she strolled up the lawn, swallows and house martins were skimming close to the ground, filling their mouths with insects, then swooping up to their mud-cup nests in the eaves above the windows. She sat on the grass for a moment to watch, breathing in the stillness and the cooling air, resting her legs, weary after her day's work with the children. As she gazed up at the house, her eyes caught a movement at one of the bedroom windows. The window opened and a figure stepped out on to the balcony above the dining room. Isa was by now about a hundred yards from the house, but even so, the figure looked small, slight, childlike. But that was not the nursery bedroom, and both the children had gone to sleep ages ago. This was the guest bedroom, which was empty this evening as Earl Roseberry and his family were not expected until the weekend. As she stood puzzling all this out she saw the child come closer to the stone balustrade. This wouldn't do. What was Miss Rutherford thinking? Why wasn't James in his bed?

She ran towards the house. As she got nearer, the child began to climb on to the balustrade. What was he doing?

'James!' she yelled. 'Get down!' By now she was panicking. 'James! James!'

She wanted him to look at her, to see she was there. She wanted to calm him and get him off the balustrade. She did not want to frighten him in case he stumbled.

And then suddenly he stepped off the balustrade, his arms wide, and fell to the ground.

'Oh my God!' Isa ran even faster to the house, screaming for help at the top of her voice, dreading what she would find as she came round the row of rhododendron that masked her view of the path. Expecting to see the body of the boy on the gravel, she was shocked to find there was nothing. Nothing at all. No child, no marks on the gravel. She looked up at the balcony. Nothing.

Mr Westfield had been in the dining room tidying the servery and had heard Isa's screams. He had gone to the window, seen her stupefied on the path and headed out to find out what was the matter. He came walking smartly towards her.

'Isa? What's wrong? Are you all right?'

'I ... I don't know Mr Westfield. I thought I saw something. Someone who needed help. But ... I must have been mistaken.'

'What did you see?'

Isa stammered through what she'd thought she'd seen.

'Ah, my dear,' Mr Westfield sighed in relief. 'Don't worry. There's no one needing our help tonight. Just you. You've seen our ghost, I think.

152

Come inside, we'll get you sorted.'

Isa was trembling and tearful. It had been so real. She had been overcome by such a sense of desperation at her helplessness to avert another terrible disaster happening right in front of her. She was overwhelmed. Mr Westfield supported her at her elbow and got her into the kitchen and into Mrs Roberts' arms, where Isa finally broke down into sobs.

Later when Mrs Roberts' shushing and soothing had calmed her, Isa was told the ghost's story. The little boy had been Edward, the youngest son of Mary and George Wardlaw, who had lived in the castle a century ago. Edward had been an unusual child, very much living in a world of his own making. From the age of three he had not really communicated with people. He made noises and pointed at what he wanted, but seemed oblivious to other people. Things were more important. He had been fascinated with insects and birds, poring over illustrations in books and copying the diagrams meticulously. One night, after being put to bed, he had got up and crept through to the guest bedroom, where he had opened the window and stepped out on to the balcony, from where he had fallen to his death. No one had seen it happen and it was not until the morning that the staff had found the body outside on the path.

Isa was still in a state of shock, for although no one had been on the balcony while she watched, she had seen replayed something that had really happened and that made ice run in her veins. She was shivering.

'Mr Westfield, I think Isa could do with some

brandy,' suggested Mrs Roberts.

'I'll just get the keys.' Mr Westfield headed through to his parlour. He returned with the bottle of brandy and poured a finger's worth in a glass.

'Here, Isa. Take this. It will help. You've had a terrible shock.' He handed her the glass.

Isa sipped slowly and felt the heat in the alcohol quickly course through her body, warming her and stilling her. She felt strength return to her legs. The fear and shock were beginning to dissipate. Mrs Roberts got her upstairs and settled into bed with an extra cover to keep away the chill. She sat down on the chair beside Isa and waited till the girl's breathing settled. Running through her mind was the vivid description the girl had given of the child: his face, his clothing, his oblivious demeanour and the manner in which he had jumped to his death, not fallen. These were details she had never had passed to her in any of the accounts of the ghost she had come across. Isa truly was a particularly sensitive girl. And tonight it seemed a curse to be so inclined.

12

Understandably Isa remained shaken for several weeks after what she had seen. It was difficult to put it out of her mind. Usually, when she was busy with the children, she had other things to focus on, but at night, alone in her room, fear and terror generated by seeing the ghost child, and memories of Eliza's death, filled her dreams. Tired from her lack of sleep, she occasionally broke down in tears. Mrs Roberts worried for her and brought it to the attention of Lady Tolquhoun, who decided to speak with Isa and had her sent for.

'Good afternoon, Your Ladyship. You wanted to see me?'

'Yes, Isa. Do come in. How are you?'

'Very well, Your Ladyship,' Isa said, surprised at the question. She had not been ill. Why was Her Ladyship concerned about her health?

'My dear, you are still looking very pale. Are you sleeping well?' There was genuine concern in Lady Tolquhoun's voice and in her face as she regarded Isa closely. 'I fear that terrible experience a few weeks ago has taken a dreadful toll on your good spirits and on your health.'

'But Your Ladyship, do not worry. I am fine through the day when I am working and I do love being in the nursery.'

'Isa, I know you are good at your work. Everything we ask of you is done to the very highest standard. It is you I am concerned for. You have been through so much recently. I wondered if you might like a few days at home with your family? It would seem to be a good time to do that, while we are here in Scotland not so far away from them. Your father, after all, has just been through a horrific time too. I think you should take a week at home, my dear. Restore your strength. We can manage here. I have already spoken with Miss Rutherford and with Mrs Roberts. Harry will see you to the station in Dunfermline. Tuesday, I think?'

Isa could not believe it. A holiday? This was un-heard of. But at the warmth of the offer she felt herself overcome with tears of gratitude.

'Oh, Your Ladyship, that would be wonderful. I am so grateful.' She dried her eyes. She would not admit to having been through a terrible time because, compared with the death of Eliza and her mother, she knew the recent terror was on a lesser scale. After all, her father had survived; she had found him – and the horrible death from the bal-cony had been long ago. Yet she recognised she had found it all distressing. A peaceful time at home would be good.

The week passed in a blur. Isa quickly took charge, cooking, washing, shopping and cleaning. Now Margaret and Chrissie were old enough to be of real help in all the household tasks. Her father was not fit enough to return to the front, but when he had regained his strength he would pick up his old job at the foundry. He took long walks along the canal and round the streets of Falkirk, meeting a few old mates who like him had been invalided out. But most men their age were away at the war, and those who were around were not fit for the drinking sessions they used to engage in, so John drank a glass of beer in the pub on his way back and had a dram before bed. It made for a peaceful family life and Isa found it very comforting. It was a return to her roots among the people she knew, whose voices she recognised and whose smiles and approval she craved. She did not have to check her speech or make sure her hair was tucked in a cap. She did not have to curtsey to anyone. She was in charge, although she deferred to her father always, as head of the house.

This time she was confident about her cooking and household skills. John looked at her moving assuredly around the kitchen with pans of stew and baking trays and saw that, although barely seventeen, she was a woman now. He'd left them all as children, struggling to be a family, ashamed at his own failure and misery, fearing they would be better off without him. Now here they were reunited, but each had matured, adapted to life without Mary. Even he, although there was still a huge gap in his life, had found a renewal of some kind from being away at war. He wanted to hold on to his life now, not throw it away, after it had been given back to him so fortunately. And it was definitely easier with Isa around.

His daughter was loath to return to Pitskellie Castle after her week at home, but she was feeling better, so she readied her few things, said her farewells and headed back. But when the household began their packing up at the end of September in order to return to London, Isa could not face the move. London was too far from home. It was alien and noisy. She dreaded the thought of the hard pavements and constant bustle of people and traffic. She had just rewoven herself into the fabric of her family and it was too painful to think of loosening the threads again to head south. Secretly she began to look in the local paper for adverts for cooks. She thought she could cope with a simple household's demands by herself, especially in the Falkirk area, where nobility were not the main guests at the family table. She listened out in the

157

shops too, in case she heard of anyone seeking to employ a cook. Then, one bright morning, as she cast her eye over the wanted ads she found it. A Mr and Mrs Sinclair, who owned the local saw-mill, were looking for a cook to live in. The wage was reasonable and they needed two references. Isa knew she would have no problem getting a reference from her tutor at the college. She wondered what Lady Tolquhoun would say. Mrs Roberts might not want to let her go either. But she had made up her mind. It had to be done.

A few days later Isa was sitting in the Sinclairs' drawing room, being interviewed for the position of cook.

'Well, Miss Dick, these references are excellent. They speak very highly of your character and skills. I must ask, though, why you seek employment here in Falkirk with us when you could be in the household of Lord and Lady Tolquhoun in London?'

'Well, ma'am, my family are here and I miss them terribly when I am in London. It is impossible to see them on days off or in the evenings as I could do here. I have realised I need to be nearer them. Falkirk is my home.' Isa was tense, worried that Mrs Sinclair was going to think she would be off again, because she had had a taste of working at the grand end of things.

'Well I must say I am impressed with your references. Let's say we give you a trial period of three weeks to see if this arrangement will suit. Can you start Monday?'

'Certainly, Mrs Sinclair. I am most grateful. Thank you, ma'am.'

Needless to say the Tolquhouns and the staff in the household were sorry that Isa would not be returning with them to London. Mrs Roberts made her promise to write and ask for any help she needed with recipes or staff, for Isa was to have a kitchen maid too. Elsie and Sally had little gifts of a knitted woollen scarf and a pretty brooch made of shells.

On her way back to the kitchen for the evening meal she bumped into Harry on the stairs.

'Isa, there you are. I've got somefink for you.' He put his hand into his pocket and withdrew a small package, tidily wrapped in brown paper and tied with string. 'I hope you like it.'

Isa was lost for words. She stood holding the package.

'Ain't you goin' to open it? I wants to see if you like it.'

She untied the string and unrolled the paper layers to reveal a box. She lifted the lid and inside was a shepherdess figurine.

'I wanted you to have one. You said you admired the one Her Ladyship has in the cabinet. This one ain't the same quali'y bu' it's a loikeness. I wan'ed to make it up to you.'

'Harry, you already did that. You apologised and you said you wouldn't let me down and you were there for me when I went looking for my father. I couldn't have had a better friend at that time than you.'

'Don't forget me, Isa. Remember me kin'ly. Not for wha' I did earlier.'

Isa looked into his earnest face and smiled. 'I'll not forget your kindness, Harry.' She paused and smiled, looking down at the ornament. 'Or your sense of humour.'

Harry knew then he had been truly forgiven.

'I'll never forget ye neiver, Isa.'

The Sinclairs' house was one of the grander buildings in Falkirk. It stood on the north edge of the town in its own grounds, surrounded by closely mown lawns and carefully tended flower beds. At the back there was a walled garden with fruit trees espaliered on the south-facing walls and bed after bed well stocked with vegetables. September of course meant there were potatoes, carrots, cabbage and cauliflower in abundance. Isa was shown round the kitchen and dining room, and then taken to her quarters. As cook, she had her own bedroom with a proper window on the top floor. It was neatly furnished with pretty curtains and a bedspread sprigged with flowers and there was a comfy armchair and rug beside the bed. There was even a proper wardrobe for her clothes and a small side cabinet for books and personal things.

She was introduced to the other staff. First there was Phyllis, a kitchen maid of about fifteen who had been trained by the previous cook for six months. Isa realised she could be helpful in showing her where everything was, and the girl looked clean and polite. She was responsible to Isa and would help prepare and serve meals and wash dishes. The housemaid, Bessie, was about fourteen and did all the cleaning. She was answerable to the housekeeper, Mrs Forester, who was formidable. Like Mrs Williams in London, she went around in a severe black dress, with a chain of keys dangling from a belt at her waist, but unlike Mrs Williams she had no respect for any other member of staff. There was no butler, as this was a much smaller team than the Tolquhouns', and in the absence of such, Mrs Forester took it upon herself to be in charge of all of them. Whether this was ever in her original responsibilities or not was irrelevant. Whereas at the Tolquhouns', Isa had seen Mrs Roberts, Mr Westfield and Mrs Williams as equals, each in charge of their own domain and giving each other that respect, here she could already sense Mrs Forester did not see Isa Dick as her equal.

She set about discovering her new kitchen, inspecting cupboards, noting their contents and considering any additions she would like to make to the supplies. The huge cooking stove, the very latest model from the Carron Works, had several ovens and three large hotplates, all kept scrupulously clean, and the heat from it made the kitchen one of the warmest rooms in the whole house. Two deep ceramic tubs with gleaming taps were at one window, with a spacious wooden draining board on either side. Isa approved of this organisation, which allowed dirty dishes to be stacked, washed in the first tub, rinsed in the second and stacked again to dry on the draining board at the other end. The kitchen table was a good size and Isa could tell as she ran her hand over its surface that it was religiously scrubbed. All in all she felt she had taken on an excellent kitchen.

Each Monday morning she met with Mrs Sinclair in the drawing room for a cup of tea, over which they would discuss the week's menus, thus enabling the ordering and procuring of foodstuffs needed. Isa and Phyllis would do the shopping at the market and local shops and Mrs Sinclair ordered any other items, which were delivered to the back door at the kitchen. Isa was glad she had some knowledge of slightly fancier fare for the regular occasions when the Sinclairs entertained. Although it was still tough for ordinary folk in the war years, the rich and the nobility always managed to get more than their official share because they had the money. Various 'tradesmen' found their way to the back doors of the big houses, telling of sought-after items that could be got for the right sum of cash. Isa was loath to get involved in these deals, but sometimes when cream was what was needed, or when there were no more eggs, or the butcher did not have a big enough joint of meat left, it was very tempting. The household budget she was given for shopping did sometimes find its way into the pockets of the back-door tradesmen.

Isa found a new confidence in her role as cook. Surrounded by her family and friends in her home town, she was no longer the isolated, strangely spoken Scottish redhead who everyone made fun of. Here she was in charge of the kitchen. She had the knowledge and the experience to command respect from Phyllis and from the Sinclairs, and she got it. She was not the lowly kitchen maid she had been when she first arrived in Cadogan Square. She took to it like a duck to water. She remembered how she had felt as a lowly member of staff in a big house, and was careful of her kitchen maid not to overburden her, remembering to thank her for her assistance with tasks and to commend her on things done well.

The Sinclairs declared themselves very well pleased with Isa's cooking and with her quiet ordering of the kitchen. Dishes always arrived steaming hot, beautifully presented, flavourful in the mouth and easy on the stomach, and guests always left replete, praising the skills of the Sinclairs' new cook. It was not long before Mrs Sinclair found herself asking Isa for her ideas for meals and giving her much more say over ingredients and new recipes, even allowing her to plan full dinner menus when they entertained. Isa loved this new level of responsibility and discovered she could cope far better than she had at first thought might be the case.

This new confidence affected her social life too. In London Isa had felt shy, alien and unsure of going out on her own to cinemas or dance halls, and truth be told there had seldom been occasions when she had the energy. She had been contented to stay in her room reading or writing letters and falling quickly asleep. In Falkirk, back among old friends and with more free time, she started attending dance lessons with Jessie's daughter, Jean. There was a dearth of young men, most still away at the war, and so the taller girls sometimes had to take the role of the man. Isa had always loved music. As she'd grown up her father and his family were forever playing the moothie or squeezebox when they met up, and they all sang. She discovered she loved moving to music, enjoying the rhythm and the swaying and the being held, even if it was by your giggling female friend. It was so relaxing. You could forget yourself and get lost in the music and the twirl of your body, the rhythmic moves in your feet. They learned the waltz, quadrilles and the polka, the liveliest one, where you dipped and twirled like dervishes in time to the fast beats of the music. Face flushed and the pins slipping from her hair, Isa was being noticed by all the young men around. But she gave off such a feistiness that most just watched and admired. Few were brave enough to approach her.

One night there was a new face in the dance hall. William Morrison had just come back from the war. He had been shell-shocked like her father and treated at Erskine Hospital. He was now well enough to rejoin civilian life but not well enough to return to the front. He was tall and strongly built, with soft brown eyes and a calm confidence. As Isa twirled rhythmically around the dance floor, William noticed her bright russet hair, her sparkling blue eyes and the look of pure pleasure on her face. What would it be to hold such a sensual woman in his arms? One who could give herself so fully to the music and to the dance would surely be even more responsive to the attentions of a man. He could not take his eyes off her.

As she left the floor to take her seat beside her friend, he intercepted her and asked, 'May I have the next dance, Miss? My name is William. William Morrison. It would be my pleasure.'

It was not often there were new young men to dance with and Isa could see he was a good height for her and well built to match her own strong frame.

'Thank you, Mr Morrison. That would be delightful.'

'And with whom do I have the honour?' he asked with a slow grin.

'My name is Isabella Dick,' she said. 'Everyone calls me Isa.'

'Then perhaps I shall call you Isabella,' he said gently, 'If I may. It is such a lovely name.'

Despite her usual reserve, Isa felt a little shiver of excitement at the sound of her full name, which no one ever used. He was right. It did sound lovely. He took her hand and led her back to the floor for a waltz. The tune was one of her favourites. She hoped he wouldn't spoil it all by constantly chatting. She found that so irritating when she just wanted to dance. He didn't. He just kept his gaze on her face, one hand firmly on her back, guiding her, and the other holding her hand gently and gracefully as he slowly swayed her to and fro in time to the music. They moved well together. When the dance ended he asked if he might get her some refreshment. They walked over to the table where jugs of lemonade and glasses had been left for people to serve themselves. He poured a glass and handed it to her while filling one for himself.

'So, William Morrison, I've not seen you here before.'

'No, I've been away at the front for three years. Not had much leave to spend at home. But I was injured, sent back. I start again at the foundry next week. They're glad because they're short right now. And what about Miss Isabella ... Dick, did you say? Not one of the famous Fighting Dicks?'

Isa blushed. 'What's that supposed to mean?'

'Oh, please, don't be offended. I know some of the Dicks that work at the Carron. Tommy and Davie and John.'

'And?'

'Fine men ... to have on your side. And I like them all fine.'

'Well that's good, because John is my father and the others are my uncles,' she said proudly.

'My, it is just as well I get on fine with them then.' William threw back his head and laughed. 'Seriously, Isabella, your father is a legend at the foundry. No other man can do as much as he does in a shift. The rest of us are in awe of his stamina. Don't know how he does it. We have our work cut out doing three quarters of what he can do. But I didn't know he had a daughter.'

'He has three,' Isa said. 'I am the eldest, then there's Margaret, who is eleven, and Chrissie, who is nine.'

'And are they as lovely as you, I wonder?'

Isa blushed again. He could see she wasn't used to male attention so he would have to take things slowly.

'Come on,' he said. 'That's a great polka tune. Shall we dance?' He reached for her hand and she complied willingly.

They had such a wonderful evening, hardly ever sitting down, and he walked her back to the Sinclairs', expressing a wish to dance with her next week if she was intending being there. She said yes and headed into the house, her heart aglow at the thought of it. What a wonderful evening. And she had been asked out on a sort of date, she believed. She was thrilled. Such a handsome man. That night she slept peacefully and her dreams were music filled with swirling figures in evening suits and ball gowns and the only face that was clear was his.

For the next few weeks they continued to meet at the dances, enjoying lovely, slow walks back to the Sinclairs' house afterwards. One moonlit night, walking along the canal, as they were approaching one of the locks, William grabbed her hand. 'Let's climb the lock. If we stand above the water we'll see the moon reflected in the canal.'

Isa dropped his hand. 'What? That's not safe.'

'I did it plenty of times when I was a wean. Come on,' he said over his shoulder, as he pulled himself up on to the worn wood. He stood and turned to face her, his arm outstretched. 'Trust me. You'll be fine.'

But Isa was adamant. She shook her head.

'Well I never had you down for a coward, Isabella,' he teased. He strode along the broad beam towards the centre. 'I was right,' he announced brightly. 'The moon is reflected in the canal. A wonderful shiny disc of light.' Still with his gaze fixed on the water, he shuffled nearer the centre.

On the bank, Isa watched. She would far rather he was on a proper bridge with railings to hold on to. There was no way she would follow him on to the lock. It was too unsafe.

William looked around to find her face. 'It is so lovely,' he called. 'If you were here beside me it would be perfect.' He stretched out his hand to her. 'Come on, Isabella.'

Isa was not enjoying this. She had not liked him

167

calling her a coward. What did he know of her life, her character? His bravado bothered her too. He was so young, a daredevil. He had asked her to come by his side. What kind of man would ask his girl to follow him in such a risky act?

'William, stop this please. I am not coming on to the lock. I want to get back.'

William laughed. 'All right. You do know how to spoil the moment. But your wish is my command.' He made a sweeping bow, lost his balance and fell in the canal with a loud splash that sent moonlit ripples from bank to bank.

Isa raised her hands to her face in horror. This was exactly what she had dreaded. She looked into the water, desperate for his head to appear. What on earth had possessed him? Had he hit his head? How deep was it here? Were there rocks? Weeds to entangle him? What if...?

Then his head emerged above the surface. He gasped for air and shook his head from side to side, his hair thick, brown and slick like an otter's.

'Are you all right?' Isa called anxiously from the bank.

'Don't worry. I'll be fine.' He started to swim towards her. As he touched the embankment he looked up and saw anger and fear written upon her face.

She offered her hand but he pushed down on his own arms, hauled himself up and got one knee on to the bank before rolling the rest of himself on to dry land. He was on his back looking up at her and he burst out laughing.

'God, Isa, you would think I was at death's door from the look on your face. I'm fine. Just wet. My brothers and I were always in the canal. Dinna fash yersel'.'

Suddenly she was furious. How dare he put her through all this worry and now humiliate her for being concerned.

'Well,' she said, looking down at him somewhat haughtily. 'If you're sure you'll be fine I'll be off then.' She turned her back on him and headed briskly along the path.

'Wait, Isabella. Let me see you home safely.'

Isa could not believe his audacity. 'Not looking like that you won't!' she called back in disgust.

How could he think she would let him come out of the canal covered in stinking weeds, dripping with water, and continue to escort her back to the Sinclairs'? What would it have looked like to have him lead her up the steps in that state? What a pathetic creature. Such a clown.

'Well, I'll see you next week, then. Won't I?'

She did not even grace his tentative question with a reply. William was over, as far as she was concerned. He was only a foundryman. After all, she didn't want the life her mother had had: washing those filthy clothes, dealing with the foundryman's lifestyle of heavy drinking and manly bravado such as she had just witnessed. No – that was not the kind of man for her. She'd seen the genteel lives of the Tolquhouns and the Sinclairs and their guests. She wanted something closer to that. A house with a parlour. Not too many children. No drunkenness and dirt. A man who could provide for her that better lifestyle.

She realised she longed for a man she could look up to, a man who took life seriously, like Mr

Sinclair for example. He knew how to treat his wife. He was always bringing her flowers carefully wrapped in paper and ribbon. He had a beautiful box of chocolates for her when they went to the theatre. He was so much the attentive gentleman. That's what she wanted in a man: some dignity, someone who dressed well, with a decent job with some prospects. Definitely not someone who would end up in the canal as he escorted her home.

So Isa decided not to attend the dance the following Saturday and of course Jeannie was demanding to know why when she next saw her in the High Street on her day off. When she heard the story, Jeannie laughed out loud in the tearoom, much to Isa's dismay.

'I do not see why you think that is so funny, Jeannie. I was black affronted.' Isa sounded so much the schoolteacher in her carefully correct English that Jeannie was set off again.

'Oh Isa. I wish I had been there. Mind you, William Morrison was absent hissel' frae the dance hall on Saiturday. He must hae been sair affrontit an aw'.'

When Isa heard this, her first thought was to wonder whether he would stay away altogether, in which case she could return. And so when Jeannie again reported him missing the next Saturday she decided she could try going back. Sure enough, William was never back there. Later she heard he had decided to go and live in Glasgow with one of his brothers and he was working in a foundry there. So Isa was able to put the incident behind her.

13

On August 6th 1918, Isa was nineteen. She found herself reflecting on her life and being grateful that her father had come out of the war alive and that he continued to keep well. She knew from Margaret and Chrissie that he was trying hard to stay sober. Work helped, and having to look after them. Margaret was now twelve and doing a lot of cooking, although Isa helped on her day off by making big pans of stew and soup and having a baking which could keep them going for a few days. Ten-year-old Chrissie was now a great help too, and with everyone doing their bit, the house in Sunnyside was kept clean and the cupboards full.

Chrissie was proving to be very bright indeed, scoring high marks in her tests and excelling in mathematics and English. Margaret was a bit of a dreamer but wrote wonderful compositions, which Isa put down to the early letter-writing she had undertaken when Isa was so far from home. She definitely had a way with words and could describe situations and people so clearly you thought you knew them yourself. Isa felt they were a credit to her and her parents, despite all they had been through. They were all made of stern stuff. Life could deal them tough blows, but somehow they just got up and got on with it. It would stand them in good stead for the future.

By the end of that month, August 27th, Isa was reading in the paper an account of the Battle of Amiens, which had begun shortly after her birthday. In July, Germany had sent 250,000 fresh troops into France to the Western Front. As a result, the Allies had made no advances and had been sore pressed to maintain their ground. But Philip Gibbs, the writer of the report, said, 'Now the tide has turned ... since August eighth the Allies have taken 50,000 prisoners and 500 guns. The Army is buoyed up with hope... Soldiers are fighting for a quick victory and a quick peace so they may get back to normal life and wipe this thing clean from the map of Europe and restore the world to sane purposes.' Isa put down the paper and paused to reflect what this might mean. Could it be that victory was now in sight? God, she hoped so.

In October that year, Isa was busy preparing pheasants for a dinner party which the Sinclairs were to host the next day. Phyllis was working at the sinks, peeling turnip, parsnip and beets. She had complained of a sore throat and feeling achy when she started that morning and was definitely under the weather, sniffling as though she had a cold coming on. Isa had reminded her to be sure and use her handkerchief to cough and sneeze into and to wash her hands before continuing with her work. Phyllis had been working away at the sink behind her when Isa heard a thump. She turned to find Phyllis on the floor. Isa dropped what she was doing, wiped her hands on her apron and bent down to the figure collapsed on the flagstone floor.

'Phyllis,' she said. 'Phyllis, can you hear me?' The girl lay crumpled and unmoving. Isa could hear wheezing. She put her hand on the girl's forehead and almost recoiled, it was so hot and moist. She took her wrist to feel for a pulse. It was racing. Isa lost no time. She rolled the girl gently on to her side and rolled the hearthrug up behind her to stop her rolling back in case she was sick and choked. Then she ran upstairs to find Mrs Sinclair. She was in the drawing room.

'Mrs Sinclair. Please forgive the sudden intrusion but Phyllis is very ill, ma'am. She has just collapsed on the floor and has a fever and a racing pulse. It has come on her so sudden. I fear she may need the attention of a doctor.'

Mrs Sinclair followed Isa downstairs to the kitchen and was shocked to find the state the girl was in. Her clothing was now damp all over, sweat was pouring off her face and her breathing was rasping. Mrs Sinclair left Isa wiping her down with cold cloths and hurried to telephone for the doctor. She called for her husband to help carry Phyllis up to her room. Isa loosened her clothing and got her changed into a cool nightgown after sponging her all over with lukewarm water to cool her down. In lots of ways it looked like influenza, except that Phyllis was unconscious and clearly her body was far more stressed. One minute she had been peeling the vegetables and next this. The poor girl was struggling for breath. When Isa rinsed the cloth in the basin she noticed the water in the bowl had turned red. Looking again at Phyllis' face she saw there was blood coming from her nose. Isa did not like the colour of her face either. This illness was very frightening in its suddenness. Phyllis, after all, was a strong young girl, used to hard physical work. How could she be overcome so quickly like this? She was starting to moan now and thrash around on the bed as though having a nightmare. Isa prayed for the doctor to come quickly.

The doctor was in his late sixties and had been retired until the war claimed most of the local doctors for service at the front and he was called back on duty. When he examined the patient and heard what Isa had observed, he advised bed rest and lots of fluids. 'It appears to be a severe dose of influenza,' he pronounced. 'We're seeing a number of quite extreme cases this year. Spanish influenza: a new, very virulent strain. So let's keep everyone else well away. Wash clothing and bed linen separately. Carry on with the sponging down and try to get her to drink as much as you can. When the fever passes, some inhalation and nasal washes can help with the congestion. She will need someone to sit with her while this high fever lasts. All being well it should break in a few hours.'

'Mrs Sinclair, if it is possible I would like to sit with Phyllis,' Isa said firmly. 'I have already been with her and I have nursed my sisters through similar bouts.'

The doctor quickly concurred that was an excellent solution, rather than exposing someone else to the germs. Mrs Sinclair headed off to show him out and finish things for the family's evening meal. Isa sat quietly in the attic room, gently sponging the overheated body. She found herself almost chanting a prayer for Phyllis to recover.

'Please, dear God, make her well.' She could not bear to be witness to another death.

She must have fallen asleep in the chair. When she awoke, an early autumnal sunlight was fingering the bedspread in weak shafts and Phyllis' eyes were open.

'Isa, what happened? Why are you in my room?' She tried to sit up but could not move a muscle.

'Don't worry. You have influenza. You were taken most unwell yesterday but the fever has broken. You're going to be fine.'

What a relief Isa felt course through her body. The doctor was pleased with the patient when he visited later that morning to check on her progress.

'You had us all worried there, young lady, but thanks to this excellent nurse,' he smiled over to Isa, 'you look like you will pull through. Well done.'

When Isa was next chatting to Jean, she told her that several in the town had been stricken by the virus; many were very ill indeed and had needed to be taken to hospital. Old Mrs McClintock from number thirty-five Sunnyside Road didn't make it but neither did some folk their own ages. 'It's a gye queer strain o' influenza that's ta'en them in their prime an aw', nae jist the aul' folks,' was what people were saying.

The influenza virus hung around all that winter and there was always someone known to be struggling with it. But the news Isa had read about the Battle of Amiens in France had indeed marked the turn of the war. On November 11th, when Phyllis was fully recovered, she and Isa were in the kitchen going about their usual Monday chores. At eleven o'clock the church bells started ringing. They rang and rang without stopping. Isa looked at Phyllis.

'Is this it, do you think? Is the war over?' Phyllis asked her.

'Let's go up and see.'

They headed upstairs and in the hallway were met by a beaming Mrs Sinclair.

'It's all over, girls. The Armistice has been signed. Thank God. Our men will soon be home.'

There were sighs of relief. Isa's uncles would all soon be home. Her father would be lifted up by their return. He had felt it, being home alone, knowing they were still at the front. It had not seemed right to him and yet he could not have gone back. It had taken long enough to get back to work. He had contented himself with his contribution to the making of munitions for government contracts at the Carron Works, which he knew were used to defend the freedom of Europe and would have been amongst the equipment his brothers and friends were using.

Through the windows, they could see people had gone out on to the streets to greet each other in relief. Phyllis, Isa and Mrs Sinclair did the same. They could hear train whistles from the stations and the foundry yards. The children were out from the school too. Workers from the foundry and the railway station and factories were running down the streets, some in tears, others shouting and cheering. 'War is over.' 'Thank God we've made it.'

By Wednesday afternoon, when Isa took her afternoon off and met Jean in the Toon café, there was a buzz on the streets of Falkirk. Everyone was excited at the thought of the men coming home and relieved at the removal of the stress of being a nation at war. People were moving around more quickly, smiling, with a new lightness in their step.

A few weeks later, when the first troops began arriving back, the townsfolk were out on the streets in strength to welcome the return of the 'Bairns o' Fa'kirk' who had been serving their country. Among them, Isa recognised school friends whom she had not seen since her father left for the war and she had been sent to Glasgow. Some were taller. Some looked stooped. Many still had disbelief etched on their faces. Isa remembered her search through the hospital wards to find her father and the dreadful sights she had seen. Great Britain's young men had made huge sacrifices for this victory. Some had paid with their lives, others with dreadful injuries or disabilities. Some would never walk, some never hear, others never see again. Many might never sleep undisturbed by nightmares or pain. The world was now at peace, but at a price.

Unfortunately there was little peace at the Sinclairs' for the staff. Mrs Forester the housekeeper seemed determined to undermine everyone. Prone to sneer at Isa, stuck in the kitchen and hardly ever upstairs, she took great pleasure in announcing how well thought-of she herself was by Mr and Mrs Sinclair, and lost no opportunity to lord it over Isa, Phyllis and Bessie. As housemaid, Bessie had a terrible time. The housekeeper was never satisfied with Bessie's work and the poor girl was hounded from morning till night. Isa hated this. She and Phyllis had become a close team in the kitchen and worked really smoothly together, but she grew to hate the housekeeper's presence and became tense at her approach. Isa quickly realised she could not stay. She began to keep her ears and eyes open for other opportunities.

It was not long before she heard that the minister of the Erskine United Free Church, Rev. Hutchison, was looking for a live-in cook/housekeeper. This would be perfect, Isa realised. There would be no other member of staff above her. She would have help in the house and kitchen with daily maids, but she would be in overall charge. She felt a strong surge of longing arise in her. She wanted this post. She still had Lady Tolquhoun's reference. Within a week she had an interview and was successful. The one hard thing about leaving was parting with Phyllis.

Isa came down to the kitchen with her bags all packed, ready to go.

'I am so sorry yer leavin' Miss Dick. I have loved workin' wi' you. Ye've learnt me so much and been sae good tae me.' Phyllis started to cry.

'Now then, Phyllis. Don't be sorry. We can still keep in touch. I'm happy to help you anyway till they get a replacement. I have something for you.' Isa passed the girl an oblong package wrapped in brown paper and tied with string.

Phyllis peeled off the wrappings to reveal a hard-backed bound notebook.

'This will be your book for when you take over

a kitchen yourself. The cook at the Tolquhouns' got me to write down her recipes and hints. You've seen my one.'

'Yes.'

'Well, you can start to write in the things you've already learned how to do. And if you need a copy of some of my recipes you can add them in. Whoever comes next, you can write in what you learn from her too. That's how it works, how we help each other.'

Phyllis opened it up and gasped, for Isa had already written in several basic recipes she could use to keep things going until the new cook was appointed.

'Oh Miss Dick, thank you so much.'

'We've been a good team together, Phyllis. You'll be an asset to the new cook. Now dry your eyes. It's not as if I'm going to Timbuktu. I'll probably bump into you in the High Street on Wednesday.'

Phyllis laughed and helped Isa with her bags to the door. She moved to shake hands, but Isa drew her into a hug. 'Take care of yourself, Phyllis.' Then she picked up her bags and headed off to her new post.

The Hutchisons' manse stood near the church in leafy, tree-lined Camelon Street alongside lots of other fairly grand three-floored villa houses over-looking the canal. Isa had never been a church-goer. When they were younger and her mother was alive they had gone to the Band of Hope, which met in the church hall. This organisation was part of the Temperance movement, which worked with Christian churches to encourage people away from the overuse of alcohol. The Band of Hope inspired young people to 'sign the pledge' that they would abstain from alcohol, and organised social occasions where no alcohol was available but there was still a party atmosphere. Her mother had been a great advocate of the movement and her father had signed the pledge under her influence. Isa remembered loving the songs with their great swelling tunes, which the adults sang out strongly with various harmonies: songs such as 'We Shall Gather at the River' and 'Bringing in the Sheaves'. She had been baptised in the church and remembered sometimes going there on a Sunday with her mother, but since her death, the work at home and then in domestic service had meant there was not much time for churchgoing. But she was not anti-church. She believed there was a God and when she was in need she prayed and found comfort. Part of her wondered if working for a minister would be any different from working for her previous employers.

Inside, the house lacked any ostentation. Furniture was solid, plain and sturdy. There was carpet in all the public rooms and heavy curtains made by Mrs Hutchison, who was a good needlewoman. The Hutchisons had two grown-up sons: Craig, who was studying to be a lawyer, and Alexander, who was not long back from service in Arabia. He looked as though he needed feeding up but he had a great sense of humour and he was soon teasing Isa in a way she found very brotherly and that reminded her of her boy cousins. Craig, on the other hand, thought himself very superior to them all and looked down his nose at everyone rather than look anyone in the eye.

Isa quickly settled in her new room, much bigger than usual with a proper window looking over the back garden. She had a rocking chair made comfy with chintz cushions, and a proper wardrobe as well as her bed and cabinet. There were two lamps, one by the bed and another standard lamp by her chair where she could read or sew. There was a little writing desk too under the window and she loved to sit there looking on to the greenery and flower beds.

Her work was to organise the household staff and meals. A maid, Lizzie, who lived out, did the cleaning and rough work and Isa had to give her the daily tasks. Isa was responsible for planning the meals, shopping for them and reporting to Mrs Hutchison every Monday morning with her plans. It was already a well-ordered household and her new employers very warm and welcoming of so young a cook in charge.

Every morning Isa and Lizzie gathered with the family in the drawing room for prayers. Everyone took it in turns to read the Scripture passage for the day and then the Rev. Hutchison led prayers. Isa was often surprised by the Biblical stories and their powerful messages and moved by the minister's humble prayers. She did not have much to compare it with, but she knew she was in the presence of a man of integrity who lived as he preached, with honesty and compassion.

One morning it was her turn to read the passage. At school Isa had loved reading aloud but she would have practised. When Mr Hutchison handed her the Bible she began fairly confidently, but soon was stumbling over unfamiliar words and place names she had never seen before and had no clue how to pronounce. The younger son, Alexander, was standing next to her and began to whisper the pronunciations to her. His older brother, Craig, just sniggered and made fun of her afterwards, repeating her mispronunciations behind her back.

Later that day the Rev. Hutchison came into the kitchen and asked to have a word with her. They both sat at the kitchen table.

'Isa,' he said, 'I realise you may not have read from Scripture before and that I may have put you in an awkward position this morning. I am very sorry. It's just that that is how we start our day here.'

'Please, sir, do not trouble yourself on my account. I would have managed better had I practised, but some of the words were completely new to me.'

'Well, I wondered if I might be of some help. Have you made your communion?'

'No sir. I am baptised, but with my father being at the war I have not taken full membership of the church.'

'Would it be something you would like to know more about? I am running a communicants' class at the church on Thursday evenings, which will start next week. You would be most welcome to attend.' The minister looked into her young eyes and saw the longing to belong. He waited.

Isa saw in his gaze his kindness and integrity, and knew she wanted to hear more. And so she began communicants' class along with several other young adults in Falkirk, including some young men returned from the war and her old friend Jeannie, who she persuaded to come with her.

The two young women now had new topics of conversation when they met in the tearoom on their afternoons off. Jeannie had found work in another big house on the other side of the town. Together they discussed the readings and inform-ation they were given about the Christian faith.

For Isa the story of Christ in the Garden of Gethsemane was a powerful one. After He had eaten His last meal with His friends they went out to a garden and Jesus went off to pray, asking them to stay awake and watch since they all knew the authorities were looking for an opportunity to arrest Him.

'Isa, I don't get that prayer. What does He mean when He says, "Father, if Thou be willing, re-move this cup from me; nevertheless not my will but Thine be done." What is the cup?' Jeannie asked.

'Mr Hutchison says it's the suffering He sees before Him, Jeannie. He feels He must prepare Himself for death but it's such a death. It reminds me of the look I saw in some of the men's eyes in the hospital when I was searching for my father. They were terrified they would get well enough to be sent back to the front. Knowing what lay ahead of them was awful. To go the first time, when they didn't know about the trenches and the shelling and the ghastly injuries and horrific deaths, was one thing. But to be asked to go back was more than many could bear. Jesus would have seen crucifixions. They all had. He knew what the

Romans would do to Him if they got Him. No much wonder it says He was sweating blood.'

'Why did He not run away?'

'I think it's because He had to stay true to Himself and His belief in what God was. If He ran away it would be like admitting defeat. That He had got it all wrong. That the old Jewish ideas were right after all. So He had to stand firm. Even if it meant they tried to destroy Him. He wanted to stand up for God.'

'What courage. I don't think I could do that.'

A few weeks later they were formally asked if they wanted to go ahead and join the church, with all the responsibilities that entailed. One or two were not sure but Isa and Jeannie were very definite. Both knew it was a solemn undertaking, but they knew they wanted this in their lives: this sense of belonging to something important, something that was changing their lives for the better, being a part of the church and working in their community to make it a better place. They were to make their vows on the Sunday at the morning service. Isa wanted her family there and so she spoke to them when she visited on her day off.

'I've got something I want to ask you all,' she began as they sat around the tea table. They were tucking in to the pancakes and jam she had made. 'I have been going to classes at the church, as you know, with the Reverend Hutchison, and I am ready now to join the church and take my first communion. It will be on Sunday and I would like you all to come and support me.'

Margaret was first to respond. 'Will we have to

do anything, Isa?'

'No. You would just sit in the congregation in the row behind us and follow the service. It would be a chance to wear your best.'

Margaret's eyes lit up at this. She enjoyed a chance to dress up in her finery although there was seldom the opportunity. 'I'll definitely come.'

'Me too, Isa. Do you get a prize for finishing the course?' asked Chrissie.

'No. No prize except knowing I belong to the church as a full member. That's enough of a prize.' Isa looked across at her father. 'You'll come, won't you, Father?'

Her father looked up at his eldest daughter and saw his wife in her more clearly than ever. She had been a spiritual woman, keen to live right and keep faith with the church. Had she been alive he might have been a better man. But here was his daughter following in her footsteps. Of course he would support her, although he did not feel fit enough to cross the door of a church after all he had done, war or no war. 'Aye lass,' he said quietly. 'I'll be there. Spruced and shining. And richt prood tae be there for ye.'

On Sunday morning the family were dressed in their best, shoes polished, the girls wearing their hats and sitting in the church pews. Isa and Jeannie sat in the front rows, along with the others who were to make their profession of faith and partake in communion for the first time. It was a bright, frosty October morning. Isa felt excited. For her this was a momentous decision that she was taking: aligning herself in full with the church, agreeing to follow Christ's teaching and work within the church for her community. She rehearsed in her head what the minister would ask each of them and what she had to reply.

The ceremony would take place after the sermon. She settled herself to listen to the Rev. Hutchison, her minister and her employer. What would he have to say to them?

'Friends, we are gathered as always to hear the Word of God, but today we have a special ceremony to perform. We are to admit into full fellowship of the Church of Christ worldwide these young people you see before us. We who have already made this commitment years previously are also called upon at this time to renew our vows in our hearts, as we recall Christ commissioning His disciples: "Go ye therefore, and teach all nations, baptising them in the name of the Father, and of the Son, and of the Holy Ghost: teaching them to observe all things whatsoever I have commanded you: and, lo, I am with you always, even unto the end of the world." So today we think carefully about the meaning of our commitment to Christ. Why is it that we took this step? What keeps us in faith?

'Perhaps the verse I just read answers my questions. Why is it we take the step of faith? Because others committed themselves to telling of Christ's life, explaining His teaching, embodying His life in theirs, and we were drawn to what we saw and heard. How could we resist this man of love, wisdom and compassion? This man who transformed the lives of all whom He met and who transforms us; who heals us, makes us whole; who enables us to live with integrity, with compassion, seeking that which is good. You first communicants have seen this. You have heard the story of Christ's work on earth and you have found yourself saying, "Yes, this is good. This is right living. These are the principles I want to build my life upon." Today you have come to publicly share your "yes" with our congregation. And you ask of us our support on your journey of faith. So all of us here gathered today make you a commitment too. We promise to share your journey, listen to your doubts and searching, encourage you when life is tough and faith is weak; and to rejoice with you in all your joy. For we are on this journey together as Christ's people.

'But that is not the only support you can rely on in this often demanding but always rewarding life of faith. For the rest of the verses I read remind us Christ journeys at our side always. When the road is safe and easy and our direction clear, but also when we are shrouded in fogs of doubt or burdened with suffering. He has promised to be with us always. He will be your guide, your, strength, your direction, and your ally. So although this step seems a terrifying prospect, to commit to live as Christ lived, He will show you the way, step by step, never moving too far ahead of you. We who have already committed ourselves to Him can testify to this and we know His promise is for you also.

'Now as we sing our communicants' hymn, "Take my life and let it be consecrated Lord to Thee", I ask our new communicants to come forward.'

Isa's heart fluttered as she rose to take her place

187

in front of the communion table. She loved this hymn and sang it from her heart, meaning every word.

When the congregation had retaken their seats, the minister came towards the new communicants and asked each one in turn to make their vows. Isa was trembling when he came to her and asked her if she confessed her faith in God, the maker of Heaven and Earth, and in Jesus Christ as her saviour and Lord.

'I do,' she said clearly. She was then asked if she promised to live according to his teaching and was she willing to commit herself to the study of Scripture, to prayer and to giving of her time and means to the work of Christ's church. She said a firm 'yes' to these too.

Then the minister laid his hand on her bowed head and she closed her eyes as he blessed her.

'May the Lord bless thee and keep thee. May He make His face to shine upon thee and give thee peace, as thou committest thyself to His service. Amen.'

Isa felt a stirring in her at these words. She was going to live this life. She had a sense of all being well and right and in balance. Much of the rest of the service was a blur as her own inner joy rose within her. She did remember that the elders in the church came and shook them all by the hand to welcome them into their fellowship.

Back home, her father presented her with her own copy of the Bible. She was thrilled. It had been so important that he support her. On Monday, back at work in the manse, Isa felt different: taller, more confident. She was no longer outside. As a member of the church she felt surer of her place in this family's household and in her community.

14

Not long after this Isa started walking out with a man she had met at Johnny Doke's dance hall in Falkirk. Peter Swan was a handsome, well-presented man who wore perfectly tailored suits and gloves to come dancing. He had caught her eye early on, but he seemed rather taken with another girl at first. After a few weeks, though, he was regularly securing several dances with Isa each week. He was not the lightest on his feet, but he did know what he was doing with most of the dances and he had a great spark in his eye. He worked in the railway as a clerk in the office at Coatbridge. It was a clean, responsible job with prospects. He always had money to take her for tea and to present her with treats. He would send her a card near their next meeting with simply, 'See you on Sunday, same time same place. Peter.' At first she found it very disappointing that there were no fonder greetings, but it was reassuring that he was looking forward to the meeting by sending her a reminder and the cards were sometimes prettily chosen. They could only meet every three weeks because of his shifts and her days off.

If the weather was agreeable, they would walk in

the Dollar Park among the flower beds and around the goldfish pond, sitting on benches to relax. The local tearooms provided somewhere warm on colder days and they were never short of conversation. Isa heard all about Peter's family: his father was a tailor employed in his brother's business, the well-known establishment of Sandilands; Peter's oldest brother, Jimmy, had his own bakery; Tommy ran a butchery in Falkirk; his older sister Alice was married with two girls, and Jeannie, of whom he was very protective, despite the fact she too was older than him, was in service like Isa.

She in her turn told him of her life and family, including the tragic deaths of her mother, Eliza and the baby boy.

'Oh God, Isa. That must have been hard on you. I knew about Eliza's death, of course. It was in the paper. The whole of Camelon virtually was on the streets for that.'

'It certainly felt like that. People were very kind immediately, but afterwards they just expected life to go back to normal. And it was for them. But it never went back to how it had been for us. We were all changed. My mother never recovered and it led to her own death, I think. It was her heart failing, but not just because of illness or weakness. It was broken. She could not bear to go on living.'

'And what about you?'

Isa was stopped in her tracks. Could she put into words what she had felt? What she still felt? She looked into his face.

'Me? I just had to get on with things. Once she died I was the one who took over running the house. I had to leave school, which I missed. It was tough at first and I made loads of mistakes, but in the end I got quite good at it. That's why I ended up in service to Lord and Lady Tolquhoun. My tutor at the college in Glasgow recommended me to them when they were looking for someone to start with their household in London.'

'You worked for the aristocracy?'

'I did. And a very fine couple they were. They took a real interest in their staff. When they heard about my situation, with my father gone to the war and my mother passed, Lady Tolquhoun told me to see her and her husband as my protectors if ever I was in any trouble. And when I found my father in the hospital and told them the story of his rescue, Lord Tolquhoun sent his car and driver round for my father and entertained him in his study. My father was very impressed with him, for he talked to him in broad Scots. They really were fine people. And he spoke out for the working classes. He voted for Lloyd George's bills on pensions for the over-seventies and tax rebates for families with children. I remember the day I saw them all dressed up to attend the opening ceremony at the House of Lords. They were fabulous in their full regalia and robes.'

'Well, I am glad you had a good experience of the gentry, but I tell you, Isa, I rubbed up against some of them in the trenches and they were none o' them any better than ourselves. Some were right idiots, I tell you. Straight into officer posts with not an ounce of nous between their ears. I once had to guide a group o' men from the back lines up to the front. That was what I did, as a runner. You had to have your wits about you and listen and smell the air and look for the telltale signs of where the worst shelling was going on so that you didn't move into a direct line of fire. There was no use mapping it out because the landscape constantly changed with the bombing and shelling. Trees were all burned, hills flattened, bunkers that were there one day were shelled to extinction another.

'Anyway, I was supposed to guide this group and lo and behold this jumped-up officer with his toffee-nosed accent wanted to tell me which way we should take. Well you're supposed to obey an officer's order but if we did obey this idiot I knew we'd all be shelled to blazes. So I drew myself up and I said, "With respect, sir, I have been a runner between the lines for eight months. I know how to read the signs. We cannot take that easterly route you used last time because the last few days that's where the shelling has been worst. And the northeasterly direction has no secure duckboards left. The mud has made those walkways impassable. I saw men slip off two days ago and lose their lives in the mud. If you take my advice I can keep you and your men safe. I know it's longer but it's safer." Well the bugger looked like he was fit to burst at my impudence.

'"Don't you know, corporal, that you could be court-martialled for disobeying a commanding officer?"

'"Of course, sir," I said, "But at least I'll be alive to attend it. You can go east or north-east if you prefer, but I will be going in the northerly direction and approaching the front further up the lines."'

'So what happened?' Isa's heart was thumping at the bravery Peter had shown in standing up to an officer. She was amazed at his confidence.

'Well, thankfully one of the men had travelled up to the front with me before, when he'd been in another unit, and he told the officer that I had a reputation as one of the best runners. Others had lost their lives in attacks, but I always seemed to know the safe routes. I was known as Lucky... So the officer backed down and said to me to lead the way. And as we headed north we saw the shelling landing heavily in the easterly direction he had wanted to take.'

'So you were proved right both by the man's testimony and by events. That must have made you feel so proud.'

'It did. But it also showed me that we ordinary working-class folk are just as able as the toffs. For all their posh accents and fancy schooling, money and inherited land, it all boils down to what can you do. In a war, your name or title or grand estate won't make you a hero. You need skills and practical courage and an ability to cope with the rough life. That's when we ordinary men could knock spots off the officers.'

He looked into Isa's face and saw there her open admiration. He knew then that he loved her looking at him like that: looking up to him as a man who was brave and strong. She was strong herself after all she had come through. To have her admiration made him feel worthy of her. He found himself wanting to look after her and to keep that light of admiration in her eyes. Even if he was not nearly as brave as he had made out.

One afternoon they had taken tea in town before going on to the dance hall. Isa was not very satisfied with their meal of chicken and mushroom pie.

'This pastry is soggy and not well enough fired. That's been cooked in too low an oven for puff pastry. I'm not going to eat mine.' She put down her fork, frowning, and looked as though she was about to complain.

'I'd like to sample your cooking some day,' Peter said brightly, to deflect the situation, not wanting her to make a fuss in the restaurant.

Isa smiled. 'Well, that might be arranged. We could meet at my father's next time for our tea before the dance. What do you think?'

'That would be grand, Isa. I'd love to meet your father.'

John Dick was keen to meet this man who had been escorting his eldest daughter to the dances for the past six months. She had told him he worked in the railway, and John thought that was a good reliable job. The brothers all had their own successful shops and the parents were respectable. Mind you, he knew his own reputation in the town would no doubt be an issue.

It had not put Peter off. He wondered what kind of man John Dick would be and arrived punctually with a bunch of irises for Isa, looking very smart and dapper, dressed for the dance in his suit, shirt and cravat with a white silk scarf. John looked down at his shoes and they were army shiny. He indicated a seat by the fire for Peter, while Isa went to fetch glasses.

'You'll have a wee dram with me, Peter.'

'Indeed, thank you, sir.'

When Isa returned, the glasses were filled and a short toast to their health proposed. Isa stuck to ginger beer. She felt rather nervous. Her mind was racing with questions. Would they like each other? Would meeting her father put Peter off her? Would either of them say something to embarrass her or annoy the other? She so wanted them to get on well enough. She was realising just how much she liked Peter Swan. Had she been foolish to let him meet her father so soon? Should she have warned him more about him? And what about the meal? She hoped the pie would turn out well so Peter could see her skills as a cook.

Once the men started chatting about the war, she went over to the stove to see to the meal, all the while keeping her ears alert to the conversation. It seemed to be going well. Peter was interested in her father's experiences at the Dardanelles. They seemed to be comparing notes about the conditions and supplies.

She reached into the oven for the pie and gently lifted it on to the wooden board. The pastry was beautifully risen, puffed and golden. She tested the temperature of the meat with a skewer and it came out roasting hot. She laid it on the table, along with a bowl of mashed potato and buttered carrots. She called them to the table. Her father cut the pastry crust and served the pie and they helped themselves to the vegetables.

'Mm, Isa – this is so good. You're right. This beats the one they served at Robertson's hands down.'

'Aye she's a grand cook, Peter. Ye'd hae a job tae find a better.' How good it felt to hear her father and her young man praise her cooking. She glowed under their appreciation.

Peter found he felt completely at ease with this big man with the huge reputation as a fighter, foundryman and soldier. In physical stature he himself with his neat, slight build felt a lightweight in comparison, but John Dick heard about his war experiences and respected him as a grown man. He did not feel he had to mind his Ps and Qs or stand on ceremony. He felt welcomed and respected.

A few weeks later, Peter invited Isa to meet his parents.

The Swans lived in a much smarter part of town but not so grand that they had servants or help in the house. Isa dressed in her best, including a new hat, and was escorted on Peter's arm to the house.

'Mother, I'd like to present to you Miss Isa Dick.' Peter looked from Isa to his mother, hoping all would go well.

Mrs Swan peered at Isa through the round rims of spectacles, perched on her sharp hooked nose, which magnified a pair of beady eyes. Isa felt as if she was prey at the mercy of a hawk, so intense was the woman's stare. No hand was proffered so Isa kept hers on the handle of her handbag and slightly inclined her head as she quietly said, 'Pleased to make your acquaintance, Mrs Swan.'

'Wish I could say the same, Miss Dick,' came the sharp reply. Isa's hackles were up. Peter had warned her a little about his mother's feistiness and set ways, but she had not quite prepared herself for this reception.

'Would your father be one of the Fighting Dicks?' The voice was laced with disapproval.

Ah, so that's what was worrying his mother: her wretched relatives and their reputation and what her son might be getting himself into. Why could she not have had a normal family? But Isa was proud of them too and knew there was more to them than their reputation as fighters.

'Mrs Swan, my father is a brother to the men known as the Fighting Dicks, but those days are long since past. He is a family man who works hard and who served his country, although he was not required to do so.'

'Oh, I know all about men serving their country who were not required to do so,' was the sharp, haughty reply. 'All my sons were in the war and Peter will no doubt have told you that he signed up underage to go off with his brothers to France. Thank God they all came home. I'd never have forgiven him if he hadn't.' She looked across to her son and smiled, the smile of a besotted mother to her favourite son, which quickly melted away on returning to his lady friend. Isa shivered.

'Well, I suppose you had better take a seat. Mind the antimacassar.'

Isa looked around the crowded Victorian room, stuffed to the brim with furniture laden with ornaments and pot plants. There was hardly a glimpse of skirting board, so heavily populated was the room with occasional tables draped in long-fringed chenille cloths. This was a house that said, 'We are respectable and of good standing.' Isa had developed an educated eye from her time serving in grand houses, especially those of the

Tolquhouns, and as she scanned the room she saw no fine porcelain pieces, just a considerable amount of inferior china littering the surfaces.

Mrs Swan herself was bedecked in a stiffly starched white pinstriped blouse, with a ruffle at the neck and cuffs, a long, dark-green tweed skirt and a small knitted shawl, needed to counteract the effect of the draft coming in under the living room door. Her husband was severe and imposing, despite his short stature, and he sported a waistcoat with the gold chain of his pocket watch on view.

Conversation in that oppressive room under the beady scrutiny of Peter's mother was not free-flowing and jovial. But Isa felt she acquitted herself well. Peter's parents seemed impressed that she had worked for the Tolquhouns in London and rather surprised that she had given all that up to work in Falkirk.

His mother questioned her. 'Why ever did you come back to Falkirk, Miss Swan, after such a good position?'

It felt like an interrogation in a courtroom but Isa felt pride rise within her at what she had done with her life, not shame or failure, as seemed to be implied in the imperious tone of the, question.

'I missed my family too much, Mrs Swan. I brought up my sisters when my mother died and to be so far away from them was too hard. And of course, when I served at the Tolquhouns' I was just working in the kitchen alongside the cook, whereas here with the Sinclairs and the Hutchisons I *am* the cook.'

Peter, sitting next to her on the couch, squeezed

her hand. He had always had difficulty standing up to his mother, but here was his sweetheart defending herself. He felt so proud of her.

When tea was served it was on a gleaming brass tray with a large china teapot and a meagre plate of finger cucumber sandwiches. Mrs Swan filled the cups one by one, holding the tea strainer over each, then resting it on the drip bowl. She asked if they required lemon, milk or sugar and added their choice to the cup before handing it on its saucer to each person in turn, her husband first, then Peter, and lastly Isa. This amused her. The pouring of the tea was pure upper class, as Isa had seen in the Tolquhouns' drawing room, right down to the sugar tongs and the slop bowl for the milk jug. But their etiquette was working class: men first. In the grand houses it would have been female guests first, then females in the family, then male guests and finally male family. What was more, the tea was stirred vigorously in circles, the teaspoon clinking against the cup. Isa knew that the true upper classes stirred the tea in a folding motion, moving the spoon to and fro without touching the cup at all. There was little sign of generosity of spirit in the whole affair and when Mr Swan had finished his tea, he tapped his teaspoon on the side of his cup and his wife obligingly refilled it, not a word passing between them.

Thank goodness Peter never behaved in such a manner with her. His charm helped her see past his surly mother and arrogant father, who was distant and made no effort to engage with her throughout the visit, as if that was all that befitted her as a domestic servant: to recognise her existence then ignore her as of no consequence. She would have liked Peter to stand up for her a bit more, though. He could have told his mother off for being so belligerent at the start, for instance. Still, she knew how difficult it could be to stand up to a parent. Her own father required careful handling at times, even when she did not agree with him or condone his dreadful drunken behaviour.

Over the next weeks and months, they spent as much time as they could together, although meetings were always so far apart, and they wrote letters. Isa's were full of the little things going on in the Hutchison household or exploits of Chrissie's or Margaret's. Peter took an interest in all their lives and often gave good advice on how to handle situations. Sometimes his letters would say how much he missed her. She gave him a photo of herself, which he carried in his wallet, and he told her he would gaze at it last thing at night and wish her goodnight with a kiss. She read that over and over to herself and fell asleep with a smile on her lips at the thought. There was a romantic streak in him after all, she thought.

After the dances, as they walked along the canal before he took her back to the manse, they would hold hands and kiss, stopping under the trees, or sitting on a bench. Isa found her body longing for this closeness, which the night of dancing had anticipated. She loved being held and kissed, seeing the hunger in his eyes which she felt rising in herself. She realised she was in love with this man.

'Isa, beautiful Isa,' Peter whispered. 'I want to take down all this glorious hair and feel it fall all around me.' He began to kiss her ear and her neck. He heard her breathing change and he slid his hand down her throat towards the dipping neckline of her dress. Reaching her breast, he stroked her over the satin material and heard her breath catching again. He kissed her more deeply and drew her closer to him.

They held each other for what seemed hours. Then Isa looked at his watch and saw it was past midnight. 'Peter, I must be getting back.'

'Isa I wish you didn't have to go. I wish we could be together all night. I miss you so much.'

'I do too, Peter. But what else can we do?'

'We could get married. I want to. Do you? I mean, Isa, would you marry me?'

Filled with their lovemaking as she was, Isa found hurried thoughts flickering through her head. Peter had a steady, clean job with prospects. There would be no dirty overalls or heavy drinking at the beer shop with the foundrymen. But if she married, what would happen to her sisters? Yet she wasn't living at home, anyway, to be available to them any more. In the pause, Peter added, 'I have £100 saved to set up house, Isa, and we could get a railway flat.'

That sealed it for her. Married to Peter, she would have somewhere for her sisters to come and visit. They could all be more secure. She would be her own woman with a home and her man at her side. A man whose income would not be sweated for among rough men. A man who would look after her, and perhaps be there for her sisters too. A man to stand up to her father. A man who made her feel fully a woman.

'Yes,' she said. And he held her tighter than ever.

Now when they met they began planning the wedding and where they would stay. Peter applied for a railway house in Coatbridge. It was a few months before he heard their application had been successful. After checking it out himself, he took Isa there on their next outing. It was small but warm in a tenement on Jackson Street, in an area where most folk were Catholic. Isa could picture bright curtains at the windows, cosy chairs at either side of the fireplace and shiny pans above the range, and some of her little needlepoint sayings framed for the walls. She could make this into a good home for them. There was a scullery, a living room, two bedrooms, and a shared toilet on the landing – better than the outhouse at home.

The wedding was to be in her father's house. Rev. Hutchison would conduct the ceremony and they would share a lunch at the house with close family. Isa was increasingly excited as the little pile of sewn garments she made for her trousseau got higher and higher. There were camisoles, slips and knickers from satin remnants she had got in the market, all edged neatly with lace from her mother's sewing basket and from neighbours who had gifted her any little piece they could spare. She had some of her mother's tablecloths and embroidered one herself with daisies round the corners. Her grandmother sent hand towels of soft cotton, which she had hand-stitched and decorated with broderie anglaise trims. Two sets of sheets were given to her by her Aunt Teenie and Uncle

Tommy, and Isa embroidered the pillowslips with white cotton garlands of bluebells, her favourite flower. Chrissie was busy on some secret sewing project that she kept hidden from the others, and when she finally presented the exquisitely embroidered table runner, Isa was delighted and promised it would have pride of place on the dresser.

One sunny morning, a fortnight before the wedding, Mrs Hutchison called her into the drawing room.

'Isa, I would like you to have this as our wedding gift to you.' She handed Isa a beautifully tissue-wrapped soft parcel. 'Would you do me the honour of opening it now, my dear? It is something personal for yourself.'

Isa sat down with the parcel on her knee. She undid the bright yellow ribbons and unfurled the pale blue tissue paper. Deep inside the many layers nestled some fine crocheted knitwear in gold and cream. Isa lifted up the garment and shook off the paper. The threads caught the sunlight and almost sparkled. It was a gorgeous crocheted chemise with a beautiful silk camisole to wear underneath.

'Oh, Mrs Hutchison. This is so beautiful.'

'I am glad you like it. Would you like to try it on?'

Isa took it to her room and peeled off her work dress. She took out the straight-cut mid-calf-length cream skirt she had thought might be suitable for the wedding and then slipped on the camisole and the chemise. She turned to the full-length mirror on her wardrobe door. Stray fronds of her bright auburn hair, which had been pinned up for work then disturbed by her undressing, lay curled around her neck and shoulders. The edge of the scooped neck was scalloped and lay smooth against her skin, drawing attention to her oval face that now seemed to have a look of her mother about it, the stillness, the dignity of the inner person beneath the façade of the good looks and clear eyes. Isa saw how the gold and cream colours complemented her complexion, warming it, giving it a glow. The three-quarter sleeves allowed her forearms to be on view and she looked down from them admiringly at Peter's diamond ring sparkling on the third finger of her left hand. At the waist there was a ribbon of pale cream threaded through the eyelet work in the chemise, emphasising her shapeliness. Isa twirled and turned to view herself from as many angles as possible. She could not believe how flattering the outfit was. She knew then this would be what she would wear on the day she became Mrs Peter Swan.

She walked back downstairs brimful of confidence and full of thankfulness for her employer's kindness and thoughtfulness. Isa could never have afforded such a fine piece of clothing nor could her best efforts as a needlewoman have created such a lovely garment. Neither her father nor Peter's parents had thought of her need for a wedding outfit. It was something her mother would have done for her had she still been here.

Isa opened the drawing room door and glided in.

'Oh my dear, you look wonderful. You're stunning.' Mrs Hutchison brought her hands to her face in a gasp.

'Mrs Hutchison,' Isa began, 'I would like to wear this on my wedding day if I may.'

'Dear girl, that's what I hoped for! It's more perfect for you than I dreamed.'

On July 28th 1922, Isabella Mary Dick and Peter White Swan were married in the kitchen of her father's house at 72 Sunnyside Road, Falkirk. The bride looked radiant in gold and cream and the groom dashing in a new bespoke suit, made for him by his father, tailor at Sandilands. The wedding breakfast was steak pie from the local butcher's, served by the bride and her childhood friend and neighbour, Jeannie Macleod. The ceremony was conducted by the Rev. Hutchison of Erskine United Free Church. Afterwards he said to Isa he had never before been served by the bride at her own wedding. Such was the low-key affair celebrating her wedding day, the day she left her father's house, left her sisters and left her work at the manse to start her new life with Peter as his wife.

Peter's working for the railway had many perks. One was the free passes he accrued, which allowed travel by rail anywhere in Britain, and which he used on this occasion to take them on honeymoon to Torquay. It was a glorious summer and they were excited to be heading off on this new adventure of marriage. They settled into the carriage, cases up on the netted luggage racks, and sat side by side, watching Falkirk's smoking foundry towers recede into the distance to be replaced by green pasture land, then rolling border country as they headed south into England. Peter treated them to meals in the dining car. Isa felt so pampered. At last someone was looking after her for a change.

Their hotel was neat and pretty and Peter had booked a double room overlooking the sea. But when they arrived, the room they were shown had two single beds. This was not what the groom had in mind for his honeymoon. He went to complain and when the staff were apprised of the situation, they came up armed with sheets to bind the two beds together. Left on their own again, the newlyweds lay down, held hands and turned to face each other. It was perfect.

Their kisses were gentle and clinging, like their goodnight ones while courting, but then Peter was roused and became more insistent. Isa responded and found a desire stirring in her, the like of which she had never felt before. They were helping each other out of their clothes. Peter was slipping her camisole off her shoulder, his hot mouth pressed on her skin. Kisses were raining down on her. Her own nakedness thrilled her. She did not need to think what to do. It was as if her body knew and had been waiting to be touched and kissed to open up like this.

Peter was assured. He knew Isa was inexperienced and that he had to go gently, but she was so responsive. It was better than he had hoped. She was gorgeous, voluptuous. He loved the way she felt in his arms, the way she moved, the way her richly coloured hair waved and rippled through his fingers as he reached up to cradle her head in his hand.

He laid her down on her back and moved on top of her, kissing her mouth deeply. He heard her breathing in his ear as he moved to her breast. She tasted of honey. She felt so ready. As he began to enter her, Isa moaned with pleasure. Suddenly, as he moved deeper in her, she gasped as if in pain. Peter was oblivious. Isa was struggling under him, clutching at him. When he finished, he flopped over at her side. It was only then he saw she was crying. Stupid. He was stupid. He'd been too hard with her on her first time.

'Oh no, Isa. I'm sorry. I'm so sorry. I thought you were ready.'

She turned her tear-stained face to his, smiling up at him. 'Oh, no Peter, no. It's not that. I just never knew I could feel such things. I am so happy.'

'Dearest Isa.' They lay at peace in each other's arms warm and secure, reliving the details of their first day as a married couple.

All too soon it was time to go home to their new flat at 74 Jackson Street, Coatbridge. Isa was so excited about setting up house. She was looking forward to buying furniture for their home. She could make things like curtains and cushions herself but she would need to shop for material. Now that she was married, of course, there was no more working for others in their houses. She would be fully employed in looking after her own.

That first night in the flat, she remembered what Peter had said about having money saved. After they had eaten, when they were lingering over their cups of tea, she spoke to him.

'Peter, I was remembering you said you had

money laid by for setting up home. I could make a start tomorrow doing some shopping for us. We could do with some curtains and cushions. I could get the material and make a start on the sewing.'

'What money would that be? I've no money.'

Isa was stunned. 'Months ago you told me when you asked me to marry you that you had £100 laid by in your trunk for getting married and setting up home.'

'Aye, well. I could see ye needed a bit of persuading. So I told you I had money. But there's none. I gave it tae ma mither fur her false teeth.' He drained his cup and set it down on the saucer.

False teeth? Isa thought. 'But your mother doesn't have false teeth, Peter,' she said, incredulous.

'Naw, she spent it on something else instead. Point is, it's no' there. So we'll just have tae wait and save. Noo, I wouldnae mind another cup.' He turned to the newspaper and signalled the conversation was at an end by hiding behind it, engrossed. Just as his father was wont to do. However, Isa was not his mother.

She was furious. She could not believe what he had just told her. He had lied to get her into his bed and his house. How could he? How could he have done this to her? She had believed he was offering her the security she had craved, a better, more comfortable life. She had trusted him. She had had no cause not to. She pushed her chair away from the table and stormed through to the bedroom. She slammed the door and tucked a chair under the handle to jam it, like she used to do when her father came home drunk. There was

208

no way Peter was sharing her bed tonight.

Peter came after her and tried the handle. When it would not move he pushed and shoved at the door.

'Isa. Isa, what are you doing? This won't make us any richer, ye daft woman. I'm yer husband. Let me in.'

'You must take me for a fool, Peter Swan. Believing your lies and getting married to you. An' all the time you've known you got me on false pretences.' Isa was practically spitting at him as she held the chair firmly under the handle.

'Don't tell me ye only married me fur the money,' he sneered angrily. 'I don't believe ye. It was surely mair than that.'

'There's no way you're sharing this bed with me tonight. You can forget it.'

Peter heard the vehemence in her voice. He never thought she'd take it this way. He'd known there would be a discussion about the money sooner or later, but he just thought she would accept it. He was her husband. It was his money anyway. What was it to do with her, really? And yet, as he stood on the other side of the door imagining her in the bed on her own, he realised he had let her down. Briefly he had felt withholding the information from Isa had given him a sense of power: to think he had used the money to his advantage with first his mother and then Isa. Yet his mother had wheedled the money off him and now here he was in this mess with Isa. He felt somewhat weakened by the whole thing.

Maybe by the morning it would all have blown over. He could give her money out of this week's wage. He no longer drank with his mates, because to snare Isa he had had to go teetotal, and so they would save more quickly. He would say sorry. They would kiss and make up. It would be all right in the morning. So he told himself as he headed back through to the living room, sat down on one of the chairs and covered himself with the fringed velvet throw his mother had given them. The chair was not comfy and the beads on the throw scratched his skin but soon he had settled into a position that worked and he fell asleep.

Isa, meanwhile, was heartbroken. Her anger had abated but she was miserable at the deception. What kind of man was he who could do such a thing? Could he not stand up to his own mother? Was his wife and their home together not more important, or was he just a mother's boy? She felt lost, at sea. On honeymoon it had been wonderful. They had been so together, so happy. Was that all a sham too?

Isa's sleep was fitful and disturbed by old dreams of trying to protect Eliza from the train. This time she was down by the track, Eliza was tumbling down the slope on the other side, Isa stepped on to the tracks in the path of the train, hoping to reach her sister in time, but the train was at her shoulder as she crossed. She woke in the middle of a scream, alone in the bed, anxious and confused. The nightmare left her with a sense of threat creeping into her life that she had not foreseen. What was marriage to Peter going to be like?

15

Sure enough Peter apologised next morning and gave her a bit of his last week's wage and some money an uncle had gifted them at the wedding. It was enough to soothe her ruffled feathers, he thought. She could still go out and buy something for the house.

He whistled as he left for work with his homemade food in his lunch box, ready for his late shift. It started at two and went on till ten. It was always busy, especially early on, with the busiest passenger trains as well as goods trains on the lines. It was hard to keep alert over the whole shift, but essential. Make a mistake telling a driver he could go ahead at a signal or checkpoint and there could be tragic consequences if another train was on the same piece of track heading in the opposite direction. He had a name in the office for being coolheaded and alert. It came from the war years, he reckoned. He'd had to have his wits about him then, right enough, as a guide leading troops to and fro between the front and back lines in the trenches. But he did not want to be thinking about that today. He was off to work, with a wife at home. Sure, they had had a spat, but it was all blown over now. He was a married man and it put a spring in his step.

Isa went down into the High Street with the money in her purse, looking for something to buy, some knick-knack, perhaps, to brighten the dresser, or a vase for some flowers. She went into the second-hand shop to have a look at the bric-a-brac. She picked up several items in turn and rejected them. Then her eye alit upon a painting. It was of a horseman holding the reins of a rearing white horse. The sky behind him was a vivid blue, with pewter-coloured gathering storm clouds. He was wearing a bright-red jacket and a large feathered hat and he was trying to get the horse to cross the water that foamed at its feet. The picture was set in a lovely gold frame and Isa was enchanted with it. It looked like the man was winning against the odds and something in her really identified with that look on the horseman's face. It reminded her of Peter's stories about exercising the working horses at the front in their rest period. He had a real fondness for animals of all sorts, but this experience with the horses had made him deeply respectful of their intelligence and beauty. She asked the shopkeeper how much it was and soon left in possession of it wrapped in brown paper and string. The shop assistant had even made a string handle for her to make it easier to carry.

Peter will love this, she thought as she headed home. The horse is so powerful and beautiful and seems completely at one with the rider. It will look good on the living room wall.

When she got home, she found a hammer and nail, chose a spot to hang it and carefully placed the painting on the wall facing the door. He would see it when he came in. Then she prepared a casserole to hotter in the slow oven in the range, ready for his late supper after his shift. She could not contain herself. This was her first purchase for their house and she was desperate to share it with him. She was still annoyed about his deception, but he had apologised and there was no way to get the money back. She realised she hated his mother more for taking the money from her son.

Despite herself she had fallen asleep over her sewing when she heard the key in the lock. 'That's me, Isa. I'm home.' Peter spoke softly so as not to disturb her if she was in bed, but then he saw the slit of light under the living room door. He opened it gently.

As he stood in the doorway looking at the painting his jaw dropped.

'What the devil is that doing in here?'

Isa's ire was aroused. 'What do you mean? It's a painting I bought for the house with the money you gave me. Don't you like it?'

'Dae ye know ken who that is on yon horse?'

'No, Peter. I just liked the look of him. He looked proud, as if he was going to win through.'

'Really? You don't know who that is? Aye right, yer faither's no' an Orangeman.' He paused. 'It's a portrait o' King Billy, that's what it is, and here we are in a tenement surrounded wi' Catholics. I dinnae think we should hiv that on oor wall. It'll scare away all oor neighbours.'

Isa's anger fizzled as she realised her mistake. 'Oh Peter, I didn't know. I'll take it down right now.'

Peter caught her arm as she passed him. He looked into her eyes intensely. 'No. Dinnae bother the now. That'll wait till the mornin'. I'm hungry. I need a kiss.' And he kissed her on her full mouth and tasted the saltiness of her sweat. She gasped as he gently drew away. He smiled. 'Now, I could fine do wi a bite to eat.'

The next day Isa rewrapped the painting and took it back to the shop saying she would like to exchange it for something else. The shop owner knew he would have no bother selling it again to one of his feisty Protestant customers and guessed Isa's mistake from the deep blush which spread across her cheeks as she returned the painting.

'Aye, it's no' to everyone's taste, that one. I have some very nice flower vases over here that might suit you.'

When she left the shop, Isa bought flowers and once back in their flat she filled the newly purchased fluted cut-glass vase with the deep-red peonies and placed it carefully on the runner Chrissie had painstakingly stitched, which now draped the dresser. Much better, she thought.

Isa was taking her turn to scrub the communal stairs a few weeks later when she had to stop as a feeling of lightheadedness swept over her. When she stood up, she found herself quite dizzy and she had to sit down on a dry step to recover herself. A neighbour, Mrs Quinn, was arriving back from her shopping.

'Are ye aw'right there, Mrs Swan? Yer no' lookin' good.'

'Just came over a bit faint, Mrs Quinn. Needed to get my breath back.'

'Ye must be goin' real hard at it, ma lass. They steps'll do jist fine the way they are. Awaw in and hiv a lie doon.'

Isa started to stand but felt woozy still. This was so unlike her. Scrubbing the stairs was nothing compared with all the physical work she had been used to in her time in domestic service. Maybe she was sickening for something.

Sharp-eyed Mrs Quinn saw she had not regained her composure. She put down her shopping then cupped her hand around Isa's elbow. 'Looks like you could use a steadying hand, my dear. I'll see you in. Now let's get you into yer bed for a bit.'

Isa let herself be led to the bedroom. Her neighbour drew back the quilt and helped her on to the bed. 'I'll jist tuck a pillow under yer feet, lass. That'll let the blood get back to yer heid.'

She looked down at the pale young woman whom she hardly knew. She could see the signs but clearly the lass did not yet know. 'I'll look in on ye efter. You get a good rest. I'll see masel' oot.'

Isa was so glad to be lying down. Her head was still spinning and she felt nauseous, but it was better now she was flat. It was not long before she was dozing.

By the time Peter had returned, Isa was up and about like normal, puzzled by her little turn but glad it had not amounted to anything. A few days later, though, she could not lift her head off the pillow without waves of nausea and giddiness overcoming her.

'Oh, Peter, I think you'll have to get breakfast yourself. I can't move without my head spinning. I must be coming down with something.'

Peter looked down at his wife and saw she was even paler than normal and there were blue half-moons under her eyes, like bruises. He felt her forehead but she was not clammy or warm. He finished dressing. 'You lie on. Ma dinner's in the cold safe is it – ready tae tak' wi' me?'

'Yes.'

'I'll see ye later.' He gave her a swift kiss.

Isa lay dozing fitfully, waking each time to nausea and light-headedness. Eventually she knew she would have to get up to relieve herself. Slowly she raised herself on her elbows then shuffled to sit upright. She sat awhile before turning to the side and swinging her legs over the edge of the bed. She waited again. She slid her feet into slippers and reached for her dressing gown. Carefully she raised herself to her feet and stood upright. She did not feel good but she had to make it to the toilet on the landing.

She held on to the walls and to furniture, slightly bent over rather than fully upright as it eased the giddiness. She reached the front door of the flat and began to descend the stairs to the toilet on the halfway landing, clutching the banister firmly as she went. She had just relieved herself and was on her way out when the nausea overwhelmed her and she fell to her knees and retched into the toilet bowl with the door still open behind her. Everything was spinning. She thought she heard footsteps on the stairway. She lifted her head to turn and saw Mrs Quinn coming down the stairs towards her.

'Oh, Mrs Swan. What a state yer in. Why didn't ye tell me?'

Isa started crying. She felt so weak. She must look a terrible sight. She started to apologise.

'Shush shush. We'll soon get you sorted. Dinnae worry. It taks a lot o' us like this. I mind when I was carrying my first I was sick as a dog every day fur the first few months. But then it passed and I was right as rain.'

Isa could not really hear what her neighbour was saying, so focused was she on coping with a new wave of nausea. At last it passed. Mrs Quinn helped her on to her feet. Isa gripped the stair rail with one hand and draped the other arm around her neighbour's shoulders. Mrs Quinn slid her arm around Isa's waist for support, and together they made it back to the flat.

Once she had got Isa settled on the bed, Mrs Quinn popped back to her own flat across the landing, took a cup of broth from her soup pot and brought it through to Isa. She got her propped up on her pillows and helped her spoon the broth down slowly.

'You need to keep your strength up, my girl. If I'm not mistaken yer eating for two now.'

'What? You mean I might be pregnant?' Isa was astounded. So quickly? She and Peter had only been married two months. What would he think? A feeling wrapped itself around her heart and clutched it. What was it? Fear? Excitement? Joy?

'And Mrs Swan, I think you should call me Cathy from now on. We twaw are gettin' to ken each other weel enough for first names I think. Don't you?'

'Thank you so much for your help. I'm Isa. It's reassuring knowing you are just across the landing. I'm sorry I'm turning out to be such a nuisance.'

'Not at all, lass. We aw look efter yin anither here. Tell ye what. When yer feelin' a bit stronger ye'll come for a cuppae in my hoose and meet the wumen in the block. We all get along fine. They'll be gled tae meet ye.'

'I'd like that, Mrs Quinn ... I mean Cathy.'

When Peter got home that evening Isa had recovered, tidied up and made a meal. She was nervous about telling him. How had her mother done this? She had never been there at the announcements to her father. When her mother had told her about her pregnancies it was later on, when she was showing, and she would just say to her, 'There will soon be another brother or sister in the house, Isa. Won't that be nice?'

When she had cleared the plates off the table, she sat down across from him. He was reading the paper.

'Peter,' she began. 'Do you remember this morning I didn't feel so good?'

'Aye,' he said, still reading.

'Well, I didn't tell ye at the time but it wasn't the first time.'

'What do you mean? Have ye no' been well?' He was surprised and looked up at her face. She seemed well enough now. Why was she bothering to give him details of an illness she had recovered from? 'Ye look fine enough now.'

'I know. It seems to affect me worse in the mornings.' She paused, wondering if he would realise the significance of that. He made no reaction. 'Mrs Quinn – she told me to call her Cathy – saw me no' weel and helped me into the house. I was very sick, Peter, after you left.'

'I'm sorry, Isa. Maybe that got it oot o' yer system.'

'I don't think so, Peter. I think I may be in for a few weeks of it ... just in the mornings...' He still had not twigged. She would have to come out with it. She took a breath, shut her eyes and blurted out. 'Mrs Quinn said I must be pregnant.'

There was a silence. She could hear the clock ticking and the sounds of the family downstairs. She willed him to be pleased.

He was stunned. Pregnant? Already? They had only been married two months. And then it sank in. There would be a wean, another mouth to feed. But this was what he had wanted: to start his own family. He got up and came round to her, took her hands and pulled her to her feet. He could see she was still waiting for his response.

'That's grand, Isa. It's just so quick. I never thought it would happen so soon.'

'I know. It fair surprised me too. But you're glad?'

He smiled. 'Of course. We've time to get organised. But we had better get you to the doctor's to see what's what.'

Isa's visit to the doctor confirmed she was indeed two months pregnant, making it a honeymoon conception. She had definitely landed in at the deep end. The flat was still partially furnished and she, a new housewife, was also in a few short months going to become a mother. Part of her was nervous, especially about giving birth. Peter insisted they would pay to book the doctor's presence at the birth in the hospital: nothing but the best for his new wife and child. Isa knew that

219

when the birth was behind her she had the experience of amusing and caring for her baby sisters to help her in the caring for her own child. Yet she knew to be a mother was different from being an older sister.

On the Wednesday of the following week, she was due to take tea at Cathy's flat. She had not yet met her husband, Joseph, as he worked shifts at the Gartsherrie Ironworks. Their two boys were at school and Isa heard their feet clattering on the stairs as they ran out to school or to play in the street. She had rested in the morning while the nausea passed. She was a little anxious being presented to several new people at once, but the women all proved to be friendly and welcoming. There was Theresa Findlay, who lived under Isa and Peter, with her husband Paul and their twin boys Freddie and James who had just started school. Isa found her very lively and voluble and was drawn to her warmth. She had dark wavy hair, which reminded her of Margaret's. Theresa looked to be ages with Cathy, in her late twenties.

Living opposite Theresa were Robert and Myrtle Mackenzie. She was tall and imposing with intense blue eyes, but the impression of severity was softened by a wonderful smile, which lit her eyes with such a sparkle, Isa imagined she could in fact be full of fun. She had two children at school and a new baby who was in a Moses basket in the living room with them. She looked to be in her early thirties and gave off such an air of capability and calm that Isa immediately took to her.

In the flat above Isa and Peter, Audrey and Michael McGillivray tried to keep control of their three youngsters: Andrew, Clare and Christopher. And opposite their family were the O'Donoghues, Matthew and Becky, who were just expecting their first like Isa and Peter.

Isa took in the simple room, just like her own but furnished properly with a dresser, armchairs, a table and chairs and a rather worn carpet square in deep reds. The windows were draped with red curtains faded at the edges by the sun. Isa saw Cathy was doing her best on a limited income. A collection of china plates was displayed on the narrow shelves of the dresser and the table was laid with a white cloth on which sat pretty, gold-rimmed pink cups and saucers and a plate of egg sandwiches dwarfed by a huge sponge cake dusted with icing sugar. The tea things were all set on a tray, ready for Cathy to pour to their liking.

When the women heard of Isa's pregnancy they were delighted. She was regaled with all kinds of advice regarding cots and bedding and where to buy a good but cheap pram. Cathy asked her, 'And have you organised the midwife? Important to get that booked in advance. We all keep them very busy around here.'

The other women laughed.

'Well, we booked the doctor for a birth at the hospital, actually,' Isa said.

There was a hush. 'Which one?' asked Theresa.

All faces were upon Isa as she told them. 'Doctor Patterson. We saw him last week to confirm I was pregnant and Peter booked his services for the birth.'

Myrtle was the first to speak. She put down her teacup and turned to Isa solemnly. 'Isa, that man is a butcher. He doesn't believe in leaving nature to take its course. He has no patience. If he is in a hurry and your bairn is no' arriving quick enough to suit his plans he'll take the knife to you.'

'What do you mean?'

Cathy took up the reins. 'Isa, it's an operation. The doctor cuts open your abdomen and pulls the bairn out through your stomach.' She wondered if she had been too blunt, as the colour drained from Isa's face.

'But why? Don't the weans just come naturally?'

'Exactly. Ye hardly ever need ony interference. We women hae been giein' birth tae wer weans for millennia wi'oot ony interference frae doctors. That's whit we've aye done, isn't it girls?' Theresa looked at the others in turn and they all nodded and 'Aye'-ed in agreement. 'The maist I ever had is a bit guidance and help frae the midwife and she's perfectly capable of goin' for the doctor if it's necessary. But I'll tell ye, Mary O'Reilly doon the road booked Doctor Patterson. She had only been on the labour ward for twaw, three hoors at maist when he scrubs up and says, "I think we'll just give this baby a hurry on now. We've waited long enough." Then he's covered her face wi' chloroform and cut her afore she has a chance tae sae yay or nay. Took her double the time tae recover frae the birth and she aye says it was the worst thing that happened tae her. She very near bled tae death.'

The women had all resumed their tea drinking and were waiting for Isa's reaction.

Myrtle laid her hand on Isa's arm. 'We've maybe hit ye wi' a bit much all at once, Isa, but it's only

222

for yer ain good. We aye look efter yin anither. We jist wanted tae let ye ken. But you and your husband will nae doot think it over. We've said oor piece. Noo, ladies. Whose place is it next week?'

Isa was stunned then terrified as she sat in the flat waiting for Peter to finish his shift. When he came through the door he knew something was wrong.

'Isa? You no been sae good again? Maybe ye should be goin' back tae the doctor. See if he can–'

Before he could finish, Isa raised her hands and said firmly, 'No. I don't want to go to the doctor. In fact after what I've heard today I do not want that man near me.'

Peter sat down and Isa reported to him what the women had told her that afternoon. Soon he was as terrified as she was. 'My God, Isa. I thought we were doing the best for you and the baby. I dinnae ken this doctor right enough. Ma mither aye had the doctor, I think, but she never had operations for ony o' us.'

'Neither did mine. And I don't want it either.'

'I'll cancel the booking and we'll get the midwife instead. As long as you're sure.'

'Aye Peter. We'll be fine with the midwife.'

They held each other close that night, both fearful of what might lie ahead. They knew the ordinary complications of births: stillborn babies, miscarriages, even mothers losing their lives, but this butchery was new and horrible to their young minds.

Their dreams were disturbed. Isa remembered her mother giving birth to the stillborn brother, whose death did not even merit a funeral but was simply hushed up and forgotten. Peter was back in the trenches amidst all the gory deaths he had witnessed: bodies ripped apart by shellfire, bloody and visceral. Then he was in their kitchen, Isa laid out on the table and the doctor cutting into her with a huge knife as though she were a side of beef on a butcher's slab.

He woke with a start. 'Peter, are you all right?' Isa's voice. He turned and clasped her to him.

'Sorry. Was I talking in my sleep?' What had he been saying?

'You were moaning, trying to say something, but I couldn't make it out.' There was no way he could tell her about his dream. It had to be pushed to the back of his mind, along with all the horrors he had seen while at the front.

'Must have been dreaming. Let's go back to sleep.' They closed their eyes and held each other close, but sleep eluded them both for a long time.

16

By early December the nausea had begun to lessen considerably. Isa had discovered if she drank some tea with a piece of bread, which Peter brought to her while still in bed, it seemed to settle her stomach. Other women had spoken of strange cravings that had taken their fancy when pregnant. Theresa had yearned for a particular kind of marmalade that her mother had made, or for weird combinations like scrambled egg with herring. Myrtle told of how some women even crave coal and suck it for the minerals in it. What Isa found herself making more of was steamed rice pudding, which she nearly always had in a double boiler on the stove, whose bottom pan she kept topped up with water while it cooked slowly. Sometimes she flavoured it with nutmeg or a handful of raisins. She would eat it for breakfast, dinner and supper. The good thing was that the milk would be protein and calcium for both her and the baby, and the rice seemed to settle her stomach too. Thank goodness she did not want to eat coal.

She began to prepare for their first Christmas in the house. She persuaded Peter to invite her father and sisters on Christmas Day, after he and her father had finished work. He had at first favoured the old way of waiting till New Year's Day for celebrating, but Isa, having joined the church and seen the ways of the Tolquhouns, was desperate for a family Christmas, so he agreed. Isa had always been working that day and she had had to wait till Boxing Day to see them. So this was going to be a very special Christmas in her own home with her family around her. She busied herself mixing ingredients for cake and puddings and preparing her own mincemeat. She ordered a large chicken from the butcher. Chrissie and Margaret were delighted they would all be together for Christmas.

They met together in Falkirk to do their Christmas shopping. Margaret had now left school and was working in a large house for the owner of a smaller foundry, Mr Cottleson and his family. She still lived at home but went each day as a housemaid to the grand house on the canal. She was sixteen, athletic, lithe and pretty, and with her glossy, wavy hair and winsome smile she was already turning heads. Chrissie, coming up for fourteen, was shy and young compared to her older sisters and depended on them for guidance. Together the three girls made a fine spectacle walking down the High Street together, chatting and laughing, sometimes arm in arm.

'So what will we be buying for your husband then, Isa?' teased Margaret. She turned to Chrissie and, winking, suggested, 'Cologne? A silk tie, or perhaps a cravat? He does like to look smart. Quite the dandy. Did I tell you the other day he pulled up his trouser leg and asked if I liked his socks?'

Chrissie giggled behind her woollen mitten. Margaret was such a tease. She was right though; they had both noticed Peter was always sprucing himself up everywhere he went. There was no doubt he was a handsome fellow but he definitely knew it.

'He never did!' Isa said, shocked. When her sisters confirmed the news with nodded heads and smiles, Isa threw back her head and laughed as well.

'What a preening Swan he is at times,' she said. That set them all off.

'But those are good ideas, Maggie. He'd definitely like that kind of thing. What had you thought of for Father?'

'Well, Chrissie and I thought we could all club together for a new pipe and some tobacco. It fairly keeps him quiet of an evening if he has a good smoke. Mellows him, I think.'

'That is a great idea. If we have enough we could get him a new pouch to keep the tobacco in. Let's head to Johnson's tobacconist first and check the prices.'

By Christmas Day the little flat in Jackson Street had a roaring log fire in the grate, paper decorations hung from the ceiling, and the cupboards and cold safe were filled to bursting with puddings, cakes, pies, sauces and chutneys. Isa was excited as she finished preparing the vegetables for the Christmas Day, evening meal, when she would be the hostess in her own home for the first time. They would gather when her father finished work at five. Peter was on an early shift and so would be back by two, when he might take a rest before the family arrived. She had everything prepared ready to cook and she had it all organised as to what order things would go on the stove, be put in the oven and brought to the table. The experience she had gained from watching Mrs Roberts organising grand meals for the Tolquhouns had stood her in good stead over the years, and in her other posts when she had been in charge of the kitchen on Christmas Day, and made this smaller affair very easy. She wanted to have time to go to church. She checked the clock. She should stop now and get on her coat. A brisk walk lay ahead of her.

As she set off along the road she was glad she had put on her boots, for falling softly from the sky were feathery flakes of snow, the first of the winter. How lovely that it was falling now for her first Christmas as a married woman. A ripple of joy ran through her and she drew her scarf closer around her to stop the icy snow falling down her neck. The church was well filled. The carols were rousing and Isa felt aglow with the wonder of the story of Christ's birth. She found herself this year focused on Mary, her reactions to the news she was pregnant, her difficult birth in the stable. As she struggled with her own pregnancy she heard the story afresh and felt a rush of sympathy for this ordinary woman thrust into an extraordinary story. At least Isa could look forward to the comfort of a clean home, a midwife in attendance and good neighbours to support her. What had Mary had? Then she realised. She had had her faith. And Joseph. And that made Isa realise that she too had the support of faith and prayer, belonging to a community of compassionate people, and also of her proud husband looking forward to being a parent as much as she herself was.

As they headed outside everything had been dusted with light, powdery snow and Isa's boots crunched on the ground as she made her way home.

The meal was a great success. Afterwards, as they sat replete around the table, they opened their simple gifts to each other. Isa had chosen a tie for Peter: not silk, as it was beyond their means, but a lovely green tweed which emphasised the green flecks in his eyes and met with his approval.

Her father was in raptures over the new pipe with its amber stem carefully presented in its wooden case.

'Aye, ye must've kent there was a crack in the ither een, Chrissie, when ye were tamping the baccie in the bowl. Weel done, lassies. My it's a meerschaum. Ye couldnae hae chosen a better gift.'

Margaret and Chrissie had found a lovely cream woollen shawl for Isa in a lacy stitch. It was light and warm and finer than any scarf she had. She was delighted.

Chrissie was beaming with joy that their gift was so well received.

'Now,' said Isa. 'This one is for you, Margaret, from all of us.' She handed Margaret a prettily wrapped package. Inside there was a box from Peterkins and then tissue paper and finally Margaret found a pair of leather gloves.

She held them in her hands then lifted them to her nose to smell the lovely leather smell. She began to put them on, ensuring each finger was fitted properly. She gazed at her gloved hands in disbelief.

'I hope you like them,' Peter said. 'I thought of them. I know you always moan about your woollen ones. We reckoned you were old enough now for a pair of proper lady's gloves.'

Margaret looked up at him then got out of her chair and came round to kiss him on the cheek. 'Thank you so much, Peter. They're just what I wanted. Thank you all,' and she proceeded round the room, kissing each member of her family and thanking them for this lovely, grown-up gift. It was as if they had recognised she was now nearly a woman.

'That just leaves you, Chrissie,' announced Isa as she handed over the last gift.

Chrissie blushed as she unwrapped the parcel. It was again a box and something inside rattled as she relieved it of its wrappings. 'Oh,' she gasped as she looked inside. Two beautiful tortoiseshell hair combs nestled in the tissue paper. 'Oh, they are lovely, Isa. Thank you, all of you. Is it all right to try them?'

'Of course. There's a mirror in our bedroom.'

When she returned with her lovely dark chestnut hair swept up with the combs, her family could all see she was on the verge of growing up, a child no longer. A thought passed through Isa's head that it was just as well Margaret was able to fend for herself and her little sister was about to follow suit, because she now needed to prepare for her own child. It felt as if these two dear sisters who she had mothered were ready to fledge: she felt so proud of them, so closely bound up in them, so grateful for them, and so glad they were nearly grown into adulthood just as she was about to become a mother herself.

As they got ready for bed that night when the others had left, Peter turned to her and said, 'Here. This is for you.' It was a small box, wrapped carefully.

'But I thought you had joined in with the shawl.'

'No. I wanted to get you something myself and I wanted to give it to you when we were just ourselves. Won't you open it?'

Isa removed the lovely patterned paper and opened the box. Cushioned in a cloud of cotton wool was a glass swan. It was cut with many facets which caught the lamplight and created shafts of fractured light as she turned it in her hand.

'Peter, it's beautiful. It's so delicate. Thank you,

Mr Swan.' She put her arms around him and kissed him, still holding it in her hand as he laid her on the bed and showered her with hungry kisses.

On Hogmanay, as the hands of the clock reached midnight, Isa and Peter were sitting quietly with a drink of ginger cordial. The gentle chimes rang out that the new year had arrived. They clinked their glasses together and kissed.

'This is the best new year, Isa,' Peter said. 'To be with you in our own home together expecting our first child.'

There was a knock at the door. Who was going to be their first foot so quickly?

Peter went to the door. Tradition said it was unlucky for the first foot over the door at the start of a new year to be that of someone with fair hair. They should be dark. So it was with great relief they discovered Theresa Findlay and her husband Paul on the doorstep. Theresa, with her dark wavy hair, was welcomed first.

'Here's yer handsel, Peter, frae us.'

'Thank ye both. Come away in and sit ye down by the fire. Isa'll put the kettle on.'

The Findlays had brought a lump of coal and a round of home-made shortbread, the traditional gifts that symbolised the heartfelt wish of your visitors that you would always have fuel for your fire and enough to eat: life's essentials. Peter showed them through to the living room and pulled out two dining chairs for himself and Isa, giving the neighbours the two armchairs by the fire.

Isa brought through a tray laden with her cake and the shortbread, glasses of ginger cordial and the teapot and tea things.

'Noo then,' said Paul. 'First things first. We'll dae the coal ceremony.'

They all stood while Paul took the coal he and Theresa had brought and put it on the fire, saying, 'A good New Year tae one and a' and mauny may ye see.'

Then they raised their glasses and toasted the New Year.

After they had drunk tea and eaten cake, the Findlays then suggested that Isa and Peter joined them in first footing the rest of the neighbours. Peter fetched a jacket and Isa took her new Christmas shawl around her shoulders and they followed Theresa and Paul to visit Cathy and Joseph across the landing.

They were warmly received by all their neighbours and it was well into the 'wee sma' hoors' of the morning before they were back in their own bed.

'What grand neighbours we have here, Isa. Ye know it relieves me so much to think when I'm off on my shift that you have these sensible women friends tae keep an eye on you.'

'I know, Peter. I'm right glad too. I feel as though they're good friends already. Cathy has been right helpful on those early days when I was so sick. And I'm glad they're all mothers themselves. They'll know what it's like.'

Peter felt heart-sorry for his wife not having her own mother to support her. He wished his mother could be more generous and affectionate towards

Isa but knew that was not likely. She was not known for her warmth towards anyone outwith the family. Thank goodness there were these other women looking out for his lovely young wife.

Peter's older sister, Alice, had offered him the use of her pram, since her family of two were now grown and their family was complete. But Peter was determined there would be nothing second-hand for his child. He and Isa would be buying their own pram. Isa remembered how her mother had just carried her babies in a sling around her chest. But she realised it would be much easier to have a pram and was so proud that her husband was willing and able to provide for his family. It made such a difference to her father's attitude at times. She looked in the shops to get an idea of prices and worked out how much she would need to save. Peter was giving her a bit extra out of the wages for getting things for the baby and she put some of this each week in an old salt jar she kept in the kitchen.

Among the poorer families, the baby's bed was often a drawer from a chest, lined with folded towels or blankets. It was warm, solid and saved the expense of a bed, for a while at least, but Peter would have none of that. His baby was to have a cot.

By the end of April when the daffodils were out in Dunbeth Park, Isa had the pram, cot, sheets, nappies, little jackets and leggings, bootees and hats all ready for the expected arrival, who was starting to make his or her presence felt. Every time Isa lay down, she would feel the baby kicking and turning inside her, digging in her ribs or pressing on a nerve, which sent shooting pain up her spine and down her leg. She had terrible indigestion and so had begun to eat only light meals, but more frequently throughout the day. At night she would prop herself up with cushions under the pillows to avoid the worst of the burning sensation of acid reflux from her stomach. All perfectly natural, the other women assured her, as they swapped their pregnancy stories.

A few days later, in the first week of May, a week before her due date, Isa started to feel a deep ache in her lower back and a cramping pain in her abdomen. It made her bend over slightly and stopped her in her tracks. Then it passed. She carried on with her dusting and polishing. Half an hour later the pains came again and she had to pause. By the afternoon, she was tired and decided to lie down. As she dozed, the waves of pain woke her then subsided again. They continued into the night and by morning were coming stronger and closer together.

As Peter got ready for work he said to Isa, 'I'll let Cathy know and see if she'll come and sit wi' ye. I'll leave the door open so she can let hersel' in. I'll phone the midwife when I get tae the office.' He kissed her and wiped the sweat from her brow. 'It'll no' be long now, lass. I'll see ye soon.' Off he went. For the brief time before Cathy arrived, Isa lay bathed in sweat, from anxiety as much as pain. This was such a lonely journey. Those who stand with a woman in labour to help her and aid her can encourage and support but they do not do the job. Isa shivered with the immensity of what lay before her and the sense of it being her task. Not

Peter's, but hers alone, as the mother. Self-doubt ran through her mind. Could she do this? Was she strong enough, brave enough? Would the baby live? Would she herself survive? She knew there was no guaranteed answer for any of these questions. It was terrifying.

She was hit by another wave of pain. When Cathy Quinn arrived after seeing her boys off to school, Isa was moaning, so intense was the clawing at her back and abdomen. The contractions were strong now. Cathy held her hand. 'It's going to be fine, Isa. I'm here now an' the midwife will be here soon. You relax now. Rest as much as you can in between the contractions. How long have you had them?'

'Since yesterday.'

'In the evening?'

'No, the first of them were in the morning. I kept going for a bit. I had to lie down in the afternoon. And then they kept on through the night.'

Cathy now understood why the poor girl looked so tired and blanched: that was very nearly twenty-four hours. She hoped the midwife got here soon. She must be well ready now, for here was yet another contraction coming. She herself had had quick labours, intense and short, six hours the longest. It struck her this was going to be hard on Isa.

There was a knock and the door opened. 'Midwife calling,' said the voice. Cathy came into the hallway to greet the familiar face of Effie Robertson, one of the local midwives. 'She's in here, Effie. Tired oot frae bein' in labour since yesterday,' she told her in a whisper.

When Effie saw Isa she realised the girl was about at the end of her strength. She ordered Cathy to fetch some broth, if she could, and to skim off the bree for Isa to sip. 'We need to keep your strength up, Mrs Swan. Now let's have a look.' She lifted up the sheet to see how far Isa was dilated. 'Nearly there, Mrs Swan, well done. I hear you've had a long, hard night but it will all be worth it soon. Baby Swan will soon be in your arms.'

In fact it took another two hours of hard slog before Isa reached the last stages of labour. She found the pain intense. Was this normal? She did not have the breath to ask. She felt so uncomfortable in the position the midwife had asked her to adopt, sitting on the edge of the bed with her feet on two dining chairs. It certainly made it easier for the midwife to see what was going on but Isa had to prop herself on her arms and she felt every contraction boring into the base of her spine.

At last the midwife announced, 'Mrs Swan I can see the head now. On the next contraction we just need your strongest effort yet and Baby will be with us for sure. Ready?'

Isa pushed with all the strength she could summon and yelled in shock as the midwife, determined to deliver the baby quickly, tugged at its head to ensure its mouth was free, and the whole body emerged. The baby was a girl and a good, healthy colour and was breathing quickly. The cord was cut and Cathy busied herself sponging away the blood and mucus covering the baby's skin, then wrapped her in the towels and blankets she had warmed by the fire.

Isa lay back on the pillows and found instant relief from the back pain even as she underwent more contractions to deliver the placenta. Soon it was all over. Effie examined the baby and Cathy washed Isa. They handed her the baby, wrapped in her swaddling. The young mother's face was lined with exhaustion but she smiled down in disbelief at what she had done. Here was the new life, which she had carried inside her for nine months and now she was lying in her arms: a strong, healthy baby. Thank goodness, for a weaker one might not have lasted the arduously long passage through the birth canal. Isa found she was crying. She wished so hard that her mother had been with her to help her, to see her new grandchild. She felt for all her mother had gone through in giving birth so many times, and that last time so fruitlessly: to have made all that effort, gone through all this pain and to have nothing at the end must have been horrific. Isa understood her mother's pain and sorrow in a new way.

The baby was heavy in her arms. She looked tired out too but peaceful, her little fists up close to her face. The midwife was back at the side of the bed. 'Now then, Mrs Swan. We'd best get the wee one fed.' She showed her how to open the baby's mouth by lightly stroking her cheek, how to bring her to the breast and encourage her to latch on and start to suck. The baby knew immediately what was required and sucked strongly. 'That's grand. Ye've a strong one there, and no mistake. She's fairly hungry. Now. That's my work done really, Mrs Swan. How are you feeling now?'

'Better. I'm so relieved she's born and healthy.

I just want to sleep.'

'Once she's finished sucking that's what you should do. You'll need as much rest as possible. Where are ye laying the wee one down?' She looked around the room and saw the brand-new cot.

The midwife looked thoughtful. 'You are so tired, Mrs Swan. To save you getting up and going to the baby we could make up a drawer and place it on the bed beside you. That way you can rest and just lift her out when she needs to feed or is looking for a cuddle.'

Cathy was summoned and got the drawer ready. Isa realised it made sense. She was not strong enough to get up yet. So the baby was laid in the lined drawer beside her mother. Cathy got Isa to take a proper plate of soup and then quietly returned to her own flat, leaving both doors open so she could hear the baby and be there if Isa needed her help. She did not like the fact that her young neighbour was so exhausted. She would need to watch her. She set to making a fresh pan of broth and an extra-large mutton stew. Peter and Isa could get a share of her family's meals for the next few days until Isa was on her feet again.

When Peter came home off his shift it was to be greeted by the wailing of his hungry newborn daughter. He looked down in awe at the tiny hands and fingers and the perfect little face. New feelings of pride filled him.

'Oh, Isa, I'm so proud of you. Look at her. She's glorious. I'm so happy.' He leaned in and kissed his wife who was more peaceful now that it was all over. She handed the baby to him.

'You're all right now, my lass,' he said to the wee one, as he cradled her in his arms. 'Yer wi' yer daddy and mummy now and we'll take right good care o' you.' Isa watched him holding his daughter wrapped in the shawl she'd been given at Christmas by her sisters and was so glad to see him already besotted. The baby lay contentedly in his arms, full from another feed, and drifted off to sleep again.

Isa, still sore and exhausted, was so thankful for her neighbour's kindness in leaving a meal for them because she could not move out of the bed. Peter ate his meal in the living room at the place setting Cathy had laid out, while Isa picked at hers on a tray in bed. She felt so different from even the day before. Then she had been an expectant mother, fit and happily tidying her house. Today she had been through a long, arduous labour, a horrific rite of passage, and had emerged on the other side sore, dispirited and feeling distant from everyone in the isolation brought by this experience, which Peter had not shared. He had left before it was really bad and returned when it was all over. How could he ever know what it was to have given life to this child? She looked into the makeshift cot. She was a mother now. No going back. How was she going to cope? Tears fell down her cheeks, hot and salty: they flooded out of her and she made no effort to wipe them away.

Over the next few days they were inundated with visitors. No one stayed too long, just enough to reassure themselves mother and baby were thriving. There were all the neighbours, some bearing gifts of food for them and little bootees or knitted jackets for the baby. Her father and sisters came and were delighted to hold the wee one and to shower Isa with their gifts. Peter's parents and family all called, although his parents still kept their distance and took minimal interest in their latest grandchild.

All were anxious to know the baby's name but neither she nor Peter had given this much thought. Now they would have to get organised for registering the birth. When she did turn her mind to the subject, Isa suddenly knew what she wanted to do. She wanted to name her new baby daughter after her mother, whose given name had been Margaret, despite being called Mary at home. Since she, Chrissie and her father often called her sister Maggie, she did not think having two Margarets in the family would be a problem.

When she suggested it to Peter, he had no issue with it, and he was quite happy to give her the middle names of Murray, which had come down Isa's mother's side of the family, and her own maiden name of Dick. It was good to include these names, he thought. Isa was relieved and seemed to find it easier to hold the baby now she had a name.

Those first few days passed in a blur of feeding, changing nappies and sleeping. When Margaret slept so did she. Her back still ached but she found it easier to get up out of bed when she needed to. Then, ten days after the birth, she decided to get up, wash and dress. She was going to get back to normal. She discovered moving around actually helped the pain in her back and she busied herself with some housework and cooking while Margaret slept. She thought she might take her for a walk in the pram in the afternoon if it stayed fine. After she had fed Margaret and had her own lunch she got the pram ready, checked Margaret was safe in the drawer bed and started to bump the pram downstairs. Cathy heard the noise and came out to give her a hand. While Cathy kept an eye on the pram down on the street, Isa went to fetch the baby and carefully carried her downstairs. She felt such a surge of pride as she pushed the pram with her baby daughter along the street. Cathy walked beside her and saw Isa aglow with the pride of new motherhood.

'This is such a precious time in your life, Isa,' she said. 'You make sure you enjoy every minute because they grow up so fast – their babyhood is over in a flash. You have done so well. That was no easy birth and yet here you are out on the street again. Lesser women would have had everyone running after them hand and foot for ages.'

Aye, thought Isa to herself. But I've no mother to do that for me. I just have to get on with it myself. Before she let her guard down and started crying she quickly changed the subject to ask about Cathy's boys. Isa certainly felt very emotional. They said that was part of the effects of giving birth. She would be glad when she got her composure back.

17

The May blossom was past and the trees in the park were once again in leaf, their fresh greens a wonderful backdrop for the summer bedding in all its red and gold. Life had taken on a new routine for Isa. She was enjoying motherhood and felt more on top of things again. Peter was attentive to Margaret when he came home and this allowed Isa a little rest if needed, or more time to cook or tidy up. In the late afternoon, Chrissie and Margaret came through by train on Margaret's afternoon off. That summer meant change ahead for them too. Margaret had big plans.

'I saw this advert, Isa. The Salvation Army is helping people emigrate to Canada or Australia. They keep an eye on you on the voyage and then when you arrive you report to a Salvation Army office and they organise accommodation and help you find work...'

Isa looked in her sister's brown eyes, wide and keen and shining from her excitement. 'But you are only sixteen, Maggie. Do you not have to be twenty-one?'

'I know. But if Dad signed the papers they would take me. I asked. They need young people.'

'But what skills would you say you had? You have only been a housemaid.'

'It's domestic staff they want. I've taken over here at home since you got married. I can cook and clean and I'd rather cook and clean in Canada than Falkirk.'

'Right. So have you asked Father yet?'

'Well, no. I wondered if you could help there. I got the papers and I think I have filled them in correctly, but if you could check them and be there when I ask him... That might help ... if you support me, that is?'

The room was quiet, as if holding its breath. Isa felt her sister's desperation to make a life for herself: to get away from the small foundry town with its smoke and dirt, and her need to be free of the responsibility for her father and younger sister. She did not think it would be easy for her in Canada, but she knew how resourceful and strong-minded Maggie was. She had no doubt she would cope whatever was thrown at her. But could they convince their father to sign the papers?

'So what's the news, then, that yer so keen to gie us, Maggie?' John Dick was sitting in his armchair puffing on his pipe after a particularly enjoyable meal, made for him by his middle daughter.

Maggie started to tell him about the advert and her plans and she took out the papers and laid them on the table.

'I need you to sign these, Father, so that I can go ahead and apply.'

John's brow furrowed as he took the pipe from his mouth. 'Yer no' thinkin' o' goin' now, surely?'

'Aye, Father. They say I can if you sign the papers.'

'They'll help her with accommodation when she arrives,' said Isa, thinking now would be a good time for her to join the discussion. 'She won't be left to do everything herself. There's work over there and–'

'And jist whit work can you dae?' John continued to grill Margaret.

'I can cook and clean and–'

'Aye, that's right, and ye know whaur ye'll be cookin' and cleanin'? Right here is whaur,' and he brought his great fist down on the table so hard that the cutlery jumped. 'Ye can forget about gallivantin' tae Canada and get on wi' keepin' hoose for me and yer sister.'

'But Father...' Margaret looked despairingly across at Isa, who shook her head as if to say there was no point in saying any more.

'Enough. I wunnae hear ony mair.'

Margaret gathered up the papers and left the room in a fury, slamming the door behind her. Isa tried to chat about the baby's progress to calm her father and the whole affair was never mentioned again.

Margaret's anger and resentment seethed within her until she found another plan, another escape away from her father. This time it involved help from Peter's family. One of his sisters, Jeannie, was working for a Professor Thomson in Glasgow. When a position became vacant for a young housemaid, Jeannie put in a word for her brother's sister-in-law and before long the job was Margaret's. It meant she had her own room in the professor's three-storey house and she had Peter's sister to keep an eye on her. Isa and Peter were delighted at having found her a position. But they were still concerned for Chrissie.

At the end of June, Chrissie came home with a letter for her father concerning her future. She had been offered a scholarship to Falkirk High, one of the very few to be granted. She had won it on merit from her outstanding results in exams. She too was nervous of her father's reaction.

When he opened the letter he could not believe it at first. It was good his youngest had done so well, of course, a matter for some pride, but she was only a girl. What did she need further education for at the High? Was it not enough to finish her junior education?

Isa and Maggie kept telling him what a wonderful opportunity this was for Chrissie. There would be no fees to pay because she had won this scholarship, which was such an honour in itself that he surely could not turn it down.

'Weel, Chrissie. Do you want tae ging up tae the High?'

'Yes, Father. It would be great to do Highers. My teachers all say they don't give out many scholarships and that it is a great opportunity for me.'

'And there's no fees.' John did not think he should be spending money on education. 'Weel, if you're set on it that's fine by me. Doesnae really matter which school yer at as far as I'm concerned.'

They thought that was all settled and were so pleased for Chrissie to be getting this chance at more advanced study and qualifications. However, they had reckoned without the uniform. Falkirk High had a particular uniform of maroon blazer with school badge, black skirt and jersey, and white blouse. She would also need a PE kit of a divided skirt and Aertex blouse. John would buy none of it. So Chrissie started the new term in August at Falkirk High as a scholarship student, without the proper uniform. It did not make her life easy. There was constant ribbing about her clothing as 'the poor bursary girl' and plenty of sniggering behind hands when she came into a room or passed other girls in the corridor.

Despite this, she continued to do well, studying French and Latin alongside Maths and Science and History. Inside, though, there was this tension. Why should she be in this position? What kind of father would say yes to her getting on, but put her in this hateful no man's land of being in the school but not belonging? Did he not understand what it did to her? A thought began to take root in her mind that she would be better away from school all together, and from home. Why shouldn't she follow in the way of her sisters and get live-in work in a big house?

Whereas Isa had sometimes challenged her father and had learned how to persuade him about things, Chrissie found she could not do this. Margaret would just stomp off and do her own thing as much as she could and she still had her sights set on Canada. As soon as she was twenty-one she would be off. She was carefully saving what she earned so she would not need any money from her father. Somehow, Chrissie just kept her head down and tholed it. Peter and Isa had her over often at weekends and on paydays to help her avoid the worst of her father's moods.

Isa had her own troubles. One morning she had

been playfully blowing raspberries on Margaret's tummy as she changed her nappy when she thought she heard something strange. She quietened herself and put her ear next to her daughter's chest. Was that Margaret's heart? It was making such a strange sound. The rhythm was irregular. She'd never heard that sound when listening to her sisters' chests, nor any other baby she had held. Thump thump, then a long pause, thumpety, thumpety, thump. Was something wrong with her dear baby's heart? Quickly she finished changing Margaret, got her dressed and in the pram and headed straight to the doctor's surgery.

The waiting room was busy. She held Margaret in her shawl and could feel the panic rising to a crescendo within her. At last it was her turn. She sat down.

'Now, Mrs Swan, what seems to be the matter?' the doctor began.

'It's Margaret. Her heart. It sounds funny.'

'Let's have a listen, then, and see if we can reassure you. Just unwrap her a little so I can get my stethoscope on her chest.' He sounded so jaunty it made Isa feel stupid, as though she were worried over nothing. Normally she would hate to be proven wrong, but today she was desperate for him to say she had worried unnecessarily.

He warmed the stethoscope in his hands then held it to the baby's chest. He listened intently. The jaunty look disappeared. Over and over again he placed the stethoscope in slightly different positions and still the frown remained.

'Right, Mrs Swan, you can wrap her up again. You were right to come. Your baby seems to have what we call a heart murmur. Was there no doctor in attendance at her birth?'

'No. The midwife came.'

'I see. Did you notice if she listened to the baby's chest after?'

'No. I was very tired and sore, doctor. I can't remember.'

'No matter. How has your daughter been? She looks to be healthy and thriving.'

'Yes, doctor, she's doing well, growing as she should, putting on weight. She's not shown signs of being unwell.'

'Good healthy cry if she needs you?'

'Oh yes. You can hear her in the flat opposite, according to my neighbour.'

'Good. Well, we may need to watch her progress carefully. I should warn you that she might find things harder when she starts to move. If her heart is not pumping at the full level she may experience breathlessness if involved in physical activity, but no point in worrying before things happen. For now, she's making good progress and we'll keep a closer eye on things as she grows. It may well be that her body will get used to the murmur and adjust accordingly, so that she will hardly know there is a problem. Do you have any questions?'

Isa was not really sure if she had been given good news or bad. He seemed to imply there might be difficulties ahead. What did she want to ask?

'This won't shorten her life, will it, doctor?'

The doctor took a breath in. 'It's too early to tell, Mrs Swan, but I shouldn't think so.'

'Is there anything I should do?'

'Well, I wouldn't leave her to cry unattended for long, since that could strain the heart. Try to keep her calm. Avoid stress in the household. Watch she doesn't get too cold or overheated. She certainly seems to be doing really well at the moment, but do feel free to see me again, should you have any concerns.'

'Thank you, doctor.' She tucked Margaret up in the pram and set off for home, relieved that there was no immediate cause for concern but pondering the possible future. Had she given birth to a child who would spend her life as an invalid?

When she told Peter that evening, they both sat for a while in silence looking at Margaret asleep in her cot, unaware of the fuss around her.

Peter was first to speak. 'Well, Isa, I don't think we should worry unless we see any change in her. She looks healthy; the doctor was pleased with her progress when he saw her; he's told us what to avoid. There's nothing else we can do but hope and trust she'll keep strong. She came through a long birth, you know. She must have been strong to do that.'

Isa felt a relief flood her at her husband's words. 'You're right, Peter. It was hard on her too. We'll just be real careful of her. And pray she keeps fighting.' Isa leant into the cot and gently stroked her cheek. 'You'll be fine, wee Margaret. Just fine.'

Margaret continued to thrive until one bitterly cold winter's night. Isa awoke in the early hours to the sounds of coughing and wheezing. She dashed to the cot. Margaret was feverish and it seemed she was struggling for breath. Isa picked her up and put her over her shoulder to help drain the fluid building up in her chest and firmly rubbed her back to loosen it. She remembered her mother doing this for Eliza, who had been prone to chest infections. She woke Peter and asked him to pour some whisky into a glass. He brought it to her.

'Good idea,' he said. 'That'll warm you up.'

'Not for me, Peter,' Isa said, exasperated. 'Now, see if there's any butter.'

Peter looked in the cold press and found the dish of butter.

'Now take a teaspoon and scrape a bit of butter on to it. Then dip it into the whisky.'

Isa took the spoon and gently slipped a little into Margaret's mouth.

'Why are ye giein' that tae the bairn?'

'The whisky will open up her tubes and help her breathing and the butter will soothe her throat. My grandmother always gave us that if we had chest colds.'

'You are amazing, the things you know. Look. She's settled.'

'I'll sit up with her in the chair to help her drain the fluid.'

'And we'll get her to the doctor in the morning. I can come with you. I'm no' on till the afternoon. You come and get me if you need a rest.'

'I will. Thanks, Peter. You sleep now. I'll be fine. Looks like she'll be fine too.'

It took a few weeks for the infection to clear, but during that time Isa watched over her baby so attentively that every cough had her in her mother's arms to ensure her heart was not under extra strain. The remedies she had seen used by her grandmother and her mother proved their worth in a new generation and soon the bronchitis was defeated.

By late summer she had begun to wean Margaret, who was constantly hungry after her milk feed. She made some rice pudding and cornflour, and some milky porridge. The baby loved every spoonful. She tried her on sieved broth and soups, which were supped up too. Isa was so delighted that Margaret continued to thrive and that there was no sign of trouble with her heart. Each time she held her close and could hear the faulty beat it still unnerved her a little.

Their first Christmas with her was lovely, and friends and family showered her with gifts of clothing, rattles and toys. Peter bought her a beautiful silver-coloured teddy bear that was bigger than her. It was soft and had beautiful eyes. Margaret was fascinated with it when they put it near her and very soon she was crawling across the room to have a closer look.

The snowdrops in the window box were just coming through when Isa had a few mornings in a row when she felt sick. At first she thought it would just be a slight stomach upset, but soon it was happening every morning and lasting for hours. She had a dreadful feeling of déjà vu. Sure enough, she headed to the doctor, who confirmed her suspicions. Again she could not believe it. She had not long finished breast-feeding Margaret. How could she be pregnant again so soon? She did not feel ready for this. Her memories of giving birth to Margaret came flooding back. She felt she was barely coping with being a mother of one child. Now there would be two come November.

What was she going to do?

Peter, of course, was delighted. For him it was all about showing his virility. He was crowing it from the rooftops. With his brothers and his workmates, he got quite carried away. 'Did Isa tell ye she's expecting again? Aye that's right. Doesnae take us two long, I can tell ye. Just two weeks merriet and we land the first and now Margaret's only jist weaned and here we are again. Powerful stuff I'm carrying, right enough.' He did not appear to notice that his wife was exhausted, sick and depressed at the thought.

This time the sickness was worse and it was difficult for her to keep food down. She tried to eat properly, for the baby's sake, but she could not face meat. Some days she could drink milk or take a piece of fish but more often only a plate of soup later in the day. As a result she got more and more tired.

Margaret was approaching her first birthday and continued to grow strong. She was now walking and blethering away in baby sounds as a running commentary to her exploration of the world. Flowers were sniffed in the park, objects lifted and examined to discover what could be done with them. Could she bite this, eat it, throw it? Would it make a sound if she hit it on the floor? Isa wanted to rejoice in her toddler's development but it was hard when she felt so tired and nauseous. Peter kept on swaggering about how the next one would surely be a boy and how he would soon be out with him in the park kicking a ball. He was all set with a name too. They would call him after his father, Robert Thomson Swan. He thought that had a grand ring.

Isa had no interest in a name at all. She just longed for each day to be over so she could lie down again and get some rest and peace. The nausea was always better if she were lying down. She was aware that she was not eating enough and that this was making her weak, but there was nothing she could do. When she did force food down she was sick and lost it anyway. When she went to the doctor for help, his advice was completely unexpected.

After he had examined her, he sat down. He paused for a moment, fiddling with his spectacles in his hands. Eventually he put them down and looked her in the eye.

'Mrs Swan, you are really unwell. Your pulse is weak and you are anaemic. The baby is smaller than usual for this stage. You are not eating nearly enough to keep both you and the baby nourished. I am of the opinion that perhaps this pregnancy is too dangerous for you and that it should in fact be terminated, in your best interests.'

Isa was stunned. She had expected to be told to rest, to be given vitamins or a diet to adhere to, maybe at worst to have to go to hospital for a spell of supervised rest. But terminate the pregnancy, not have the baby?

'Doctor, I don't understand.'

'Mrs Swan, you cannot sink much lower or your own life will be endangered. That is what I am saying. At present you and your child are just coping and no more. But if the sickness continues and you cannot eat or keep up your strength there is a danger you will lose the baby, or indeed that your own health will be in jeopardy.'

'There must be something else. Tell me what to eat, what to do and I'll do it. I can't take my baby's life, I can't...' Isa's voice trailed away into quiet sobs.

The doctor asked his wife to telephone Peter at work to come for Isa. There was no way this woman should be trying to get home herself. His wife took her through to their living room, made her tea and waited with her until Peter arrived. When he saw Isa, paler than ever, slumped in the chair with anguish written on every line of her face, he knew there was terrible news.

'Isa,' he whispered, getting on his knees beside her and putting his arm around her. 'What is it, lass?'

She could not speak. She held on to him and cried tired tears. The doctor came through to find him and gave him his assessment of the situation.

'Take a few days to think it through and talk it over with your wife. But I must impress upon you how poorly she is. She is not in any fit condition to go through birth as she is now. She will need help to regain her strength. If you can get someone to stay and look after her and your little girl, cook nourishing food for her and do all the heavy work in the house, she might have a chance. She has a strong spirit. But right now the body is weak. Look after her, Mr Swan.'

Isa and Peter were both determined there would be no abortion. When they told the family, Margaret left work immediately to stay with Isa. She saw her sister was utterly dispirited and tried everything she could to cheer her again. She got

254

out the best bed linen and made up the bed. She got Isa into one of her prettiest nightdresses and combed her hair. She picked flowers in the woods and filled jars and vases everywhere. She dusted and polished everything until it shone. She looked up Isa's cookery books and her old notes from her time in service, finding recipes for invalid cooking: poached fish in parsley sauce, steamed chicken and spinach, tasty soups and milk puddings. With the rest, company and good food, Isa began to revive. Margaret discovered she really liked looking after someone. Being a housemaid was all right, but caring for someone was more rewarding. She could see her older sister reviving under her care and it felt very good.

In a few weeks, Isa was on her feet again but Margaret did all the work in the house and looked after her little niece. Isa saved her energy for walks on sunny afternoons through the autumn leaves in the park. She was glad to be better again, but still rested most of the day. By the end of October, she felt well enough to do some cooking, and at this point she told Margaret to head back to work. Jeannie had said they could do with her back as soon as she was able and Isa felt ready to take on most of her duties again. Her sister made her promise to do no cleaning, to leave that to her, and she would come on her afternoon off.

So Isa and her daughter settled in to a new routine of resting together in the middle of the morning and again in the afternoon. Sometimes Isa would read to her while they lay on the bed, but sometimes she would sing Margaret to sleep and then fall asleep herself.

Then one morning, late in November, Peter was getting ready for an early shift and came through to the bedroom to find his wife panting and clutching her abdomen.

'Peter, I think I've gone into labour.'

This was a bit earlier than expected. Since his wife had never given him the details of the experience of Margaret's birth, and he had not been there when it was getting tough, Peter headed off quite cheerily, saying he would telephone for a midwife from the office phone. Then he closed the door behind him and hurried down the stairs.

Little Margaret had woken up and came through to her mother's bedroom sleepily.

'Up, Mummy,' she said. 'Up, up.' Her little hands grasped at the bedclothes as she tried to clamber up on to the bed. Normally her mother or father would have stretched out to pick her up by now and draw their delightful eighteen-month-old baby girl into their arms. This morning, though, all her mother could do was groan.

'Margaret, go and get teddy and some books and bring them through beside me.'

Off Margaret went to her bed, returning with her teddy and some cloth picture books. Now her mother reached down and helped her clamber on to the bed. Isa got her settled behind her, surrounded by some cushions. It was all she could think of managing at this point. Perhaps when there was a bigger gap between contractions she could go and get a neighbour.

'*Aghhh!*' she groaned, as the pains gripped her and the urge to push overwhelmed her. Surely the baby was not going to be born so soon. Last time the contractions had gone on for over a day before the final stage came. But what she was feeling now was definitely the urge to bring forth her child. What choice did she have? She got herself into the birthing position, knees up, feet close to her hips, leaning back on the pillows. She gritted her teeth in her shut mouth to stifle her moans. She could not give rip to her cries with her baby daughter on the bed beside her.

Again the contractions gripped her body and she let herself push as she wanted. Then she lay back exhausted on the pillows. When she had recovered her breath, she sang to Margaret. 'Rock a bye baby on a treetop.'

That was as far as she got before she was overcome by another wave of contractions. Little Margaret's piping voice hummed in the background and was something for Isa to hold on to in the dazed state that she was now in, all her effort concentrated on birthing this new child into the world.

'*Aghhh.*' At last she felt it pass from her, aware of the emptiness in her and of the slipperiness between her legs. She let her knees sink down on the bed splayed apart and looked down at the bloodied body on the sheet. She bit the cord and took the baby up to her chest. The little mite was already making tiny cries, not the strong, loud cries her sister had made on her entrance into the world, but tiny weak sounds. All the same, it was proof that her lungs were working. Now she needed to suck and feed and stimulate Isa's milk, so she was brought to the breast and made a few gentle tugs before falling asleep. Isa covered her with the top sheet on the bed and then covered herself up with the blankets.

Beside her, sheltered by the cushions, Margaret babbled away, oblivious to what had taken place in such proximity. Somehow her mother had managed to protect her from the strangeness of it all, and in looking after her, Isa had protected herself from the horror of the situation. She had given birth alone, with her tiny daughter on the bed beside her. Who would have planned such a thing, allowed such a thing? Why had her husband walked out of that door so easily this morning and left her in this situation? Why had they stupidly let her sister Margaret go back to work when she could have been here with her? She sank on to the pillows exhausted, wanting so desperately to cry but not allowing herself to do this in front of Margaret.

'Cooee. Midwife calling.' Isa heard the front door opening and footsteps in the hall.

'I'm in here,' she called weakly.

'Oh, Mrs Swan. I'm too late. How are you my dear?' The woman was shocked at the state of the new mother. Her face had the unhealthy pallor of ash, her hair was wetly plastered to her head and every part of her exposed skin was slick with sweat. Still, she quickly recovered herself to reassure her patient. 'I'm so sorry I wasn't here for the birth. You must have been so quick. Let's have a look at Baby and then we'll check all's well with you too.'

Isa was so relieved to have another person there with her, she felt herself relax for the first time in hours.

'My daughter. She was in the bed beside me. I should ask my neighbour to mind her for me.'

Then the midwife saw the clever but makeshift arrangement this poor mother had made to protect her toddler while keeping an eye on her during her labour. She was overcome with compassion and respect for her.

'I think I shall go and fetch her right now. Across the landing is it?'

Isa nodded. Within seconds, Cathy was in the flat, whisking Margaret into her arms and showing her to her new baby sister.

'See, Margaret, here's your new baby sister. Look how she's sleeping nicely. Why don't we go through to my house for some cake?'

Cathy squeezed Isa's hand. 'You are an amazing woman, Isa Swan. You rest. When the midwife goes, tell her to knock on the door and I'll be right back.'

Isa thanked her and smiled wanly from the bed. It had all been so quick she could hardly believe what had happened to her. The midwife helped with the delivery of the placenta and checked the cord. All was well. The new baby was not strong but then she herself had not been well. Hopefully they would both gain in strength now. She was just so glad it was over, too exhausted now to cry. The next hours were hazy as she drifted in and out of consciousness. She was vaguely aware of some panic around her, but she knew the midwife and Cathy were there and they would have to sort it all out, for she certainly could not help them.

What had transpired was the midwife could not stop the bleeding after the birth. Isa had haemorrhaged. She lost a lot of blood before the doctor managed to get it stopped using an injection of ergot. He wished he had been called sooner, so that he could have administered the injection prior to birth, which might have prevented the haemorrhage altogether. He was very concerned for his patient, considering how poorly she had been previously.

'I'll be keeping a close eye on you, Mrs Swan,' he told her. 'You get that sister of yours back to look after you. I don't want you moving around for ten days at least. You've to get your strength up. You've lost a lot of blood. I'll be in to see you tomorrow.'

When Peter was sent for, he hurried home, expecting to find his wife all wreathed in smiles holding his son in her arms, as he had been imagining throughout the months of Isa's pregnancy. Instead he was met with Isa's abject weakness and another baby daughter.

'Another girl!' he exclaimed in disgust. He did not look at the baby properly, nor did he come closer to see his wife. There were no tender words of comfort or joy. He simply turned on his heels and left. He grabbed his coat and hat again, and left to walk off his deep disappointment.

Why had he boasted so much about his virility, and of his future fathering of sons? How would he hold his head up now with the men at work, or with his brothers? He would be made to feel a fool. His father would sneer that he was not up to much. Daughters and granddaughters were not the thing that brought prestige. Only sons: strong, healthy sons to carry on the family name. He felt weak, useless, such a failure.

It was with a heavy heart that Peter went back through to the bedroom on his return. Isa was in bed, nursing the new daughter. She was pale, exhausted. Her glorious hair, dulled to brown and matted with sweat, lay tangled in clumps over her shoulders. She looked up at him with a fierceness in her eyes, the fierceness of a watchful tigress ready to pounce should she be required to defend her young. Peter almost backed away. The silence hung over him like a blanket smothering the breath in his chest.

'Aren't you going to look at your daughter?'

He could not. Not without anger and pain and failure flooding out of him and disgracing him even further. 'I'll sleep in the other room. Do you need anything?'

'From you? I don't think so.' Her voice was cold, her tone scathing. 'I managed to give birth to your new daughter while your older daughter was on the bed beside me. I was on my own when the baby was born. I cut the cord and got her to my breast before the midwife even arrived and Margaret played beside me on the bed, through it all. So, no, I don't think I need anything from you.'

He was cut to the quick. He had behaved abominably, but he could not help himself. He did not know how to apologise or how to tell her what he felt. What did she know about his family and his upbringing and what was expected of him? Yet he knew what she told him reflected poorly on his organising for her and Margaret. As he lay on the spare bed his mind was filled with gloomy doubts about himself as a father and provider and as a man. He had badly let everyone down. He buried his head in his hands and wept bitter tears.

Isa was furious. She held her new daughter in her arms and gave in to the tears she had held back through the agony of the birth, the stress of having Margaret on the bed beside her and then Peter's dreadful rejection. What had possessed him? Could he not see there was no way to control what nature ordained? Boy or girl, it was beyond anyone's wishes or plans. Was it not enough that they had two healthy children and that she was still alive herself, despite the doctor's fears and the terrible haemorrhaging? That had felt almost like death. She had felt herself slipping into a dark, peaceful oblivion. No more pain. No more tiredness, just utter peace. It had felt good. If that was death, there was nothing to be afraid of. What held more fear was staying alive and living this life of endless struggles and sorrow. Peter had asked perfunctorily did she need anything, and anger and dismay had prompted her bitter litany of grievance at his abandonment of her, his distance from her.

Yet she did need things. She needed him to take her in his arms as he had done at Margaret's birth. She needed his love, his reassurance that they were close, together in all this. But because this child in her arms was not a boy she was denied his comfort. What a mistake it had been to marry this fickle, immature, unreliable man. She thought of her own parents, close and strong together, influencing each other for good, supporting each other. She remembered the warmth there was between them, her father's compassion towards her mother

262

over the loss of their baby. He had never complained about a lack of boys in the family.

Her sorrow and longing was overwhelming. The tears dripped on her new daughter's downy hair. Gently she wiped them away and kissed the baby's tiny head. The maternal instinct arose in her and strengthened her. She would have to accept her lot and soldier on like she always had. Life had decreed that she lose her mother when she was but a child herself, yet she had survived and become a mother to her two sisters. She had been thrust into the adult world early but had learned its ways. She had not given up. Nor would she do so now. She would tell Peter to send word to her father and sisters, and to his family, and they would rally round. He would soon see what she was made of. Isa Swan was one of the Fighting Dicks after all. They did not give up; they fought. But she would never forget what he had done today.

'Come on, lad, chin up,' said his brother Jimmy, when he called in at the weekend to see the baby. The two men were in the kitchen by themselves. 'It just gies ye an excuse tae try again, lad. It's no' the end o' the world.'

'I wish we had aborted it now, like the doctor said. What a waste. If we'd got rid o' this yin it wid hae bin easier tae try again for a boy.' Jimmy could not believe his ears. What was wrong with his brother that he could think such an abominable thing?

'Peter, for God's sake. Abortion?'

'What of it? When I got that French lassie pregnant in Normandy when I wis on leave, that's what she did.'

'You did what?'

'You heard me fine. I wasnae the only one snared like that. It was happening all the time during the war. She was fine after. God, why did we no' do like the doctor said?'

Jimmy was shocked. He could barely take in what Peter had just confessed. His brother had just been a teenager throughout the war, yet he had been through this personal trauma on top of everything else. What had it done to him? He could not believe the callousness.

'Peter, dinnae say that. Ye've got twaw healthy girls. That's grand. And ye love making a fuss o' Margaret. Now ye'll hae twaw tae fuss o'er.'

'I wanted a boy. A boy tae call after ma faither. A boy tae carry on the name. What use is another girl? That won't cut it in ma faither's eyes, tae just be the faither o' girls. You've got a son, so has Tommy. But me – just girls. Useless. That's what he'll say. Useless.'

Jimmy knew his brother was right. That was his father's view. But he also knew it was not a healthy one. He put his arm round his younger brother's shoulders.

'What does it matter what the old devil thinks? I know you're a man with guts. You fought in the war and came through it alive. That took courage and intelligence. You're good at your job. You'll be promoted to controller soon. Who cares what Father says? You don't need to produce sons to be a man, Peter. You need to think about your lovely wife and girls. They need you to provide for them. That's what being a man is all about.'

18

Margaret arrived that evening, Peter having telephoned from work to the professor's house in Glasgow. She had quickly packed her things, caught the early evening train and hurried through the dark, wet streets to tend to her sister. She knew immediately there was more to the situation than Isa's weakness. The tension was almost palpable between her sister and her husband. They hardly looked at each other and both directed their remarks to her alone, not to each other. As to the cause she had no idea. But she tidied up, prepared some food and sat quietly by her sister as she slept. When the wee one woke, she held her and rocked her for a bit then brought her to Isa to be fed. When the baby fell asleep at the breast Margaret changed her and held her till she fell asleep again, laying her down gently in the cot.

'Had you thought of names for her?' she asked Isa. She was unprepared for the sobs coming from her sister. 'Isa, what on earth is the matter? You know you can talk to me. I can feel there's more to this than you being exhausted after the birth. Tell me what's wrong.'

'It's Peter. He was desperate for a boy. Wanted to call him after his father. We've no name planned for a girl.'

'Well, why not call her after his mother? Janet, isn't she? That's nice enough. Will she not be pleased if you do that?'

'If she's ever pleased. But it won't be enough for Peter.' Isa gripped her sister's hand. 'Oh Maggie, I'm terrified he'll be at me to try again. I could not go through this again. I thought I was dying this time, Maggie. Margaret's birth was longer and harder and more painful, but this time I was so ill all through the pregnancy and then lost so much blood. I don't ever want to be pregnant again.' She paused, pulling at the bedcover. 'In fact,' she blurted, 'I don't want Peter to come near me again.' She broke down and her sister took her into her arms and held her, stroking her hair and her arms and soothing her.

'Let it out. You've had such a hard time. Let it all out. We'll not let you down, Isa. I'm here for as long as you need me. It'll be all right. We'll soon have you strong again and you can put all this behind you. Peter will be all right too in a few days. He's disappointed right now, but he'll come round. He dotes on Margaret and he'll dote on Janet too – if that's what you call her. He'll be pleased at that suggestion, I'm sure. Don't worry. It'll be all right. You need to get some rest.'

She helped Isa settle down.

When Isa had fallen asleep, her sister tiptoed through to the other bedroom, where Margaret was cuddled down beside Peter.

'Peter?' Maggie whispered.

'How is Isa?' he asked.

'She's sleeping now. I think I should stay with her and help with the baby through the night if you are all right here with Margaret.'

'That's a good idea, Maggie. Thank you for

coming. You get some rest yourself. I'll see you in the morning.' He rolled away from her and put his arm round his older daughter's small, strong body protectively.

Margaret slipped back through to the other room where she lay down quietly on the marital bed by her sister, placing her arm gently on her shoulder reassuringly and falling into a light sleep.

The doctor, true to his word, called every day for the next ten days, ensuring his patient was making some progress, checking with Maggie on her diet and taking a look at tiny Janet too. He was not too sure she was entirely thriving as she should and warned Maggie to let him know if she noticed her not feeding well. Isa's pulse was weak the first few days but then began to pick up. She was able to eat the carefully prepared food her sister brought to her and felt some strength returning. But her hair, which had lost its rich hues, was impossible. Try as they might they could not get the tangles out of it. Isa was too exhausted to be bothered with combing it and one morning she asked Maggie to bring the scissors and a bath towel.

'Isa are you sure you want me to do this?' Maggie looked at her hesitantly.

'It's got to be done, Maggie. I can't get it sorted or washed like this.' She paused. 'It will grow again anyway. Come on, let's get it over with.'

Maggie took the scissors in one hand and a clump of her sister's hair in the other and began the long process. As the matted clumps of hair fell, dull and brown, on the bed around her, Isa felt the weight going. She was shedding a part of herself.

What was she losing? A major part of her appearance was her hair – its length, its volume, its colour. It was always the thing most commented on by Peter. He loved brushing it for her and watching her pin it up. She remembered her mother brushing it by the fire when she was little. Tears welled up and spilled down her cheeks. This was hard.

When it was finished, Margaret helped her wash the short crop and towel it dry. Isa finally faced herself in the mirror. She could not believe what she saw there. Who was this woman? Oval faced, translucent complexion telling of exhaustion, staring pale-blue eyes flashing like ice in sunlight and spiky brown hair. She looked shocked. The youthful Isa was gone. Staring back at her was a more mature woman: a mother of two children, someone who had been through troubles, each of which had left its marks on her – wrinkles round the eyes and mouth, furrowed lines in her brow, and now this brown, lifeless, short hair.

'Well, Maggie. It's done. Thank you.' Isa swallowed hard. There was a long pause.

'I don't think I should go in for hairdressing though, do you?' Margaret smiled tentatively and Isa, tears in her eyes, laughed and fell into an embrace with her.

When Peter returned, Margaret saw him first as Isa was sleeping. She told him what they had had to do.

'She was really upset about it, Peter, but we could not get the tangles out any other way. It will grow back.'

Peter was crestfallen when he saw his beautiful

wife shorn and still pale and weak, yet he put on a brave face and tried not to mind. He was still reeling from the disappointment at not having his longed-for son.

He and Isa hardly spoke or spent much time together, since Maggie was there as mediator to cook, clean and mind Margaret, and Isa was still confined to bed. Only perfunctory remarks passed between them, such as Peter giving information regarding his shifts and Isa telling him of purchases to make on the way home. All such communication was clipped and brief, as though being given to a servant or employee. It made Maggie very sad for them.

When Chrissie called in to visit after school one day, she brought exciting news.

'Father asked me what I wanted for Christmas and I asked if we could have a dog. And he said yes! I can't believe it. I thought he would laugh. But he's going to pay the licence.'

'That's wonderful, Chrissie,' said Maggie, delighted for her. 'You've always wanted a dog. What kind will you get?'

'We'll pick one from the home in Stirling this weekend. I don't mind. Maybe a Labrador or a collie. Something that will be good with the children too, so I can bring him round to visit here. That will be all right, won't it?'

Isa was tired and not showing over much interest but she realised this would be good for Chrissie, since Maggie had well and truly left home now and Chrissie was on her own with her father. 'Of course it will. I'm so glad, Chrissie. You'll love that.'

John took his youngest girl to the dog home that weekend. Together they walked round the cages, looking at the various animals. Some were terrified and cowered at the back of the kennels. Others were up at the fencing barking and growling with voices made hoarse through constant use in their nervousness. But one beautiful black Labrador caught Chrissie's eye. He stood proud with his tail wagging looking eagerly into every face as if to say, 'Take me'.

Chrissie looked into the dog's eyes and said to her father, 'Let's take this one.' He too had noticed the animal's calm bearing.

'Let's ask to have a look at him and find out a bit about him,' he said sensibly.

They discovered the dog had not long come in to the kennels because his owner had suddenly taken ill and was in hospital, with little hope of recovering to the level of being able to care for him again. He had been well cared for. Chrissie was thrilled when her father said to the kennel maid that they would take him. He was brought round to meet them. In no time at all he was licking Chrissie's hand and wagging his tail. She clapped his silky head and rubbed under his chin and behind his ears, instinctively knowing what he liked. She was proud as Punch walking home with him on the end of a piece of washing rope, which would have to do until she got a lead.

Chrissie had known as soon as she saw the way the dog held himself amidst all the confusion and yapping of the other dogs that his previous owner had understood the dog's nature perfectly when he had called him Noble.

'He is a handsome dog and that's a fact. Ye were lucky there, ma lass. Definitely the best of the bunch. Now what do ye say to a walk in the park to show him off?'

'That would be grand. This is the best Christmas present ever. Thank you, Father.' Chrissie was beaming. John was all aglow from seeing her so happy. What a difference a dog will make to our lives, he thought. It will be grand, right enough.

Over the next weeks, Chrissie developed a new routine of rising earlier to put on the breakfast porridge to simmer while she took Noble out for his first walk of the day. Even when it was bitterly cold and wet, she still loved this task that allowed her out of the confines of hearth and home and into the air. She walked along Dorrator Road towards the edges of the town, where she could let Noble run in the fields. After school the first thing she did was get the rope down from the hook at the back of the door and call Noble to her. After making a fuss of him she would loop the rope through his collar and be off. Once in the fields she began to train him to stay and sit until she called him, to fetch sticks, and to walk close to her heel. He was quick to learn and delighted to please his mistress and so was easy to train. Chrissie discovered a new happiness and comfort with Noble, who helped compensate her for the loss of her sisters at home. And comfort was much needed, for life with her father was not easy.

He was going through another heavy drinking phase and would often return home noisy and demanding. She hated it. There was no one else to share the burden of humouring him or deflecting him from something that was getting him all worked up. She could not relax in her father's presence when he had been drinking for fear of what he would do or say next.

One night he staggered into the kitchen holding on to the door. Chrissie was finishing homework by the lamplight before going to her room and had not noticed how the time had passed. Normally she would be in bed as early as possible, but the essay for English had been taxing and it was not quite finished.

'Dinna tell me yer still at they bloody books o' yours. Guid's sake, lass, ye'll ruin yer een writin' in the dark.'

'I'm nearly finished, Father,' she said quietly, keeping her eyes on her work.

'Whit dae ye mean, nearly finished? Yer finished the noo. Get that stuff off the table and mak' yer faither a cup o' tea.'

Even as he strode over to, the table, Chrissie bundled her papers and books together and clutched them to her chest.

Her father had slumped into the armchair by the fire. She scurried through to the bedroom with her papers. Noble got out of his bed and followed her back through to the kitchen. By now her father was struggling to get his boots off, his strong working hands fumbling with the laces, which he had in his drunken state managed to get knotted several times.

'Chrissie, help me get these boots off my feet.'

She knelt down and patiently loosened the knots while her father stroked Noble's head. The dog had a good calming effect on her father, yet another way he helped lighten this troubled household.

Just when Chrissie's pulse rate was settling back to normal, her father suddenly sat upright.

'Noo, whaur's the tea! I askit ye tae mak' me a cup o' tea!'

Immediately she rose to her feet and went over to see to the kettle. It was not far off the boil. She got the tea-caddy down from the shelf and spooned three scoops into the pot to make it strong as he liked it, without waiting too long for it to brew. She looked in the cake tins for something to offer him. She found some ginger parkin. She put everything on a tray and carried it over to the table.

'Here we are, Faither. Tea is served,' she said lightly, hoping to keep a quiet atmosphere.

'Tea is served?' he mimicked derisorily. 'Whit airs and graces is this ye're pittin' on? That bloody Fa'kirk High makin' a lady o' ye, is it? A lady wha winna remember her low beginnings in a foundry cottage? Aye, I can jist see it. A right little Miss Hoity Toity.' His workman's hand, powerful from all its hard use but clumsy, reached out for the cup. Whether his drunken state had blurred his vision or he was not concentrating properly, he ended up knocking the filled cup of hot tea from the table to the floor, where it just missed Chrissie's feet. Although no harm was done she yelped in shock and Noble was on his feet at her side nuzzling his head into her hand and licking her in reassurance. When John continued his tirade, the dog turned to face him, his shoulders nudging

Chrissie further away from danger and a deep throated growl of warning emanated from him as he faced her father. Instinctively he knew who was vulnerable here. Although the big man stroked him lovingly at times, he knew Chrissie was his mistress and the one he must protect. John quietened.

Her confidence briefly strengthened, Chrissie left the room with Noble. Then she sat on the bed, shaking and weeping, while Noble licked her hand and whined in sympathy.

The next day when she came home from school, she took Noble and a few pieces of clothing in a bag and set off for Coatbridge to see Isa. When she and Maggie heard her story they both said she must stay there for a few days. They would manage fine. The one problem was that Peter would have to return to the marital bed. Isa had known she would have to deal with this sometime. It might as well be now. Chrissie certainly needed some respite from their father. She shuddered to think of her being just sixteen and handling him on her own.

She cuddled her baby daughter protectively. There was such a sour feeling to everything right now. There was a hatred and aversion to Peter for his carelessness and lack of love. He was not the man she had thought he was when she married him: he had lied to her about his savings; he had been callous when she went into labour; and in rejecting his new baby daughter, he had rejected her too, blaming her for not giving him a son. And yet Isa desperately needed comforting. She wanted to be held. She wanted him the way he had

274

been when they courted, when they had been on honeymoon: attentive, humorous, admiring her, laughing with her, thinking up trips and treats for her. Was that Peter not still somewhere inside her surly, distant husband?

The three sisters set the table, looked after the children and made the meals. Janet was being called Netta by her big sister and the family liked the sound of that, so Netta she became. Little Margaret loved the dog and he put up with his tail being held and a toddler running after him because he was with his mistress. The women were relaxed with each other and Isa began to heal in their company.

They set up the marital room with Netta's cot on Isa's side of the bed and Margaret's at Peter's. Chrissie and Margaret shared the spare double bed and Noble slept on a rug at Chrissie's side of the room.

Having the children in the room with them helped Peter and Isa cope with the arrangement. He had no problem with sharing his home with Isa's sisters but the lack of privacy meant it was hard to talk about personal things. In some ways that allowed them to carry on dealing with basic practicalities like meals, shopping, caring for the children. But it left wounds untended, which kept paining them both. He was disappointed, yet knew he had to accept his new daughter. He could hold her now and nurse her if Isa were busy with wee Margaret. He knew there was a coldness between him and his wife, which he had caused by his poor behaviour, but he could not bring himself to apologise. To do so would be to admit to full culpability and part of him knew that Isa had her own guilt in the affair. She should have known he would be disappointed and offered some consolation. She had made her heart hard towards him, he felt, and was going to make him pay dearly for his natural manly disappointment. She was expecting him to win her back with apologies and gifts and promises and he wanted none of it until she saw things from where he stood, as a failure in his father's eyes. If she could just see where he was coming from it would help him bridge the gap between them. Without that first move he could not see how to make things right.

Isa of course was in retreat from him and on the defensive for her girls. Where was her husband as protector of their welfare? How he had let her down. She could not understand his reaction on the day of Netta's birth. There had been no words of comfort for her in her exhausted state, no desire for the details of the harrowing experience, no sympathy for her pain. Not even a glance at his newborn child. What kind of man was he? Cold, callous, selfish and utterly unreliable, was her conclusion. This would not be kissed away in the morning. There was a split in their relationship as if a fissure had opened in the ground between them, leaving them stranded on either side of an awkward chasm.

Chrissie could not just stay in Coatbridge if she was to be at school in Falkirk. To have a few days away was one thing, but indefinitely it could not work. As they were trying to sort something out, John Dick arrived at the house on Sunday afternoon. After taking tea and fussing over his grand-daughters, he then announced that he would be taking the dog back with him to Falkirk.

'What?' gasped Chrissie.

'You heard,' John stated firmly. 'Noble will be coming back with me. I paid for him, the licence is in my name and he belongs with his owner.' John bent down to pat the dog's head and Noble wagged his tail. The others were stunned. What would Chrissie say now? She said nothing and left the room. Her father finished his tea. Margaret gathered the tea things on the tray and took them through to the kitchen.

A few minutes later Chrissie emerged from the bedroom with her bag packed.

'If Noble is going home with you then I'm coming too,' she announced.

'That will be grand,' said her father. 'It's where you belong, right enough.'

His was the only heart that was filled with joy that day: he was getting his housekeeper back, as well as his youngest daughter. But the others were all fearful for Chrissie returning to his volatile temper and demanding behaviour.

Chrissie was also facing pressure at the school. Although she was doing well in all her subjects and on course to do well in her Higher exams, the taunting had been incessant and she still felt she did not belong at the High School. With her father's controlling behaviour at home as well, she was now at the point where something had to change. Since she could not change her father or leave him, and since he insisted on having the dog, she decided she would have to leave school and find a job. So she began looking in the papers for some work.

Eventually she found an advert for a cleaner/ housekeeper for the owners of an antique shop in Falkirk. She took an afternoon off school feigning sickness and went to the interview, slipping on a jersey over her schoolgirl shirt.

She stood outside the shop briefly, looking in at the window, which was stuffed with all manner of objects covered in dust. Everything looked as if it needed a good polishing. There were tea sets and vases, oil paintings and little bureaux, lace cloths and silver cutlery. She was desperate to put the stuff in order and present it nicely. She pushed open the door and a little bell tinkled. There was a musty smell, a tang of iron and brass not cared for. Behind the desk there was a balding man in a worn brown overall peering at a ledger through round rimless spectacles. These he took off in his right hand as he looked up from the counter.

'Good afternoon, miss, and how may I help you?'

'I'm Miss Dick, here about the interview for the post of cleaner/housekeeper.'

'Ah yes, Miss Dick. Delighted to meet you. Do come through. My sister has some tea ready, I think. This way.' He pulled back a green velvet curtain and in doing so released thousands of dust motes into the afternoon shafts of sunlight. He coughed and motioned Chrissie under the curtain through to the parlour. Like the shop this room was cluttered with stuff, all layered with dust. There were three chairs and a little table in the centre like an oasis amidst the chaos. On it were some china cups and a plate of cut fruitcake.

His sister had ginger hair held up with pins, some of which were coming undone, causing the hair to fall about her face and neck in wisps, which on a younger, prettier girl might have been considered charming, but on this middle-aged, harassed creature just looked dishevelled. She motioned to Chrissie to take a seat and began to pour out some tea.

'Now then, Miss Dick. Tell us something about yourself.'

'Well. I am seventeen. I live here in Falkirk with my father. I have experience of housekeeping and cooking from looking after him. My mother died a long time ago and so my sisters and I took over the running of the house. I can launder and sew too. My sisters have learned a lot in their jobs as cooks and housemaids and have passed on what they learned to me. I am hard-working.' She paused. What else could she say to convince them to give her a job? 'You have beautiful things here, but it must be so hard to keep them all clean.'

'Indeed,' said the man. 'And which of our beautiful things took your eye?'

'I loved the china you have in the window, with the dark patterned bands and gold trim round the rims, but the gold could be gleaming if it was washed in soapy water. Then it would catch the light in the window and customers would stop to look. And there was a lovely brass plate that would just shine if it were rubbed up with brass polishing paste.'

The man looked at his sister and she smiled.

'Sounds like we have found our cleaner/housekeeper, my dear,' she said. 'When can you start?'

Chrissie was overjoyed. She had a job, and moreover a room above the shop if she wanted it. She was not completely sure about that, though. Her father might insist she came home to look after him. Yet she was nearly seventeen. At least she would have somewhere to come to get a break from him.

Her father surprisingly made little fuss about the job. He was glad she was leaving school, having thought it a waste of time anyway for a girl of her station. She was meant to be out working. The wage would always be handy. He was even amenable to her staying over the shop during the week while she was working.

'But I'll be in by to walk the dog and make the tea, Father.'

'That'll be grand.'

Isa was not so pleased. She tried to persuade Chrissie to go back to the school and finish her Highers, reminding her of how well her teachers said she was doing.

To her great surprise, her young sister burst into tears.

'I know, Isa. But I'm sick of all the teasing about being a poor scholarship girl. I've had enough. And Father is grand when he's sober but he's at the drink more now and I'm fed up having to hide away in my room when he comes home from the beer shop and of having to listen to all the shouting. I want a live-in job where I have somewhere to sleep away from home.'

Isa saw that her young sister whom she had mothered since she was a toddler needed an immediate solution to her problems. Reluctantly she agreed Chrissie should try the job.

Very quickly Chrissie was given a free hand at the shop, and in the living quarters, since the brother and sister really had no idea of how to get on top of the chaos. In a few days all the objects on display in the window had been carefully washed, scrubbed or polished and artistically replaced in a tasteful display, which now caught the eye of passers-by. There was more tinkling of the shop bell than there had been and the joint owners were very pleased. Chrissie gradually and systematically worked her way around the shop, dusting, polishing and rearranging. She had mixed her pastes and rubs according to Isa's instructions and had every kind of cloth and duster and brush that was available in the hardware store. Thus equipped, she was doing her best to get on top of the dirt and clutter.

Isa and Margaret were curious about the brother and sister she worked for and kept asking for stories about them. Chrissie was always happy to recount escapades she had seen or overheard.

'Well this week on Tuesday, the wuman was through in the parlour and the fella was at the books on the counter when the shop bell went and—'

'Don't you know their names, Chrissie?' Isa interrupted.

Chrissie suddenly realised she didn't. 'I just call them the wuman and the fella. They only ever call themselves Brother and Sister, as far as I can see.'

'Did they not introduce themselves to you

when you first met?'

'No. I don't think so. I've never heard them address each other any other way.'

'How strange,' Margaret mused. 'How do you address them when you're speaking to them?'

'I just say "ma'am" and "sir". They seem quite happy with that. Anyway, on Tuesday the fella was at the books, the doorbell pinged and in came this gent all dressed up to the nines with a briefcase. The fella looked up and his face fell when he saw the man. Then the customer said, in an almost threatening tone, "You know why I'm here. Is it ready?" Then the fella went through to the parlour and came out again all nervous with a small parcel wrapped in brown paper and string. 'Here you are, sir,' he said to the gent, handing over the parcel. There was such a look of fear in the fella's eyes and a gloating in the gent's that just made me shiver watching them. I mean if it was just a normal transaction why all the secrecy and menace? I think it was very strange. Goodness knows what was in the parcel to create such a fuss.'

'You fancy yourself as an amateur sleuth, Chrissie,' laughed Margaret. Isa joined in. But Peter interrupted the amusement of the sisters. 'What was the parcel like, Chrissie?'

'Just small and squishy-looking, not hard.'

There was a pause as they waited for Peter's verdict.

'You know, that could be extortion money he was handing over. I've heard it's rife just now. Business owners being asked to pay money for being protected by a gang and if they don't agree the gang smashes up the shop or steals goods

282

until the owner realises he needs to pay them to stay in business. I don't like the sound of that at all. I think we should go down and have a look at this shop and these people you're working for.'

When they called in that weekend, the brother popped his head round the curtain.

'Ah, it's yourself, Miss Dick. And who have you brought with you?'

Isa came forward.

'My name is Mrs Isabella Swan and this is my husband Mr Peter Swan. Miss Dick is my sister. And you are?'

'I am Mr Andrew Hebblethwaite, proprietor of this establishment.'

The green curtain twitched and the ginger head of his sister emerged.

'And this is my sister, Miss Evangelina Hebblethwaite.'

'Co-proprietor of this establishment,' she declared, with a frosty smile towards her brother.

Chrissie gave them a tour round the shop and then showed them her room above it. It was full of furniture that the owners were in the process of refurbishing. There were paintbrushes and cans of varnish and the air was full of chemical smells and dust. Her bed was just a camp bed squashed into the corner of the room. When Chrissie saw the room through the eyes of her family she realised she had been a fool to accept this as fit accommodation.

Isa looked around the room aghast. 'Chrissie, pack your things. This room is no fit place to be sleeping, breathing in all these fumes.'

Back downstairs Isa demanded to speak to the brother and sister.

'My sister, Miss Christina Dick, is in your employ as cleaner and housekeeper and you have supposedly provided her with accommodation.'

'Indeed that is correct. She has the use of a bedroom above the shop.'

'It would appear that she does not have sole use of this room because it is being used to restore furniture. It is in fact being used as a workshop. Hardly suitable accommodation for an employee.'

'Miss Dick seems to find it satisfactory.'

'Not any more, she doesn't. Unless you have it cleared out and fitted properly as a servant's quarters I am afraid my sister will no longer be in your employ.'

The brother and sister stood stunned. 'But we have no other space for the furniture.'

'Then in that case... My sister is no longer in your employ.'

Chrissie, still somewhat bemused, was taken out by the elbow and propelled along the street by Isa and Peter.

The search was on for a better position for Chrissie and it was not long before one was found with a family called the McKays who were looking for a general maid. They lived in a smart two-storey house in Falkirk near the canal. Mr McKay was a commercial traveller and often away from home on business. His wife did not like to be in the house herself, so she was glad to have a live-in maid with her, especially at night. The house was close to her father's home in Sunnyside, so Chrissie could still walk Noble and attend to her father when her work at the house was completed. It was a perfect solution and Chrissie was soon happily instated.

Isa and Peter had settled into a pragmatic relationship while Maggie and Chrissie had been living with them, but now that Netta was weaned and Isa's strength was returning it was Maggie's turn to think of leaving them. She was still determined that Canada was her goal as soon as she reached twenty-one and that was now only two and a half years away. She was taken on again at the professor's house, where Jeannie Swan still worked.

Meanwhile young Margaret was a strong toddler, able to walk along beside the pram in which Netta was sleeping. She proudly told everyone, 'Margot's got a baby sister now.' Isa liked nothing better than to be out with her two girls in the fresh air, talking to Margaret about everything they passed, encouraging her to pick daisies, ask questions, look under stones, examine and delight in the world. In these situations she recovered a sense of her own innocence, which she had so quickly lost as a child herself but which was now returning to her as she saw the world through the eyes of her daughter, whose natural curiosity led her to new discoveries every day. She saw again how things grow, wither, die then grow again, and she reflected on how that was true in her own life. She wondered if it would be true in her marriage. Could it recover from this period of death and withering?

Peter was a good provider and a good father. He

had got over his aversion to his second child's gender and was now able to hold her and comfort her as he had done with Margaret. He was even starting to hold Isa and ask for more than kisses but she was terrified. She could not bear to become pregnant again, nor to have to go through a birth. As a result, her body closed off as soon as he came near her in that way. She asked him to be patient and he trusted all would be well soon, but the tension between them was often taut.

Isa focused on her and Peter becoming a strong team for their family, providing a good home and guidance for them. That would be their shared goal, she decided.

There was the chance of a promotion for Peter at the station at Inverkeithing. She would encourage him to go for that as he could earn more and work his way up to even more responsible posts. She would focus on using everything she had learned to give her girls the best start in life she could, drawing on all her experience in bringing up her sisters and all she had seen in the Tolquhouns' household. Her girls would be independent and have the manners of the gentry. Peter's extra earnings would be saved to pay for music lessons and elocution lessons. No one would know by looking at their behaviour or listening to their speech that they were the grandchildren of a Falkirk foundryman. They would be able to move in the best circles. She wanted them to have a career so that they would be independent of any man. That's what she wanted for her girls and she would fight tooth and nail to get it for them.

19

One of the immediate advantages of the move to Inverkeithing was the house on Spitalfield Road that came with the job. It had three bedrooms, making it easier for Chrissie and Margaret to come and stay, a living room, scullery and bathroom and a front and back garden all to themselves. Isa was over the moon. Now that Netta was moving around independently, she and Margaret would have a safe place to play. Isa got Peter to fix a garden gate with a tight catch that the girls could not open. Then she could relax as she worked in the kitchen and the children played in the sunshine. Even on winter days they would spend some time outdoors, warmly wrapped up in coats, hats, scarves and gloves.

The two girls were becoming good playmates for each other but they were very different. Isa had only to raise her voice and Margaret would stop in her tracks. She sought peace and wanted to please her mother, and only needed to be told once not to do something, responding to the definite tones in her mother's voice. As a result she was rarely smacked or punished. She seemed to enjoy her role as big sister, looking after Netta and including her in her imaginary play. She would nurse her doll and sing her songs, then pass her to Netta and encourage her to do the same. Netta, however, could not sit still for long and loved to be on the move, exploring every physical aspect of her environment. She especially loved the garden, but not in the way that Isa and Margaret did. These two would be busy weeding the flower beds, Margaret gathering the earthy weeds up in a basket and taking them across to the compost heap. Her mother would tell her the names of all the flowers and show her how to recognise the weeds. She demonstrated how to pull them up by the roots, using a trowel to ease them out if necessary, so that the plant would not re-grow in the same place later. Netta had no interest in flowers and weeds. She wanted to look under the stones for creepy-crawlies and watch their wriggling bodies twist and twirl across her hands or run through her fingers. She would hold up worms and admire their length while Margaret ran away screaming in loathing of their writhing.

As soon as she was able, Netta loved to climb and jump and explore the world physically, moving through it confidently, as would a pioneer. Her older sister was much more timid in her approach and was held back by her mother's fears and commands. When Netta wanted to leave the garden and go into the fields and woods, Margaret said, 'No we mustn't. Mother will give us into trouble.' While Netta was very little she had to content herself with being pulled back into the garden by her stronger older sister.

On her seventh birthday, Margaret was brought into the kitchen and stood before her was a large, mysterious object shrouded in a sheet. Her parents sang 'Happy Birthday' then pulled off the sheet to reveal a bright-red tricycle with a basket, ribbons on the handlebars and a shiny bell. She was thrilled. She could not wait to take it into the garden and try it out. She sat upon the seat, held on to the handlebars, got her feet on to the pedals and began to go round the garden path. What a lovely feeling to be on the move without her feet touching the ground. She cycled slowly and cautiously, looking straight ahead to ensure she kept to the path. Her father walked by her side, trotting a little when she went faster.

'You're doing grand, hen,' he encouraged. 'Isn't this great?'

'Yes, Daddy. It's wonderful.'

Netta eyed the trike jealously, craving the movement, longing for a turn and a chance to go fast on it. Margaret was moving at a walking pace. Netta thought, What is the point in that? A bike is for making you go faster. At five and a half she was already the little adventuress in the neighbourhood. Margaret was very proud of her new possession and, unlike most of her other toys, which she was made to share with Netta, the trike was to be hers alone, at least for now, while Netta was so young. When she finished playing with it she always put it away in the shed as her parents had asked and shut the door to keep it safe and away from her sister. Netta watched every move she made on the trike, waiting for the opportunity to have a turn herself. And then one day she got her chance.

They had been playing in the garden together, Margaret on her trike and Netta with the dolly's pram, circling round the path that bordered the patch of grass, when their mother called Margaret in to the kitchen. Margaret got down off the trike and ran inside. Immediately Netta saw her opportunity. As soon as Margaret was indoors, she left the pram, jumped on the tricycle and made for the street. The gate latch was now just within her reach and she knew how it operated. She pushed the sneck back, lifted up the lever and pulled open the gate.

Spitalfield Road ran down the hillside towards the bay. Netta pedalled fast and soon she was sailing downhill, ribbons streaming out their bright hues, the wind in her hair and a smile on her face. It was wonderful. An open tourer car passed her by and came to a stop ahead of her at the bottom of the hill. A tall man got out, came on to the pavement and stood right in front of her, his legs apart and his arms open to catch her as she came at him full tilt, screaming in delight. It was the doctor.

'Hello, Doctor Gibson,' she piped.

'Hello to you, Netta Swan. What on earth are you up to? I'm sure your mother doesn't know you're doing this.' He was imagining what might have happened to this feisty child had he not been there to break her speed as she hurtled on into the road behind them.

'I know. I'm not supposed to. It's Margaret's trike. But I just had to. It's so good. I want to go again. Will you catch me?'

'Oh, I don't think that's such a good idea. We need to get you back home to safekeeping. Come on. Hop in.' He opened the car and got her safely ensconced, loading the bike in the boot. Netta could not believe it: first the trike ride, then a car ride. What an amazing day she was having.

When he arrived outside the house, the doctor was greeted by Isa, who had been into the garden and had found Netta was missing. She was at the front door anxiously scanning the street.

When she heard what had happened, Isa was very grateful to the doctor for bringing her child home but she was mortified that he had had to do so.

The doctor headed off as he had patients to visit and Isa took Netta indoors. As soon as the door was shut the tirade began.

'What on earth did you think you were doing? How many times have I told you never to leave the garden?' Isa shook Netta by the shoulders until her teeth rattled. 'Get in there.' And she pushed her into the living room. Margaret was standing aghast.

Isa brought Netta over near a chair, sat herself down, turned Netta face down on to her knee and began to smack her.

'You will not do that ever again. You naughty girl. Do you hear me? I said, do you hear me?'

In between the gasps Netta whimpered out, 'Yes, Mummy.' But the smacks continued. Isa was so angry, so humiliated, so furious at Netta for showing her up as an incompetent mother that she laid into her until her hand was too sore to continue. By then Netta's backside was red. Margaret was cowering behind the settee with her hands over her ears, crying for her sister, feeling every blow as though she were the one being punished. If she had only put the trike away or taken it in with her or taken Netta in with her to the house this horrible thing would never have happened. She hated it. She felt sick. She wanted it to stop. Then she heard her mother's voice.

'Now go to your room. No more playing today.'

Margaret came out from her hiding place and followed her little sister up to their room. Once there she held her in her arms and they cried together.

'Why did you leave the garden? You can take the trike any time, you know. I don't mind sharing.'

'But it was wonderful outside, Margaret. I went so fast. And then the doctor brought me home in his car.'

Margaret held her little sister. Tears from her own eyes spilled on to Netta's hair. 'I hate it when Mummy hits you. I wish you wouldn't be naughty.'

Netta snuggled in closer. 'I always try to be good. But the bike was so wonderful. I don't mind the smack.'

Margaret couldn't believe her ears. She had been terrified imagining the pain, frightened of her mother's anger and longing for it all to end.

Margaret held Netta close till they both fell asleep on the candlewick cover, finding peace and security in each other's arms.

Downstairs, Isa was exhausted and burst into tears. What kind of a person was she, who could let her little sister be killed on the railway line and then let her own daughter nearly lose her life on the road? How could she be forgiven for such irresponsibility? She had to make Netta see she must do as she was told. She had to try harder to keep her child safe. She must be a better mother.

That summer they went on the train to Scarborough and took rooms in the town. It was sunny if sometimes breezy and the girls had wonderful days on the beach, building sandcastles with elaborate walls and towers, helped by their father to fill pail after pail of sand to make fine turrets. Then they fetched water to fill the moats. On a particularly hot, bright afternoon they had a ride on donkeys along the sands, their father proudly holding the reins of both animals as he posed for Isa to take a photo of them: he in his tweed plus fours, waistcoat and jacket, the girls with their cute short bobs and summer shirts and shorts. For Isa this was the epitome of happiness: to see her husband as the proud father of his two daughters.

On the last evening they went to Peasholm Park to see the fireworks in the gardens. They had been walking around before it got dark and Margaret had loved all the bright colours and fabulous scents of the flowers. When they took their seats for the fireworks, however, she was terrified by the noise and the way the sky filled with red and blue light and sparks and by the smell of burning that surrounded her. Fear overwhelmed her and she shook and cried.

'Peter, I think you'll have to take Margaret back to the lodgings.'

'What? I want to see the display. It's spectacular, they said. I'm not missing that.' He turned to Margaret. 'Come on, lass, there's nothing to be scared about. Stop yer greeting. Come on. Be a big girl.' But Margaret was terror-struck and was hyperventilating.

'Peter,' Isa hissed, 'she's too frightened. Her heart, remember. You'll have to take her back.'

He knew he could not afford a shouting match with Isa to get her to change her mind. Not in front of all these people. There was nothing else for it. With great reluctance he got up, took Margaret by the hand and led her out sobbing along the row of seats and away from the fireworks display, which he had so longed to see. Then he walked her quickly away from all the noise, shushing her. Once out of earshot he gave vent to his anger.

'What a baby you are. I thought you were more sensible than to be scared of fireworks, for goodness' sake. And you've spoiled the night for me too. Did you think on that when you started yer greetin'?' He was furious and it was a long walk back to the lodgings for Margaret, struggling to keep up with him, berated all the way, but at least this was something she knew how to cope with.

On Peter's weekends off the family made a trip to Falkirk on the train and visited the two sets of grandparents. In the morning it was John Dick's in Camelon, where the girls were given a sixpence each to spend on sweets. Margaret could take her little sister by the hand and walk round the corner to the shop, where they stood for ages eying the garishly coloured sweets in the tall glass jars. There were bright fluorescent pink sticks of rock, black and white striped humbugs and dusty white bonbons. There were long, sticky black strips of liquorice and jellies in strong reds, blues, greens and yellows like the colours in their paint-box at home. Often they liked to choose some-thing different, but sometimes they just wanted their favourites: Margaret loved caramels and Netta preferred liquorice.

Back at Grandfather Dick's house there would be steak pie for lunch and great stories, some-times even singing. They loved it when he sang and played the accordion. They would all join in the ones they knew. 'Ally bally ally bally bee, sit-tin' on yer mither's knee, greetin' for a wee baw-bee tae buy some Coulter's candy.' That was a great one to sing when their mouths still remem-bered the aniseed or caramel tastes of the candy their grandfather's sixpence had bought for them.

Netta particularly loved the freedom to rum-mage through her grandfather's things. One Saturday she had been through a drawer in the bedroom chest and came through holding some-thing metal and shiny.

'Look, Mummy, what I found. See?' She came closer and held up her hand. 'It's rings that fit on all my fingers.'

Her mother was shocked. What her innocent child had in her hand was a knuckleduster.

'Ah now, lassie, that's no' really for playing wi'. Gie it tae your granddad.'

Obediently Netta returned the knuckleduster to her grandfather, who slipped the contraption into his pocket as he would have done with a coin. Isa and Peter were struck dumb. In her mind, Isa saw her father's hand made a weapon mashing into the face, head and stomach of an opponent. She had had no idea he had been involved in such dirty tactics. Peter had not quite realised the harsh significance implied in the title the 'Fighting Dicks'. His father-in-law clearly had been involved in some rough stuff. He was unsure whether this raised or lowered his estimation of him.

In the afternoon it was over to the other side of town to visit the Swans on Major's Loan, a posh area near the Royal Infirmary. This was a very different experience and not one the girls relished much, for they had to be on their best behaviour and sit primly in aprons their stiffly formal grandmother had laid out for them as soon as they were in the door. Sitting on the edge of uncomfortable chairs, they had not to speak unless spoken to, while they listened to the boring adult talk all around them. If it was a Sunday they were given books to read about saints or Bible stories. At first they liked the pictures, but compared with the books they had at home many of these were too sad and filled with children suffering. They were supposed to make them grateful for what they had and sympathetic to those who were suffering, but they just made Margaret want to cry and made Netta feel sick when she was old enough to read them. One amusement they did have here was listening to the conversations as the hospital visitors passed the house and waited at the nearby bus stop. They heard about operations and tests and reports on patients' recoveries, all delivered in knowledgeable tones, as though the visitors were the doctors.

When the clock chimed five in the afternoon it was time for tea. Grandmother Swan would bring in the tea things and pour each cup laboriously, using the tea strainer, topping up with milk, dropping in delicately the sugar cubes lifted individually with tongs and even stirring it for each person. By the time it finally reached them it was often cool. Then there were the plates of bread and butter to be eaten first before the cakes. Isa had them under strict instructions to take only one cake no matter how many were left on the plate. To take more would be seen to be rude.

It was always a relief to leave in time for the evening train home and to be able to relax with their parents. Even their father seemed glad to get out of his former home.

By October, Maggie was getting ready to leave for the big trip to Canada, as she was now twenty-one and had her savings ready. She had her ticket at a reduced rate because she was travelling by assisted passage to meet the needs of the Canadian cities for domestic servants. Isa and Chrissie had been helping her sew a suit with a skirt and fitted jacket in a chestnut-brown tweed flecked with green, which complemented her skin and hair so well. She bought a thick wool coat, the best she could afford, and two pairs of strong shoes. Isa and Peter made her a gift of a trunk. She was all set. It was with a heavy heart that Isa travelled with her by train to Glasgow and then on to Clydebank, where the ship stood ready. The gleaming white SS *Montcalm*, built at the local John Brown's shipyard, towered high above the quayside, its two black elliptical funnels spaced widely apart, giving it a pleasingly balanced silhouette.

'I can hardly believe you're doing this, Maggie.

Off to Canada. It's so far away.' Isa was determined not to cry. Her sister was so excited. She must not dampen it with tears.

'I'll write to you every week, Isa, with all my adventures.' Maggie was amazed to have got to this point. She had longed for this since she was sixteen but now that she was beginning her trip to a new life, she was glad she was older, wiser and more experienced. She had worked as a maid and housekeeper and had looked after her family when they had needed her. She felt ready for anything.

'You make sure and wrap up warm when winter comes. It's bitterly cold then, you know.' Isa's voice faltered as the emotions rose within her. For it felt that she was not just saying goodbye to her sister but was witnessing her first fledgling leaving the nest completely and sailing far away without her, to the other side of the Atlantic. Her sense of loss was compounded by her years of mothering her dear sister. Would they ever see each other again? Her heart ached, her throat tightened and she felt hot tears in her eyes.

'I'll be fine, Isa. I have to do this: try myself out in new pastures. I can only do it because of you, because of all that you showed me. Because of watching you cope with everything when Mother died. You made me strong, you encouraged me. But I need away: from Falkirk, from Father. I need to prove myself.'

They were near the gangway now and a porter had approached to help with the trunk. Maggie turned to face Isa and they moved nearer into a long, close embrace. 'I'll make you proud of me, Isa,' Margaret whispered. 'Take care of Chrissie.'

Isa did not want to let go, but she dropped her arms to her sides slowly and smiled through the tears as Maggie stepped on to the gangway. The porter walked ahead with the heavy luggage and Maggie walked steadily behind him. At the top she turned round and gave Isa such a cheery wave with her gloved hand. Then she set off along the deck towards the Salvation Army officer, who was waiting to welcome his passengers aboard. Isa then watched as Maggie followed her trunk and disappeared out of sight.

Isa felt as though a part of her body had been wrenched away. She felt suddenly empty and lost as she stood disorientated on the quayside. What on earth lay ahead for Maggie? What if there were storms? Would she be all right? And when she arrived would she find a job? Would all the guarantees of shelter and work materialise? How would her dear sister manage over there on her own, so far from family and friends? Tears were streaming down her face. Suddenly she shivered. She took her handkerchief and wiped her eyes. She should not start worrying so far ahead. She had important things to get on with herself. This was Maggie's journey and she had to let her go and trust God to look after her. She had to return home to her girls.

The winter of Margaret's seventh year was very damp and the smog over Inverkeithing was thick. She had several chest infections that hung around for weeks, taking ages to clear. Isa knew to dose her with *ipecacuanha* wine and glycerine, which soothed the cough and allowed her to sleep at night. Isa set up a bed in the kitchen in the warmer air from the stove to make it easier for her to breathe. Netta missed her sister not being beside her in their shared room. She worried for her and listened out for her coughing, but Isa made an excellent nurse for them when they were sick. She was attentive and drew on all the knowledge she had gleaned over her years of mothering her sisters and watching the nannies in the nursery at the Tolquhouns'. She carefully planned health-giving meals, laid cool cloths on their brows, tempted them with refreshing drinks and their favourite foods, and thought nothing of sitting at their bed-side telling stories, singing or just quietly keeping them company. Both girls loved her most at those times and she felt so needed and glad to be their mother. Under this wise and watchful care, Margaret made a good recovery.

Isa was dusting the top of the cupboard in the hallway when she heard the post drop behind the door. She went to the mat to pick up the pile of mail. Leafing through the envelopes, she found one with the longed-for Canadian postmark. She rushed through to the sitting room and sat on her favourite chair by the window. At last, news from Margaret! It had been six weeks. She savoured the moment, holding the letter and looking at the writing. Carefully, she ran the edge of a knife along the top of the envelope, gently opened it up and pulled out the sheaf of thin blue paper.

Dear Isa (and Peter, Chrissie, Margaret and Netta),
    All is well! I am settled in a job and have good lodgings nearby. But there is so much to tell. First the journey. The Montcalm *was very comfortable and all*

*the staff were wonderful, no matter what we pas-
sengers requested or fancied wrong, they could never
do enough for us. My room had two berths and I
shared it with a lovely girl, Miss Theresa O'Sullivan
from County Clare in Ireland. She too was travelling
with the Salvation Army, as were about another fifty
or so. I do like Theresa very much and still see her, for
we both are lodged in the same women's hostel for the
present. We discovered a love of reading and writing in
common and spent many happy hours on deck walking and talking about what we had read and of our
plans when we arrived.*

*Our berths were comfortable and spacious. I had
thought we might be very cramped, like the sleeper
compartments on the trains to London, but we had a
bit more floor space than that. We had our own sink and
there were washrooms along the corridor where we
could book a bath if wished. I had two while aboard
and luxuriated in the warm water, imagining the
Canadian adventures ahead of me.*

*There was also a small library and writing room,
which I spent time in and where I began my diary,
which is helping me write this letter! The first-class passengers had access to a much bigger one, which we were
not allowed to enter. It may well have been larger and
more lavish, but I had no desire to sit amongst books
and passengers when I could be on deck with the wind
in my hair, filled with the joy of sailing. I wanted to
remind myself that I was on board a ship travelling
across the Atlantic to Canada. After all, one can sit in
far greater grandeur in the Carnegie Library in Dunfermline!*

*On the morning of October 15th, seven days after we
had left Glasgow, while out on deck I noticed flocks of*

gulls following the ship's wake; and then on the horizon, still faint and far off, the blue smudges of land ahead. After that it was a matter of hours before we were sailing south of Anticosti Island and entering the mouth of the St Lawrence Gulf. In every direction there was land: a mixture of promontories and peninsulas of the mainland of Canada, and the islands in the gulf. I walked round and round the decks, craning past lifeboats and funnels to get the best views of my new home. I was thrilled to bursting point, my heart hammering inside me in a most lovely way. But I had to tear myself away to get ready to disembark as we approached Quebec City.

Female Salvation Army officers, in their distinctive navy uniforms, with the red ribbons round their bonnets, awaited us on the quayside and Theresa and I made our way over. Our names were ticked off their list and once the others who had travelled with us were disembarked we were taken in a fleet of cars and buses to the Citadel in the town centre. There we were shown round, and registered with their agency for finding employment as domestic servants. That first night in the hostel I shared with five others, including Theresa. We were all tired but excited.

In the morning we began looking at possible jobs from the requests received by the agency and from adverts in the papers. I spotted one for the manageress of a laundry and thought that might be different. I took the details, checked the maps and set off, dressed in my suit, my new shoes, coat and hat since it is chilly here. It was only a forty-minute walk along streets laid out straight as rulers in easy grids. At every crossroads there was a signpost clearly naming each street and so it was not long before I found the establishment. It was down a flight of steps and was marked by a bright-blue sign with 'Dawson's Laundry' on it in white letters. I rang the bell, was warmly greeted and escorted into the interview room. A very smart, efficient, middle-aged woman introduced herself as Mrs Graham. She asked if I had done laundry work before and of course I said yes, for I have: I've washed for Father and Chrissie for years. I know how to boil water, grate soap and iron. She obviously liked the look of me and there were no other applicants – that's why we are here after all: unemployment at home and not enough workers here – so she told me I had got the job and then showed me round the premises.

The first area was kitted out with washtubs, boilers and scrubbing boards, and was hot and steamy. But there were also electric washing machines which rocked to and fro, agitating the clothes without the use of a dolly. The next room, slightly cooler, had more sinks for rinsing and huge pairs of rollers that looked capable of mangling carpets. Next came the drying room, which was like entering a desert or an oven, it was so hot and dry. It was filled with racks and clothes on rails of hangers but it also had electric drying machines the like of which I've never seen. The next section was filled with ironing tables and pressing machines. Finally we came to an area where the clothes and linens were wrapped, ready for pick-up by customers or delivery by the vans. It was a big operation and I could see there were all kinds of machines I had no idea how to work. What had I got myself into? She was keen that I start as soon as possible so I said I could start the next day.

After I left her I wondered how on earth I would ensure everything ran smoothly. What we use back here bears little resemblance to this professional business set-

up. How could I have been so naïve? But on the way back to the hostel I suddenly knew what I would do.

Next morning, I went down into the basement to watch the women at work. They were skilful workers and did everything so quickly I really could not follow it all. I got talking and asked them how long they had worked in the washroom. Did they ever take turns anywhere else in the laundry? They seemed surprised and told me everyone stayed with the same part of the job. It was as I thought. As I went through the other rooms, I raised the same questions and got the same answers. At the end of the day I called all the women together briefly and asked them if they might not be getting bored with doing the same part of the job all the time? Did anyone fancy a change, since I was willing to try them out in new positions? Several said yes. So I got them swapped round and then got experienced people in each section to train them how to use the machines. I watched these lessons too and that's how I got to grips with the whole process. The workers were more motivated and we completed orders more quickly and efficiently, even receiving several commendations from customers.

I am so happy to have a good post, comfortable lodging and good friends. All is well. So you do not have to worry about me. I am so glad to be here. I think of you all often and hope you are all well. Look after each other.

Love Margaret

Isa laid the letter on her lap and sighed in relief. She had thought Margaret would do well. Her independent spirit and real self-reliance had come to the fore. She was sociable and adaptable and she loved adventure and thrived on new things. This was such a reassuring letter. She had arrived safely and found work, lodging and friends. Isa felt relief flowing though her and suddenly realised she had been carrying tension in her body about how this venture would work out. Now she felt it dissipate. Her sister had done it, broken away to a new life, which she was going to shape with her own choices and skills. She folded the letter carefully and tucked it in the letter rack beside the clock in the kitchen. It would be read several more times that day, she knew, and she wanted to know exactly where to find it.

20

When Peter told Isa in the spring about another post coming up in Burntisland on the Fife coast she quickly realised this would be far better for Margaret. Falkirk, Coatbridge and Inverkeithing were foundry towns with soot-filled atmospheres. The cleaner air and fresh sea breezes on the Forth shores would be healthier for her chest condition.

When they started to look at houses, Isa thought they should go for something a bit bigger. It was not long before she found the perfect home in nearby Aberdour, a pretty village along the coast. It was an upstairs flat in a solid sandstone villa with four bedrooms. The generous sitting room had a grand fireplace and two big windows looking out onto the quiet street. The kitchen had a lovely window overlooking the garden, a large range, a recess for a bed, a huge pantry and a separate scullery for the sink and cooker, leaving enough space for a dining table and sideboard. In the bathroom the bath was boxed in and there was a medicine chest on the wall. Isa could see that the family could do well in this house.

'But do you not think it's too big, Isa? After all, the girls can share a room. What do we need a third or fourth for, or a dining room for that matter?' Her husband was beginning to think she had ideas beyond herself.

'Peter, I've got plans. We can let the spare rooms and take in boarders. The back one is big enough for a double bed and a single. We could have a family in there. I could do their meals for them and make extra money. It would pay the extra rent and give us some to save.'

When he thought about it he was still unsure. 'If we have something smaller the rent will be less and then we can still save,' he reasoned.

Isa could not believe he was going to try and stop her plan. Why could he not see the huge possibilities for them all? He was such a cautious, passive man. Why had she not seen this before she married him and had his children?

'Look, Peter, I've made up my mind. This is the house I want. I'll make it work. I know what I'm doing. Just trust me. This will be a fine home for us and it will help us make our way up in the world.'

'What do you mean *you've* made up your mind? Don't I get a say in this? It's my wages that will be paying the rent, remember.'

Isa was furious with his putting down of her ideas.

'Why can't you just listen to me? If we followed your plan we'd still be back in Coatbridge and you would just be a clerk. Haven't I been right so far? Haven't all these moves been for the good? We need to do this for the girls. They need education, music lessons, decent shoes and clothing. They are just children now, but they will grow and need more from us. This will help us save more quickly for them. I want them to have more. More than I had. I want them to be secure. We'll do it together. You *and* me. The boarders will be my contribution.'

Her eyes were flashing; her voice was firm. Peter felt beaten, not by Isa's argument but by his own guilt at how he was not enough for her. She always left him with that sense of having let her down. Why was she not satisfied with his provision for her and the girls? He did overtime and night shifts to increase his earnings. They could do perfectly well on his wages. But it would never be enough for Isa and her grand plans. He looked at her face and saw the determined set of her jaw, the fierce intensity in her eyes.

'All right, we'll give it a go – but mind, we'll need to keep a close eye on our finances, and if we don't make enough, we need to pull out quickly before we lose money over it.'

'Of course, but we won't lose money. We'll make money, I promise you.'

When they moved in, Isa looked at each room surveying their present furniture and working out what else they needed. She saw too what did not look right in this grander setting and began to look at second-hand shops and in the papers for house sales and roups where furniture was auctioned. In this way she furnished the dining room with a beautiful table with turned legs and Queen Anne chairs. She found a piano for the sitting room ready for the girls' music lessons and for sing-songs like she remembered having as a child at her father's family gatherings. She bought beds and bedside cabinets, wardrobes and pieces of carpet, which she cut to size and trimmed with cotton edging. She used ends of material and sewed cushions. Very soon the house was ready. She had a blue room, a pink, a creamy yellow and a green. There was a spare bed in the kitchen recess. She could let out one or two rooms and had the accommodation for feeding people too. Everything had been freshly painted and she was as proud as could be of her new home. She was climbing up the social ladder, no doubt about it. Peter had to be got round on almost every idea and plan she had, but she was fit for him and was learning how to work him and together they were going to succeed.

She sat in the garden on the grass and looked up. Between the neighbouring rooftops there was a little patch of bright-blue sky right above her poppy-fringed lawn. Isa breathed in slow and deep. This felt so right, lying under this patch of sky. A peace she did not often feel crept over her and she felt cradled, safe, secure. At last she had found a purpose and a place where she could breathe easy and be herself. She felt herself smile. Was this happiness?

She wondered how she should go about advertising the room for rent. Perhaps a card in the shop windows would be a good idea. She talked to Peter and they tried out different wordings for adverts.

A few afternoons later, Netta, now nearly six, was coming back from the beach. She was skipping and singing to herself when around the corner she almost collided with a couple carrying a suitcase.

'Oops, sorry,' she said and giggled. 'I nearly knocked you over.'

'Don't you know you should always look round a corner before you run?' The woman laughed kindly, in a delightfully different accent Netta had not heard before.

Netta eyed the suitcase. 'Are you on holiday?' she asked, wanting the lady to speak again.

'Indeed we are. Do you know where we could stay for a little while?'

'Yes. I'll take you.' She skipped ahead and took them along to a lovely sandstone villa with the name Willowbank in the glass fanlight above the door.

'Here we are,' she said opening the door and calling through the hall. 'Mummy, I found some people who want to stay.'

The couple stood aghast on the doorstep. The child had brought them to her own house. How were they going to explain themselves?

Isa came to the door in a smart brown dress. She had swiftly taken off her apron when her daughter had told her people were at the door who wanted to stay.

'Oh we are so sorry, ma'am. We met your charming little girl and asked her if she knew somewhere we could stay and she seems to have got confused. We thought she was taking us to a hotel, not to her own home. Please forgive the intrusion.'

Isa heard the American accent. 'Oh, no, that is quite all right. I do in fact offer accommodation. We have a bedroom to let and I can do full board if you wish. Is it just for the two of you? Would you like to see the room? I'm Mrs Swan, by the way.'

'Oliver and Sarah Grant,' said the young man, politely raising his hat as he did so. 'Yes, please. We would prefer a room to a hotel, to be honest.'

Isa led the way and watched Sarah Grant eye the tastefully decorated green room with its candle-wick bedspread and satin cushions and the lace drapes at the window. She showed them the bathroom with its gleaming black and white tiles, explaining the cost of a weekly bath and towels if they were required.

Then she took them to the dining room, where she could serve them breakfast, lunch and high tea if wished. They were delighted. Isa had her first boarders. Her business was starting and no advertising had been needed for her first customer, just the word of her 'charming daughter'.

St Fillan's church in Aberdour was one of the key centres in the village, whose worshipping population was split between it and the Catholic church of St Joseph's. Such was the strength of village identity that both denominations joined regularly for fêtes and fundraising events, and there was no animosity towards those who prayed through a liturgy with the priest as opposed to sitting quietly in their seats led by the minister. Isa and her family were warmly welcomed and she was quickly accepted into the Women's Guild and the sewing circle, where the women helped each other fit the items they were working on, pinning up hems, tailoring tucks and sorting out each others' lives while they worked. Sometimes they mended cushions for the church or sewed new pulpit falls. When youth organisations decided to put on shows they were especially busy, fitting costumes according to the tale to be told.

On a Sunday morning, Isa, Peter and the girls would walk through the gate, up the long drive through the cemetery, flanked by swathes of lavender, to reach the church. They would sit on a row of rush-bottomed chairs, the girls' feet dangling over the wooden frames. Netta loved to trace the diamond pattern woven into the rushes with her finger. There was a shelf attached to the back of the chair in front of them where they could place their Bible and belongings. In front of them was the carved wooden pulpit where the minister stood to give the sermon, and the altar where the two tall silver candlesticks were placed. Margaret loved to look at the windows and was fascinated by the Nativity scene, where Mary was almost clapping her hands in joy while Joseph smiled down on Jesus, and the animals lay beside the baby so peacefully. When the Sunday school teacher had told them the story of Jesus' baptism by John, she remembered the picture in the window of both men standing in the river and the dove coming down from the sky. There were thistles growing by the river in the window, just like here in Scotland. Netta's favourite window was the one depicting Jesus welcoming the little children and telling the adults not to keep them away from him. She wished adults would remember that and not keep telling her she was too noisy, too fidgety or too naughty when she came home untidy from her outdoor play. She didn't think Jesus would mind any of that.

The family all loved singing and Isa was proud to be there, showing off her daughters in their beautiful outfits made by herself, her husband with his good job by her side. But she was there for more than that. She wanted to be rid of the weight she seemed to have carried around inside her since she was eleven, but she did not have the words or the time to delve into the darkness that dogged her. Her father's behaviour was part of the weight: she wished he was kinder and would drink less. Her disappointing marriage was part of the burden too: she wished Peter loved her better, that she could be closer to him. Her role as mother, which mostly gave her great joy but which at times seemed to tear her apart, this too caused her much pain: she wished she did not lose her temper with the girls, that they would not let her down so much. And then there were the old burdens for which she had never found solace: Eliza's death, her mother's grief and decline. How was she to pray for release from all of this? So she came longing for comfort, to feel free of this emotional pain. She had no other way to tackle it. She just had to live with it. Keep carrying it, simmering inside her. Work at keeping it subdued.

Aberdour was a good place for them. Margaret's chest was not nearly so troublesome in the fresher air and gentler climate. Both girls' health was strengthened by the sea breezes. They all swam regularly in the sea and the exercise showed in their lengthening limbs and rosily tanned skin. That first summer in the village Chrissie came to stay with them and found work hiring out the bathing huts. These lined the beach in bright pastels with candy-striped awnings. Chrissie had the enterprising idea of serving hot drinks to people after they returned from their swim. She got a Primus stove and a kettle, obtained permission from a house-owner near the beach to use her garage tap for water, and persuaded Isa and the girls to carry kettles of water from the garage over the rocks down to the shore, where she brewed Bovrils, teas and coffees for grateful bathers when they came out of the waters of the Firth of Forth, which never could be called warm. She could keep all her profits from the hot drinks to supplement her fee as ticket seller for the beach huts.

It was great that summer for Isa and the girls to have Chrissie's company. They spent most of it out of doors on the beach. The two senior sisters chatted and laughed near the huts, scrubbing them out at the end of the day and rehearsing old memories, while the two younger sisters ran in and out of the water, collected shells and seaweed and built castles, around which elaborate tales were told of princesses, wizards and dragons.

Isa was so pleased that Margaret and Netta

never competed with each other but cooperated in all their exploits. They built their castles together as a joint project and shared the joy on completion. They never fought over toys, Margaret as the elder being always willing to share. Their main delight was in each other, and most of their play took the form of make-believe games and dramas where they each took a role: shopkeeper and customer, for instance.

Isa's drawers were raided for stockings, scarves and handkerchiefs to set up a draper's shop on a little table in the hall. Isa watched them one rainy afternoon. Margaret was the shop assistant, bringing out items for inspection for the attention of a very particular customer who knew just what she wanted.

'What about this lovely blue scarf, madam? It brings out the colour of your eyes very nicely,' suggested Margaret in her most correct shop-assistant tones.

'No, I don't think that's what I want today. Show me something else,' Netta said haughtily, handbag draped on her arm and nose in the air.

Margaret folded the scarf neatly away and brought out instead a pretty lace-trimmed handkerchief, a tiny square of fine lawn for tucking into a bracelet at a dance, hardly a handkerchief at all.

'Ah, now, that is very pretty,' sighed Netta admiringly as she unfolded the tiny quarters and surveyed the whole work of art in all its glory. 'I think I shall have this.'

'Very well, madam,' said Margaret and she refolded the handkerchief into its minute squares and popped it in a paper bag. 'Although,' she lapsed into her naturally pragmatic self, 'I think if you blow on it that will be the end of it,' and they both dissolved into fits of giggles, while their mother joined in. She felt her heart swell with love, glad to see her girls close and companionable like she and her sisters had been.

Sometimes when they had seen films at the cinema or had stories read to them, they re-enacted favourite scenes. After seeing a film about Dick Turpin, they had mounted the garden swing and swung it as far out as they could near the garden wall, where they lashed the stones with a cane – the one their father had used to stake up the drooping poppies Isa loved so much – yelling, 'Onward, Black Bess!' as though they were really mounted upon the gleaming black back of the horse.

Isa did not always appreciate their exploits. She gave permission for the use of the drapery and for tins to set up grocer's shops. She was glad to have them help her cook and bake. But the outdoor messy games when they came in with school uniform or best dresses muddied or torn were not well received. After the first spanking, Margaret never dared slide down hillsides or climb trees again, terrified in case something got damaged or dirty. But Netta was a tomboy and loved to pit herself against physical tests. Once she had made the first mucky mark she knew she would be for a telling off and so she might as well thoroughly enjoy herself since the punishment would be the same anyway. She would regularly come home after playing on the beach or in the woods with grazed knees, muddied knickers or torn clothes. This exasperated Isa as it meant more washing and mending that she saw as unnecessary. So Netta's joyfully wild afternoons of play often ended with her over her mother's knees and being sent off to her room in disgrace. Somehow it all seemed to roll off her like water off a duck's back. But for Margaret it was a nightmare and she dreaded coming home after Netta had fallen and torn something. She had to endure the punishment and felt the blows empathically.

One particular afternoon, Chrissie came back from a walk to find Isa laying into Netta, her niece's slight body hanging limply over Isa's knee as her mother continued to smack her.

'Isa,' Chrissie shouted. 'That's enough.' She came over and lifted Netta from her sister's knees. The poor child could barely speak or stand. Chrissie took her through to her bedroom and laid her on the bed. She stroked her head and soothingly spoke to her.

'I'm sorry,' whispered Netta. 'I know I'm very naughty. I'm sorry...'

'There, there. It's all passed. You get some sleep now. I'll bring you some tea later.' She waited at the bedside until the poor child was asleep and peaceful.

She came in to the living room and shut the door behind her. Then she turned to her sister. 'Isa, this has to stop.'

Her older sister turned angrily. 'Don't you tell me how to look after my children.'

'Isa, you'll kill her one day with beatings like that. It's not right. It's too much. You never did that to Maggie or me.'

'Netta's not like you two. She keeps doing such dangerous things. Today she was swinging from a branch above the cliffs. I saw her from the harbour. My God, she could have fallen and broken her neck or been drowned in the firth.'

'So she arrives home safely and you beat her to within an inch of her life? It doesn't make sense, Isa.'

Suddenly Isa burst into spasms of tears and sobs. 'Chrissie, I don't know what comes over me. It's like my mind is just taken over and I don't know what I'm doing. I just lash out.'

Chrissie came over to Isa's side and pulled her close.

'I couldn't bear to do her harm, Chrissie. I'm trying to protect her. She has to learn to stay safe. I keep thinking...'

But Isa could not go on and speak of her fear of losing another child in her care. When it rolled over her, she drowned in it, losing her reason, all sense of proportion. What if Netta had fallen onto the cliffs and died? How could she live with herself then? Every incident where her own children came close to danger led to the nightmares of Eliza's death returning. Again she relived the last moments of her sister's life and convicted herself anew of her death. No one understood this burden she carried. It was never spoken of. Isa repressed it in herself, but the nightmares were vivid and the emotion they aroused was raw and real, undiluted by the intervening years.

Her anger was exacerbated by other troubles. She had had no relations with Peter since Netta's birth, six years ago. She could not stand another pregnancy and the doctor had warned them both that it would not be wise. Peter still wanted to come to her and said he would use protection, but Isa found she had no faith in that idea. The two of them were much too fertile to risk that. But abstinence was not good for either of them. It made Isa bitter and edgy and she found fault in almost everything Peter said or did. She was aware of a seething energy within her. Somehow when Chrissie was there it was easier, because she had emotional support from someone who understood her and to whom she felt close. Peter came home tired at the end of shifts and wanted a meal on the table and peace and quiet to sleep. If he had been on night shift this was not easy. Isa tried to keep the girls quiet with books, jigsaws and colouring books on wet days and on good days they cleared off down to the beach. It all added to her stress and sense of being out of control.

And for Peter the enforced abstinence fuelled a hunger for sex and closeness that grew and grew. Sometimes after a shift that ended in the evening, a group of men in the office would go to the railwaymen's club in Burntisland. At home he never drank, but when out with the others he had a dram and a pint to relax and join in the laughter and banter. Behind the bar there was a very attractive barmaid of Peter's age who clearly had taken a fancy to him. She knew he was married, but that was not what she wanted. Just a bit of excitement every now and again would do her nicely. Peter was very dapper and polite, and had a good line in patter. She noticed a lovely twinkle in his green eyes and a smile that lit his face when he laughed. When she saw him coming in, she took time to refresh her lipstick and to fluff her gold-brown curls at the mirror behind the bar.

'Well, Peter, how are you this evening?' She greeted him with a warm smile.

'All the better for seeing you, Maureen,' he said in jest.

'And what will it be tonight?'

'The usual whisky chaser if you please. You're looking well, as always,' he ventured.

'Why, thank you, Peter. The effort's not wasted then.'

'Don't tell me that's all for me?' He caught her gaze, then allowed his eyes to wander over her shiny hair, creamy complexion, the carefully painted red pout, and her curvaceous figure, wrapped closely in deep-blue velvet. He looked back to her sparkling blue eyes, his hunger almost leaping across the bar.

She saw it in him. She leaned over the bar and held his gaze.

'I finish soon. We could go somewhere, if you like, after your pint,' she whispered as she placed the glass on the counter.

Peter raised the glass to his lips. The beer slid down his throat and he felt himself renewed, invigorated. After the years of enforced celibacy at home, there was no way he was going to turn this down.

21

That autumn, Isa's health was again a source of concern. She was having 'woman's troubles'. Every month she would be laid up for a week in pain, with terrible abdominal and back cramping, as if in the early stages of labour. She would lose so much blood that she could barely function for several days afterwards. The weakness and enforced bed rest was getting her down.

Despite his wife's incapacity, Peter's mood remained positive. He began to be quite adept at helping around the house when Isa was not well. There was no softening between them, though. She would undress for bed in the privacy of the bathroom and once she got into bed Peter went through the same procedure. They had become protective of their naked bodies as they held themselves back from each other. There was little intimacy left. No sharing of secrets or dreams. Just the routine exchanges required to keep the household going. Off-season, there were no visitors lodging with them either and no other adults to take the pressure off the lack of communication.

Isa noticed Peter seemed to be doing overtime, yet there was no difference in her allowance for housekeeping. She tackled him about it one evening when the girls were in bed.

'Peter. You worked overtime on your day shift three times this month and you had two extra night shifts.' She paused.

Peter, who had been reading the paper, felt suddenly on guard. Isa heard it in his reply.

'There's been a lot of goods movement on the lines this month. Must be the build-up to Christmas. Factories moving their stock down south for the shops in London. That's the direction most of the trains are going.'

'I wasn't questioning why you were working extra. It's just that usually we'd save the extra. You would ask me to bank it or you would give me extra in the housekeeping. We could be putting by for Christmas ourselves.'

Peter had to think quickly. 'I've no' had the extra pay yet, Isa. They're giving it out at the end of the month. Some new wages clerk has created a new system. Basically means the company get our money for longer, along with the interest.'

'What a nerve! Did you not get any chance to be consulted?'

'Are you serious? You know what the railway company is like. All decided from on high and we just have to like it or lump it. But don't worry. When I get the extra at the end of the month we'll bank it, right enough.'

He thought he had done pretty well there, thinking all that out on his feet.

Isa was left with a strange feeling of being kept in the dark. She almost believed Peter's explanation. It seemed to make sense. Yet why had he not told her of the new arrangements? That was the kind of thing that would have annoyed him, for he was good with money and would have seen the implied benefits for the company at the men's expense. Why had he not come home complaining about it the very first he had heard of it? Perhaps it was a sign of how much wider the chasm between them was becoming.

Margaret and Netta had music lessons through in Dunfermline on a Saturday morning. Now that Margaret was nine and eminently responsible, they sometimes took the bus themselves if Isa was poorly. They loved this. Travelling on their own turned the familiar experience into an adventure, even though it was a short run from Aberdour. They wore their thick winter school coats with colourful berets, their music satchels resting on their knees.

Dunfermline was very familiar to them. This was where they came to swim in the winter when the sea got too cold. Afterwards there was the lovely treat of a poke of chips from the little Italian café near the swimming baths. If Chrissie was with them, she used to hide her chips in her pocket since to be seen eating chips out of a poke on the street was deemed very common by her peers. She would walk along swinging her arms nonchalantly, then surreptitiously put her hand into her coat pocket, draw out a chip and pop it quickly into her mouth. Netta and Margaret thought this was hilarious.

Pittencrieff Park in Dunfermline, known to the locals as 'The Glen', was also a favourite haunt for the family. Many Saturday afternoons might be spent walking through the woodland, buying paper bags of peanuts with which to feed the squirrels and perhaps stopping for refreshments in the tearoom on the hill. The girls thought it the grandest place, with its round tables, linen cloths and waitresses in black dresses and lace aprons taking their orders for scones and cakes.

One Saturday morning in December, they were walking back from their music lesson swinging their satchels and humming snatches of the tunes they had been learning when Netta glanced across the street and started to wave, but then dropped her hand to her side.

'Margaret, look over there. Is that Daddy?'

Before she even looked, Margaret began, 'Daddy is working today.' But she looked anyway and there, on the other side of the street, was a man the spitting image of her father, in his best coat and hat, with a woman on his arm she had never seen before. The children were used to big family gatherings with both sides of their family and Margaret knew that woman was no aunt, cousin or sister. But she was also sure her father was supposed to be working in the station in Aberdour. It was very confusing. Both children sensed they should not wave or call or cross the street and ask to be introduced. In fact it was all so strange they just wanted to move as quickly as possible. Had they been mistaken? Could the man have been someone else? But in profile his nose had that funny hook shape caused by a fall their father had had when young, which had broken his nose. And his hat and coat were the ones that hung in the hallway behind the door. The confusion left them sick and troubled. They spoke in whispers on the bus home.

'I don't think it could be Daddy after all,' said Margaret in her big-sister voice after a while. 'He said he was going to work.'

'But it looked so like him, Margaret. We will just need to ask him tonight when he gets home.'

Margaret felt as though her insides were draining away. Instinctively she sensed danger in that course of action. She did not understand why, but she knew they had to keep quiet. They could not ask him. They could not tell their mother.

'Netta, that's not a good idea. They'll just think we're stupid, mistaking a stranger for our own father. It was a coincidence. That's all.' The big word seemed suddenly reassuring. Yes, it was just a coincidence.

Since his promotion to chief controller in Burntisland, Peter had had a telephone installed. It was a condition of the post that he must be contacted in any emergency. An extra advantage was that prospective boarders could also telephone a booking ahead of their arrival. It stood on a neat little wooden table, draped with an embroidered cloth, in the long hallway between the doors to the sitting room and the girls' bedroom.

Netta loved getting to the phone first and answering in the phrase her mother had taught them. She could sound quite grown-up, she thought.

One afternoon, just in from school, she had dropped her bag on the floor and was unwinding her scarf from her neck when the phone rang. She picked it up.

'Good afternoon. You're through to Willowbank. How may I help you?'

The woman's voice on the other end was unfamiliar.

'I would like to speak to Mr Peter Swan, if I may.'

'I'm sorry, he's not available but I can get Mrs Swan for you. Just hold the line.'

Before she could put down the phone to call her mother through the voice at the other end became harsh and sharp.

'What would I want to talk to her for?' And the phone went dead. Netta felt all strange inside. It did not feel right. There was something in the way the woman had spoken which left her uneasy. She went to find her mother in the kitchen.

Isa was busy making pastry for a fruit pie. She always found pastry-making soothing: the careful sifting of fat and flour, the mixing in of the water, then the kneading and the glide of the rolling pin over the paste.

'Good day at school, Netta?'

'Yes, Mummy. It was fine.' She paused. 'I answered the phone right now.'

'Who was it?'

'I don't know. It was a bit strange. She asked to speak to Daddy but when I said he wasn't here and asked her if she would like me to get you, she was very rude, Mummy.'

'What did she say?'

'She said...' Here Netta took a breath and mimicked the woman's voice: '"What would I want to talk to her for?" Then she put the phone down.'

Isa laid down the rolling pin and sat back in the chair. Who would speak in such a tone about her? She was on good terms with the neighbours and the church people. She had not fallen out with anyone in the family.

'Netta, think carefully about the woman's voice. Was it anyone you knew?'

Netta knew this was important, but no matter how much she tried she could not recognise the voice. 'No. I didn't recognise her, Mummy.'

'Do you think it could be a wrong number?'

'No. She asked to speak to Mr Peter Swan.'

Isa said nothing but her face was ashen.

'We can tell Daddy when he gets home and he will maybe know.'

A chill gripped Isa's heart. 'No, I don't think you should worry about that. I'll talk to your father. Do you hear me?' She continued firmly, turning Netta to look at her. 'I will talk to him. You get on with your homework.'

Netta headed through to her room and sat at her little desk. She knew her message had upset her mother. It had made her feel strange too. But she was glad her mother was going to sort it out. She got her books out and was about to start her maths exercises when suddenly she recalled the same uneasy feeling she had experienced that Saturday in Dunfermline when she and Margaret had seen someone they thought might have been their father with a strange woman. Could this woman, the woman on the phone, be the same one? What was going on? Why had she been so rude about her mother? She could not wait to talk to Margaret. She would feel better when Margaret was home.

In the kitchen, Isa too was mulling over things. She remembered the strange smell of perfume on Peter's shirt last week as she had picked it up to wash, which he told her had been caused by new soap in the cloakroom at work. He said he'd had a washdown at the end of his shift because he'd been so tired. Then there were the extra shifts without any sign of more money coming, and now this phone call from a woman who wanted to talk to him but definitely not his wife. She could only see one way to read all the evidence and she did not like the conclusion it pointed to.

She did not notice that she had put the pie in the oven, cleared the table and washed the dishes, as the certainty mounted within her that Peter had now betrayed her with lies and subterfuge to have an affair. She stood with her hands in the soapy water, shut her eyes and let the pain spill out of her. All her life she had had to be strong in order to cope with what life threw at her, but she was a mess, really. She knew herself to be fragile, a series of broken, jagged pieces trying to be a complete person, but struggling to hold herself together. There was so much pain, so much self-doubt, so much guilt, such a desperate sense of failure. She had failed to protect Eliza. She had failed to look after her mother. Her father had been so disappointed in her as a substitute mother for her sisters he had been thinking of putting them in a home. And look at her now! Her husband was deserting her for another woman; her sister had to intervene to prevent her from harming her own child. What kind of person was she? She had so much wanted to be someone who would be respected, admired, someone who was capable. But it seemed all she was capable of was letting everyone down.

She stumbled through to the hall, her hands still dripping wet, her feet in house shoes. She grabbed a coat and headscarf from the hall stand and went to open the door. Netta came out of her room on hearing the door, expecting her sister's arrival.

'Oh, it's you, Mummy. I thought it might be Margaret.'

Isa wiped a hand across her face and turned away from Netta.

'Are you going out, Mummy? Will I get my coat on too?'

'No. You stay here. I have to go.' Her mother sounded so strange: there was anger in the sharpness of her voice, but she was almost sobbing. As she wrenched the door wider, she added, 'It's the only way.' Then she stepped out and slammed the door shut behind her.

Netta was stunned. What did her mother mean – 'It's the only way?' Why was she leaving Netta on her own? Anxiety made her heart beat faster. She opened the door to see where her mother was headed, just in time to see her turn the corner in the direction of the station. Was she going to catch a train? Was she planning to run away? Was it because of that woman? She stood on the doorstep, unsure, anxious for what seemed like hours but was only minutes, then she caught sight of her father returning from work, carrying the shopping he'd been asked to pick up on his way home. Netta ran out on to the street and flung herself at him.

'Daddy! Daddy!' she cried out in distress.

'What's got into ye, lassie? Dinnae cling tae me like that.'

'Daddy, there's something wrong with Mummy. A lady phoned for you and said she didn't want to speak to Mummy, and now Mummy is running away.'

'What?' He spoke sharply. 'What do you mean Mummy is running away?'

'She put on her coat and said she had to go and it was the only way. Daddy, who is the lady? Why does she not like Mummy?'

'Which way did your mother go?'

'She went down the street and turned left. She might be going to the station.'

'Come on! We need to catch up with her.' Peter dropped the shopping on the doorstep. He ran through in his mind all the different trains that might be coming into the station. Where might his wife think of going? How had she found out? What the hell was that silly Maureen thinking of, phoning his house? He'd never given her his number.

Netta was speeding on ahead and he was a little out of breath behind her. He paused briefly to catch his breath. He had to keep going. He had to get Isa back.

Netta ran on ahead and as the road rose to form the bridge over the railway line, she saw her mother sitting on the bridge parapet, her legs over the side. Suddenly she realised what her mother intended to do.

'No. No, Mummy. No!' she yelled and ran as fast as she ever had done, right up to where her mother sat, and held her arms tightly around her mother's waist, burying her head into her side.

'Mummy, no,' she sobbed. 'No, you can't do this. We need you. We love you. I won't let you do this, Mummy.' She began to tug at her mother to try and pull her off the bridge, but it was as if Isa was in a stupor and could not work out where she was or what was happening.

Peter was at her back now, physically hauling her off the parapet. He swung one leg back round and got the other over too then pulled her into his arms, sobbing.

'My God, Isa, what were you thinking? How was I going to live without you? How was I going to live?'

In a soft, tired voice, Isa said, 'It wasn't my fault ... not my fault.' Then her voice faded and she passed out in Peter's arms as Netta held on, her arms tightly wrapped around her mother's waist.

Isa lay still, on her back, tightly wrapped in the white sheets and green hospital blanket. Occasionally she opened her eyes and looked up at the ceiling, drifting in and out of a drug-induced stupor. In moments of clarity, she remembered and relived the day of the phone call, the strange, unreal walk to the bridge. The cold stone under her hands, the cement dust in her fingernails. Looking down at her slipper-shod feet dangling over the parapet and the shiny metal rails below her. The vertigo coming over her in waves, like something magnetic: drawing, pulling her towards those gleaming rails. Then her mind would lapse into fog again.

The doctor ordered rest and treatment for pernicious anaemia. Her blood count was severely low. He attributed the depression in part to her physical condition but wanted to keep her under safe observation until she was stronger.

Peter and the girls came to visit but often she was asleep or staring at the ceiling, oblivious to their presence at her bedside. Neighbours were helping with the girls.

Guilt made Peter especially anxious and attentive. He brought flowers or fruit every day and his gifts piled up on the locker and filled the ward's flower vases, completely ignored by Isa. She still swooned in swirling memories and odd glimpses of her present reality. When the doctor was happier with her physical health, the medication was gradually reduced so that she had longer periods of awareness. It was then that she started to piece everything together.

One night, Peter came to visit on his own. Isa was awake.

'Isa,' he whispered. 'Oh, thank God. I've been so worried. How are you feeling?'

'Peter.' She spoke hoarsely, her voice unused in weeks. 'Who is she?'

His heart sank.

'Isa, you know you are the only woman for me.' It was a struggle to stop himself from weeping.

She leaned on one elbow and pulled herself higher up the pillow. 'No more lies, Peter. I need the truth. I want the truth. You owe me that much.'

He looked at his hands gripping his knees. 'It's over, Isa.'

'That's not what I asked.'

'But it's done.' He looked up angrily. 'I told the stupid bitch never to phone me. It was only ever about sex for both of us. Not an affair. We're not in love. It meant nothing.'

'I need to know. I have to walk down the street, go into shops, go to church. I need to know who she is. I can't be suspicious of all my neighbours.'

There was a long pause. Peter reached for Isa's

hand but she snatched it away. He dropped his voice.

'It was Maureen at the railway club bar in Burntisland. You don't know her. She knows it's over.' He looked up at her, his eyes openly pleading. 'Isa, please.'

'Please what?'

'Let's put this behind us. We can–'

She cut across him, a new strength in her voice. 'I want a divorce.'

22

Peter knew he could not handle things on his own. He walked round to the McKays' home to ask for Chrissie. They went for a walk and he told her everything.

'I know I was wrong to go with Maureen, but she practically threw herself at me and Isa would never let me near her.'

'You knew Isa was terrified of getting pregnant. She was told she could lose her life if she tried to give birth again.'

'I know, Chrissie, but I told her she didn't need to get pregnant. I would have made sure of that. There are ways–'

'I don't want to know. That's between you and Isa. You say she's asked for a divorce?'

'Yes, but Chrissie, I don't want a divorce. It's over with Maureen. It never was anything serious. I just want to get back to normal. I can't lose

Isa and the girls. Please help me. Help me get Isa to see sense.' He began to tremble. 'I can't bear it, Chrissie. I want her as my wife. No one else.'

Chrissie looked at her distraught brother-in-law and realised that he was speaking the truth. 'I'll talk to her. We'll work on her together.'

Isa was still frail. The doctor had ordered that she rest even when she came home. He prescribed a daily bottle of liver extract, liver ash and iron. Margaret hated the smell of it when she poured it into a glass for her mother to drink. Isa had to hold her nose to allow herself to swallow the foul mixture.

Margaret tried some cooking. She made scrambled eggs for her mother's breakfast and set it nicely on the best china. She picked a flower from the garden and put it in a tiny rosebud vase on the tray. Isa appreciated the trouble her older daughter was taking. She remembered when she was a child herself and her mother had nursed her when she was sick. The thought made her sad. She had been without her mother's love and guidance for most of her life. Had her mother lived she knew her life would have been very different. She would have kept her father sober. She would have saved his huge wages and moved them out of the tiny cottage into a bigger one. Isa would have finished her schooling and been employed as a secretary, perhaps, or a teacher.

But there would still have been Eliza's death. Isa was beginning to realise that Eliza's tragedy was the key to understanding her own troubled life and relationships. She went over in her mind her anguished recollection of her life as she had stood at the sink in the aftermath of the phone call for Peter. It had led her to believe that all the pain and heartache she had experienced was her punishment. How could she expect happiness when she had caused so much tragedy? Eliza had died because she had not kept her safe. Her mother had died of a broken heart as a result. Her father had turned to drink and soldiering to escape his grief. She was not a good wife. Peter would not have needed an affair if she had loved him properly. She was not a good mother either, for she was far too strict with her daughters. But how could she know how to be a good wife and mother when her own mother was not here to guide her? If only she had brought Eliza safely home that day.

She had convinced herself she had to bring this all to an end, draw a halt to the endless chain of consequences that all went back to that tragic day. That was why she had grabbed her coat and left. That was why they had found her on the bridge. But she had not made the jump. She had to remember what had stopped her.

As if groping through mist, she felt the return of that insight she had had as she tried to find the courage to jump. As she had sat on the bridge she heard again her mother sobbing into her father's arms just a few nights after Eliza's death. 'I should have got Belva to look after them. I'm a bad mother, John. I didn't organise properly for my children. I should never have left it to Isa.' At the time, all those years ago, only days after the tragedy, Isa had thought her mother blamed her for Eliza's death. But on the bridge, when she replayed the words again, that was not what she heard. Her mother had blamed herself for not making the right arrangements, for being a bad mother. She had never blamed Isa. This was what had come to her on the bridge.

She shut her eyes and lay back on the pillows as the tears came. 'Oh Eliza, I am so sorry,' she sobbed. 'So sorry.' All the guilt, the weight she had carried with her since the day of her sister's death could be suppressed no longer. It racked her. Exhausted, she lapsed back into weakness and felt the room recede, all sense of time and place dissipate. She felt a featherlight pressure on her arm and a voice she had not heard since childhood softly murmur, 'I'm safe, Isa. Don't blame yourself any more.'

She opened her eyes, knowing there would be no one physically in the room, that nothing in it had changed, and yet aware that she had had the most profound experience of her life. A deep peace fell over her and wrapped her in sleep.

Chrissie came. Isa revived in her helpful, calm presence. She tidied up, cooked, took the girls out, sat quietly by Isa's bed with her sewing. One afternoon she broached the task Peter had set her.

'I'm so glad to see you improving, Isa. You aren't nearly as pale as you were. Your appetite is better too. You are getting stronger every day.'

'I do feel better. But Chrissie, are the girls all right? They are so tentative when they come to see me.'

'They don't want to tire you or upset you, so that probably makes them careful, but don't worry. They just need you to get better.'

Isa clutched her sister's hand, her face anxious and intense. 'I want to get better for them. I have to. I can't believe I nearly left them motherless, Chrissie.'

Chrissie took a deep breath. 'Thank God you are still with us.' She clasped Isa to her. They held each other wordlessly. Isa was quiet and her face relaxed as Chrissie drew back from their embrace. Chrissie was worried she might raise the issue in the wrong way, or too soon, but it had to be said. 'And Peter. What about you and Peter? He told me, Isa, that you had asked him for a divorce.'

'What!' Isa's bright eyes flashed at Chrissie. 'He had no right. That is something between him and me. He'd no right getting you involved.'

'Isa, before you go off on your high horse, listen to me. He is worried sick about you, about the girls, about the family. He wants to make it work. He begged me to help him. He'll do anything to sort things.'

'You know he was having an affair? That the woman even phoned the house and spoke to Netta–'

'Yes, he confessed to it all and said it was the biggest mistake of his life. He's finished with her. He doesn't go to the railway club any more. He knows he made a huge mistake. But Isa, we all make mistakes. Sometimes we just need another chance to show we can do it right.' She paused. 'Do you remember what Dad always said when you burned the dinner? "Dinnae greet, lass. We can aye hae a bit bread and cheese. You're only learning. Mistakes are easy made. Don't give up. That's the real mark of success. To give it another go." And you did, and you became so good you earned a living from your cooking. Nothing comes easy. We have to work at things, even relationships. We're none of us perfect.' Chrissie paused. She saw Isa was quieter. 'I'd best go down and see to the tea.' She hesitated, then bent down to kiss her sister's pale cheek, before leaving the room.

Isa lay back on the pillows. Why was she asking Peter for a divorce? Because he was far from perfect? She knew that even more so now: he was weak, easily influenced, unreliable. But he was the father of her children. He was generous, earned good money, worked hard, lived soberly. She knew he loved her, in his own way; he just wasn't all that she had hoped for. She had wanted to look up to someone who was principled and she had not seen Peter's tendency to hide behind lies when it suited him until it was too late. But maybe she wasn't all he had hoped for either. She had withheld her body from him and, with it, her love and respect. Could she blame him for turning to another woman? She thought of her own withering self-analysis that had taken her to the bridge parapet. She was not perfect: not a perfect wife, not a perfect mother. Peter had as much right to be disappointed in her as she had to be in him. But did that have to mean the end of their marriage?

She paused in her train of thought. Had she not just received the most amazing gift of forgiveness from her sister? What a release, to let herself receive that and find some healing from the lifelong pain of guilt she had carried. Was she about to load Peter with a similar burden of guilt about his affair by making it end their marriage?

What had he said to her when he had hauled her off the bridge and held her to him, before she passed out? 'How was I going to live without you? How was I going to live?' These words surely were his declaration of love, and they called forth a strong response in her, a recognition that this was also her own question. How could she live without him?

A shaft of sunlight streamed through the window on to the counterpane. She was aware of its warmth on her body. It felt like a thaw, like she was coming to life again. She turned to look out of the window. Amongst the wintry grey cloud, a patch of blue sky was emerging. She needed a new start: new vigour, new commitment. This life had been given to her at birth: she had not chosen where it would be lived, nor into what circumstances or family she would be born, and it had not been an easy life. In fact it had been so hard she had sometimes despaired of it, and only weeks ago she had almost thrown it away. But here, now, she realised that was no longer her desire. This was her second chance, her fresh start. Instead of destroying her life she could make up for past mistakes by how she lived now: by gifting Peter with the unconditional kind of forgiveness she had received from Eliza. Her life was not just hers after all: she had daughters who needed their mother, a husband who needed his wife, and sisters whom she had mothered, who were all willing her back into life. Wordlessly, she let her longing for renewal shape itself as she lay in the sun's warmth until she knew for sure.

'Peter,' she called.

ACKNOWLEDGEMENTS

This book is an imagined account of life in the early twentieth century for my grandparents Isa and Peter. So my first thanks is to them for inspiring this story. To my mother, Margaret, and my aunt, Netta, I owe a huge debt of gratitude for their carrying the family story and passing it on to me. When I began this project, after my mother's death, my aunt had lost her sight, but as I wrote each section I read it out loud to her and she gave me her feedback. Sadly she died without knowing that the book was to be published, but she had heard the whole of the first draft. Her encouragement inspired me to seek publication.

Early on in my research when I was trying to establish the facts about Eliza's death, I was put in touch with Sandra Reid at Falkirk library, who found newspaper reports, death certificates and a coroner's report, which helped to authenticate the account of Eliza's tragic death, for which I am hugely grateful.

I am indebted to my first reader outside the family, Helen Watt, and to ex-colleague Liz Young from Denny who discussed the written form of the braid Scots with me, thus allowing a more accurate portrayal of the Falkirk dialect.

My husband, Alan, has encouraged me from

the start and early on saw what needed to be elaborated upon, refined and honed. Without his guidance and encouragement, the project would have been a much lesser thing.

Isabel Jackson

The publishers hope that this book has given you enjoyable reading. Large Print Books are especially designed to be as easy to see and hold as possible. If you wish a complete list of our books please ask at your local library or write directly to:

Magna Large Print Books
Magna House, Long Preston,
Skipton, North Yorkshire.
BD23 4ND

This Large Print Book for the partially sighted, who cannot read normal print, is published under the auspices of

THE ULVERSCROFT FOUNDATION